The Curious Magic
of
Buckeye Groves

Jennifer
Enjoy! ☺

Maura

Maura McCarley

ISBN-13: 978-1502585035
ISBN-10: 1502585030

Library of Congress Control Number: 2014919268
CreateSpace Independent Publishing Platform, North Charleston, SC

Dedication

I dedicate this book to my father, Robert Eugene McCarley. He died on August 19, 2014 two days after his 83rd birthday. He was the kindest man I ever knew, and from him I inherited my love of nature and trees. The last time I visited him in Iowa, June 2014, we went for a walk together and found a beautiful old Red Oak near his home. It was a portal tree, as evidenced by the split down the center. Peeking into the darkness through the split, it appeared to lead to intriguing places. I am grateful that I was able to share this with him before he left.

Dad, I didn't know you would pass through your own portal so soon after. I feel you with me every day now and I love you.

Acknowledgments

This story would not have been written were it not for the impact Peter Kingsley had on my life. I have him to thank for pointing me toward Awareness, which led me to experience reality in a way which has transformed my life. Although the story and the characters are fiction, many of my experiences that came from my work with Peter informed this story.

There are many others to thank for their contributions. My husband Pete patiently put up with listening to my story over and over, and he supported me financially and emotionally. Janice De Jesus was my writing teacher; her classes inspired me and she taught me much about this craft while I was writing. My weekly writer's group members Ana Galvan, Ceci Pugh, and Charles Burke encouraged me, gave me great feedback and kept me going; without them, I am not sure I would have finished either the story or the editing process. Marguerite Rigoglioso, good friend, provided inspiration with her pivotal work on Virgin Births. She also introduced me to Theresa Dintino, who edited my story and provided the honest feedback and suggestions I needed to make this a much better book; without her, this would have been a much poorer story. I want to thank my editor, Cris Wanzer, for her amazing skill as an editor. Her edits and suggestions refined this work in so many ways and the design is part of her beautiful work.

My women's circle, Karla Donohue, Sandra Vaughn, and Viola Lew-Simcox have been my loyal and constant cheerleaders. Other people in life also deserve thanks: my parents, Robert and Jenna McCarley, have provided life-long support and love. My daughter Megan provided her skill as an artist to help me with graphics for marketing, and her boyfriend Marcus Ervin has given ongoing computer support—both encouraged me along the way with interesting plot discussions and ideas. My cats, Avatar and Scamper, provided daily cuddling and laughter. Finally, and not least, I want to thank the trees: the buckeyes (and their fairy friends) which were the original inspiration for this story, and all the great trees I have ever met.

Table of Contents

Part II ~ The Encounder

Chapter One 1
Chapter Two 18
Chapter Three 31
Chapter Four 41
Chapter Five 52
Chapter Six 57
Chapter Seven 61
Chapter Eight 69
Chapter Nine 75

Part II ~ The Awakening

Chapter Ten 87
Chapter Eleven 97
Chapter Twelve 106
Chapter Thirteen 111
Chapter Fourteen 116
Chapter Fifteen 121

Part III ~ The Journey

Chapter Sixteen 137
Chapter Seventeen 150
Chapter Eighteen 159
Chapter Nineteen 169
Chapter Twenty 174
Chapter Twenty-One 183
Chapter Twenty-Two 187
Chapter Twenty-Three 192
Chapter Twenty-Four 199
Chapter Twenty-Five 209
Chapter Twenty-Six 216
Chapter Twenty-Seven 225
Chapter Twenty-Eight 232
Chapter Twenty-Nine 234
Chapter Thirty 235
Epilogue 236

Prologue

Six women in flowing white tunics stood around the dying tree. Where the tree's bark had once gleamed white, it was now a faded gray. The flowers that made a circle around the tree, marking the place where the women now stood, were wilted. The once shiny, silver backs on the tree's leaves had yellowed and leaves were dropping to the ground. The women, standing in silence now and locked in worried gazes, cried tears of grief and astonishment. They were at a loss for what to do.

Too many of the portal trees were gone. The music, once a harmonious, pleasant background symphony, had grown dissonant. The signs of instability could be felt all around them. Many of their people had disappeared, and grove after grove of trees had burst into flames. The sacred mountains, once locked in place, now moved from location to location, and it became dangerous to stay in one place for too long. They knew their sister was on the other side, but the signs were not good. If this tree was dying, surely it meant the other tree had already died. And what of their sister? Had she given birth to the child?

The women took each other's hands. Palm to palm, the spiraling, magical energy of each mingled together. They sent healing energy to the tree, hoping to save the tree on the other side, but it was too late. The grove burst into flames. One by one the women disappeared as the ether swallowed them up. Not even a wail marked their passing.

Part I

The Encounter

Chapter One

irabel Mairead McInness stared out the window of
the bus as it pulled away from the station in Billings,
Montana. She could see the reflection of her dark
almond-shaped eyes in the window and she grimaced at the
sharp angles of her face. Memories of kids teasing her about
her "whore-red" lips surfaced, uninvited. Her reflection
reminded her of how unusual she was—something she was
never allowed to escape in her rural world. Mirabel hungered
for a more tolerant place. Montana felt backwards, as though
it still belonged to the last century. Even Billings, much bigger
than her home town, retained that backwards inclination. It
was already ten years into this century, and Mirabel didn't
foster hope that it would catch up anytime soon, so she was
going to a place that was already ahead.

Nevertheless, Mirabel's stomach churned with nervous,
writhing snakes. She had never traveled far from home. Now
she was going on a grand adventure, away from her unhappy
childhood, as fast as she could. She contemplated her name
and the restricted life she had known so far. Mirabel loved her
name in all its strangeness because it was one of three gifts she

had gotten from her mother. She didn't know why her mother had named her Mirabel, and she never had the chance to ask her, as her mother had died long before she was old enough to wonder. The other two gifts were left for her after her mother had passed; a silver acorn and a bottle of glitter.

The acorn seemed too big to be an acorn, but her father said it was an acorn and she didn't know enough to argue. It had a clasp holding it shut with a tiny lock and no key, so she couldn't ever open it. On the old bottle of glitter, scrolled writing spelled out *Hawthorne Drug*. Both gifts rested in an old powder box her father had given her, without ceremony, on her sixteenth birthday. Her father never explained why she had the bottle of glitter, but Mirabel imagined the bottle held real fairy dust. Because there was no one to argue with her fantasies, it became fairy dust to her. She never opened the bottle, saving it for someday in the future when fairy dust would be needed, although she could never quite imagine what it would be needed for. But it made a good story, which brought her a measure of happiness in her otherwise melancholy life.

Mirabel knew the story of her mother's last night by heart. It was impossible to escape because of her father's nightly ritual.

"Yer ma was not a good driver," he would start. "She drove off the road, smack into the old oak tree. Musta hit her head on the steering wheel…died instantly. Wer a good thing for her, I s'pose. Musta felt no pain t'all." Mirabel knew the whole "no pain t'all" mantra was his way of trying to reassure her in this morbid ritual, but it had the opposite effect for her. "No pain t'all" he'd say, over and over, until his head sank onto his chest and his words became too slurred to understand. Eventually, he'd sink into a stupor, and the sickly sweet smell of body sweat tempered by whiskey would permeate their home until morning came. Mirabel would bury her head in her pillow, avoiding the smell as best she could before she fell asleep.

"No pain t'all" became a constant background rhyme in Mirabel's head throughout her lonely childhood years. Her father never recovered from his grief over the loss of her mother, and Mirabel's gut twisted with heaviness as her father drank away each night. Her heart ached, too, devoid of a mother's bedtime stories, kisses for ouchies, and especially shared wisdom that could have eased the trepidation of first blood. Instead, she had to figure out what to do by asking the woman who worked at the drugstore. She had skipped school that day, terrified that she was dying. When she confronted her father with the terrible news, he stammered, "Yer got yer blood, girl. 'Tis no good thing. I wish yer ma was here, but I s'pose I'll take you into town to git some supplies and Old Nelly at the drugstore can tell you what you need to know."

It was an agonizing memory. She had stuffed toilet paper in her panties, but the blood had leaked through and stained her pants on the way to town. Her father made her go into the store anyway and talk to Nelly, who took her into the back, sent her to the bathroom with some supplies, and told her to wash her pants out while she found something else for Mirabel to wear. Now, years later, Mirabel sat on the bus, still stung with embarrassment by the incident and wishing for a mother once again.

When she was still in grade school, Mirabel entertained herself with alternative stories about her mother. She attempted to fill her emptiness with charm, to fill her void and stave off the biting loneliness of her childhood years. Mirabel didn't hate her father; he was not a bad man, but he had little time for her on the Montana ranch and his whiskey always seemed more important to him than her. He spent his days herding sheep, and often camped out with them. On the evenings when he was home, he was consumed with grief and alcoholism. Mirabel was left alone to spend her days carding wool, knitting, and keeping house in the little shed they called home.

When she wasn't doing chores, she wandered the wilds surrounding their home, wading streams and finding special trees to dance around. Her favorite had been a grove of white-barked aspen near a stream. The grove was a magical place. To Mirabel, the trees were more than trees; they were guardians to other worlds, and if only she knew the right words, she would be able to pass through to a magical world filled with elegant, bewitching women. The trees whispered to her in a familiar language that hovered on the edges of her understanding. Placing her hands flat on the papery bark, sparkling energy swirled in her palms. She imagined that her mother was one of the women waiting for her on the other side, if only she knew how to open the tree.

Often, when she was in the aspen grove flitting in and out among the trees, dancing and twirling with a crown of flowers on her head, a fawn-colored deer would come to visit her. It would walk right up to her and gaze into her eyes, mesmerizing her. In her memory, it seemed that the deer would speak to her inside her mind. She would say, "Mirabelis, my little one, does the man treat you well?" Mirabel remembered feeling shy and nodding a timid yes. Sometimes she would cry and tell the deer, "I wish I knew my mommy. Why can't she be with me? Do you know her?" The deer would bow her head and implore her to be patient, telling her that one day she would know everything and cross over into her magical world. Now, sitting on the bus and steeped in memory, Mirabel chuckled inwardly. *I was an imaginative child.* It seemed to her that she had found clever ways to salve her loneliness.

During her high school years, Mirabel studied hard, read a lot, and worked at expanding her vocabulary. She plotted to leave her small community of McClave, Montana, for California as soon as she was out of school. She wanted to leave behind all the wariness and unkind teasing from the small-town people she had grown up with. She longed to go somewhere where she could fit in, and the San Francisco area struck her as such a place. It had a reputation for attracting oddballs and misfits. Although her father herded sheep for wealthier ranchers, he always saved some wool for her, which she carded, spun, and knitted into fanciful gifts that she sold in the nearest, larger town. She managed to save enough money over the years to cover a few months' rent and Greyhound fare. Soon after graduation, she bought a backpack, filled it with her meager belongings, and walked to the nearest highway. She hitched a ride into Billings and caught the first bus to California.

• • •

Mirabel arrived in San Francisco a day and a half later. As she exited the bus, she sniffed myriad unfamiliar smells that surrounded her; sewage mixed with salt air and engine exhaust. A little overcome, she choked up. She wanted to cover her mouth and wished she had a scarf, but she acclimated quickly. Excited by her adventure, and a little daunted, she wandered the streets aimlessly for a while. Her first task was to find a cheap place to stay, and it was getting late, so she headed into a small market. A bored girl with pink hair, a nose ring, and tattoos sat behind the counter. Mirabel approached her.

"Hey," the girl nodded.

"I need a place to stay, not too expensive. Do you know where I might go?"

"Yeah, check out the hostel. It's cheap. It's on Taylor."

The girl directed her to the Amsterdam Hostel not too far from Union Square. Mirabel skirted around vagrants and beggars as she followed the directions given to her. A man with dreadlocks, wrapped in a dirty green blanket and mumbling to himself, passed a little too close for comfort and she nearly gagged as his rank body odor assaulted her nose. She eventually located the hostel, opened the door, stepped into the lobby, and let out a sigh of relief, happy to be out of the unnerving street life that was beyond her experience. It would take a little getting used to. The hostel was the right price, but it didn't allow for much privacy, and Mirabel was surprised to find herself missing Montana as she settled down for the night.

Over the course of the next week Mirabel tried to find a place to live in the city, hoping such a different environment would help her escape the lingering sadness in her life. But the numbers of homeless vagrants only added to her melancholy, and she had underestimated how hard it was going to be to find a place without the security of a job that most of the landlords required. Even the tiniest, rinkiest places in San Francisco were a far cry from her current financial capabilities. So, she expanded her search to Berkeley and Oakland, also without any luck.

On a whim one day, Mirabel decided to take the local transit train, and she picked Walnut Creek as her destination. She liked the name. *It sounds so pastoral.* On the way, the train went through two long tunnels set apart by stations in between; one went under the bay, the other traversed through the coastal mountains that bordered Berkeley. The train finally emerged from the last tunnel and stopped at a station called Orinda. Mirabel looked out the window. Hills sprinkled with wooded areas and open space rose up beyond the station parking lot. Her shoulders relaxed. *This is more like it.* San Francisco was interesting, but she could live out here. There were trees, open vistas, and she saw much more nature. As the train traveled to the next stop, Lafayette, she continued to take in the scenery out the window. A two-peak mountain dominated the landscape and moved closer as the train sped toward the next stop, Walnut Creek.

Mirabel stepped off the train in Walnut Creek. She couldn't smell sea air, but also couldn't smell sewage. She looked over at the mountain and its foothills, then at the suburban city as it spread out before her below the raised platform. Terraced buildings, very modest in height compared to the skyscrapers in San Francisco, bordered the north side of the station. The downtown area, filled with one- or two-story shops and restaurants, spread out southeastward from the station. It was attractive, neat, and safe. With her backpack on her back, Mirabel went down the escalator and exited the station. She sighed with relief that she didn't have to go back to the city to retrieve her things. Now that she was here, she knew she was meant to stay.

Mirabel stumbled across a Motel 6 not far from downtown. She walked into the lobby to find a young woman fighting with the printer.

"How much for a week's stay?" Mirabel asked.

"Two ten," the girl slurred, still intent on picking scraps of paper out of the printer.

Mirabel pulled out the ever-shrinking contents of her wallet and handed over the cash. Soon she was settled into a drab room with a lumpy bed and curtains that didn't quite shut, but she didn't mind. *At least I have a place to stay for a week.* She pulled out her best outfit and changed clothes. It was time to explore and see if she could find some work downtown. She worried about her dwindling savings.

Mirabel wandered back past the train station and made her way down Main Street. She ambled past restaurants filled with well-dressed patrons waited on by white-aproned servers carrying trays full of wine glasses and simmering food. It was an alien world of wealth and privilege quite outside her small-town experience. She trembled, overwhelmed and suddenly shy, but continued down the street, determined to overcome her roots and step into a new story about herself. *I'm from Walnut Creek now, and I will survive.*

An eclectic mix of shops beckoned as she made her way through town. When she grew tired of walking, she found her way into a busy coffee shop where she found a long line of customers attended by two harried baristas who were trying to keep up.

Mirabel waited in line, and when she got to the counter she said, "Looks like you guys could use some help."

"Yeah, you know anyone? We just lost a barista this morning."

"Well, I'm looking for work. How do I apply?"

Later that day, Mirabel fell onto her lumpy Motel 6 bed and thanked the stars for her luck. *I have a lot to learn about coffee. It's a different world here.* Montana didn't have baristas that she knew of. In Montana, coffee was made in a drip machine and poured from the pot into white diner cups and doused with a lot of sugar to improve the taste. But the coffee shop manager had promised to train her in the art of making coffee drinks. Mirabel just had to trust that she was capable of learning this art.

Her job provided her the necessary security to rent a small, furnished studio apartment within walking distance of her job and downtown, and she was able to move out of the Motel 6 after a couple of weeks. Mirabel kept a tight budget, with barely enough for rent, food, and utilities, but she had succeeded. *I have escaped Montana.* She wasn't disappointed about not living in San Francisco. Mirabel learned to enjoy the quirkiness of the San Francisco vibe where the people were as colorful as the city, but Walnut Creek felt like home. There were refreshing glimpses of that quirkiness in Walnut Creek, too—especially among the other baristas she worked with. They accepted her for herself, and she had never experienced that kind of belonging before. Soon the other baristas became her friends. She'd never really had friends before. Life was new and interesting.

One day, after she was settled into her new place, Mirabel set out to explore more of downtown Walnut Creek. She strolled down Main Street and wandered in and out of shops, lollygagging wherever it pleased her. She found a cupcake store and browsed the enticing rows of colorful confections, finally choosing a chocolate velvet cupcake. Her mouth watered as the clerk neatly packaged it in a pretty pink box, which she promptly discarded so she could sink her teeth into a cloud of chocolate bliss. Chocolate sprinkles and buttercream frosting lined her lips as she left the store.

Wiping her mouth with the back of her hand, Mirabel made her way down the street again and turned into an enclosed alley full of hair and nail salons. Coming out on the other side of the alley, she was enticed by a window full of fairy statues and crystals. She looked up to a sign posted above the door that read *Mystic Dolphin*. Entranced, she opened the door and entered, a wave of sage and cedar scent wafted over her, calming her. A colorful and eclectic array of statues, crystals, and ritual objects lined wall shelves and glass cases. Jewelry hung from display racks on the counter. Bookshelves adorned a nook at the back of the store and two stuffed chairs and a table sat in the middle of the book area. Mirabel circled the store, pausing and picking up objects, then putting them back before moving on.

A young woman helped a customer at the counter, and Mirabel barely noticed when the patron finally left, leaving her as the only customer. Mirabel picked a hanging crystal fairy off a hook and admired it, wishing she had more money for such things.

The young woman came up beside her and said, "She's a lovely one, isn't she? I've been eyeing her myself."

Mirabel glanced over and smiled at the young woman, noticing her warm brown eyes and kind face framed by shoulder-length, wavy brown hair. She wore a beautifully draped, asymmetrical tunic over a long, full skirt in the same unusual watercolor pattern of muted purples and greens. She was not a tall woman, but stood half a head taller than Mirabel, who was by most standards smaller than most people she met. Mirabel could see hints of her full, curvy figure under the draped tunic, adding to the woman's aura of compassionate softness. As she stood near, Mirabel could smell lavender. Her shoulder's relaxed in this woman's presence. *She's flowy, like her clothes.* "Yes, she is lovely," Mirabel replied, now looking at the fairy.

"Would you like to take her home with you?"

"Oh, yes I would, but I am afraid not today."

"Well, I am sure she will wait for the day when you can. My name is Janey. Did you come in looking for something special today?"

"Oh, no. I saw the fairies in the window and I couldn't resist. I didn't know this was here. It smells so nice in here and I like to look at everything. I wish I could afford to buy something today, but I can't."

"Tell you what. You can have that fairy, on me, today. I can tell she wants to go home with you."

"Oh no, I couldn't."

"Oh, I can see she's as smitten with you as you are with her, and I don't know why, but I think we're going to be friends. I can feel these things sometimes."

"My name is Mirabel." At first she resisted taking the gift, but caved when she looked at the fairy again. "Okay. Thank you, Janey, it's so kind of you. You won't get into trouble, will you?"

"Oh no, I get a discount and she's really not so expensive. Besides, I'm good friends with the owner. Come on, I'll wrap her up for you."

Janey wrapped the fairy in tissue, then a person came into the store to pull her away. Mirabel explored the candles while Janey waited on the customer. There were so many colors, and each candle had a sign underneath. There was a yellow candle in a tall glass with a picture of a crown on it, and words that read *Crown of Success;* another was purple with a picture of a fist and tied hands, and it read, *Command, Control, Compel.* Bemused, Mirabel continued to scan the other colorful candles.

"Candles for everything, huh?" Janey giggled from behind Mirabel.

"How do you know what to do with them? Do they really work?"

"It depends. We advise people on how to use them, and even do readings on the candles after they burn all the way down, to see if the spells worked."

"Fascinating." Mirabel turned to Janey. "Would you like to meet me for tea sometime?"

Would I love to meet for tea sometime! Janey thought as she stood there, gazing at this woman named Mirabel. *A magical name.*

Janey had noticed the slender, graceful Mirabel as soon as she had entered the store—her long, dark hair that fell to her shoulders in gentle waves; and her unusual eyes, which were almond shaped and framed by lush lashes. The irises were dark brown, almost black, but as the light hit them, they appeared to be deep purple. Janey took in her pale, fawn skin and heart-shaped lips that needed no enhancement as they blushed red, naturally curving up at the corners. There was something indefinable about her that screamed exotic and foreign, but also radiated magic. The proportions of her face were not quite right and her body was sylph-like, on the edge of being implausible.

Standing in the radiance of Mirabel's gaze, Janey noticed a stillness creeping outward from her center. Her existence suddenly became suffused with vibrancy and her feet the roots to eternity. One moment in Mirabel's presence and Janey's heart was forever bound. Mirabel embodied something that Janey longed for her entire life, and she wanted more. At that moment, Janey had decided to buy the fairy for her because there was something fragile about Mirabel, and Janey suddenly wanted to protect her. When she wrapped the fairy in tissue, she silently recited a protection mantra before handing it over to Mirabel. So, when Mirabel asked to meet her for tea, Janey jumped at the opportunity.

"Yes, I'd love to. Can we meet tomorrow? I don't have to work."

• • •

Mirabel and Janey sat outside the cantina across from the Mystic Dolphin.

"I've never had Mexican food before," Mirabel shared.

"Really? How have you never eaten Mexican?" Janey raised her eyebrows.

"Oh, we didn't have Mexican restaurants where I grew up."

"Where was that?"

"Montana. McClave, Montana, to be exact."

Somehow, Mirabel and Montana didn't seem to belong to the same world. Mirabel was full of surprises.

"What was Montana like?"

"Oh, I didn't get away from the ranch much. I used to go to the aspen grove and dance and play fairyland when I was little. I loved the trees. I'll tell you a secret. It was like they whispered to me, only I could never understand what they were saying."

Wow, I think I've found a true sister, Janey thought. "Mirabel, that's amazing. I always feel like the oaks whisper to me. Everybody always acts like I am crazy when I try to talk about it. I finally gave up telling anyone. I used to think someone would share my experience and explain it to me, but that never happened. I'm so glad we met. I don't feel so crazy now." She giggled. "Would you like to go meet my favorite oaks someday?"

"I'd adore that. When can we go?"

"Let's go right now. There is an amazing old oak at Ruth Bancroft Garden not too far from here. I'll drive."

• • •

Janey and Mirabel stood under the magnificent oak.

"If we want to approach the tree, we have to wait until the staff is out of sight," Janey said.

"Why?"

"They have to protect the roots from all the people. But I know this tree loves me. We've had several conversations and I'm careful. Just do not step on the roots as we move in toward the tree." Janey glanced around and didn't see any of the staff. "Okay...the coast is clear."

Janey and Mirabel reverently approached the tree. Janey placed her hands on the trunk and said, "Hello, Grandmother." She nodded at Mirabel, and Mirabel placed her hands on the tree as well.

"Meet my new friend Mirabel." Janey looked at Mirabel. "I can hear whispering and I feel her..." Janey patted her belly, "right here. Do you feel anything? I think she likes you."

"It's not like my aspen, but yes. Mostly I feel it in my palms. They tingle and I feel... *rooted* or something. I feel like I can almost understand, but then I can't quite grasp it. Oh, all trees are special, aren't they Janey?"

"Yes, they are. And I totally get the 'not being able to grasp it' thing. I feel the same way. But I think we all have a resonance with one kind or another. Someday I *will* understand their magic." She looked up at the tree. "Thank you, Grandmother." Turning and walking away from the tree, she waved at Mirabel. "We'd better step away before the staff comes back."

Mirabel reluctantly stepped away. Just in time, Janey and Mirabel made their way around the tree, acting innocent as a staff member passed by.

"Do you have any questions about the tree?" she asked.

"Oh, no, I've been here many times," Janey replied. "But thanks." Janey sniggered as she moved beyond earshot. "What they don't know won't hurt them. I don't think they understand this tree as much as they care for it."

Together the new friends walked toward the car.

"It's so nice to have a friend I can share this with...and who understands. Growing up, I didn't have anybody to talk to really. Thank you, Janey."

Janey took Mirabel's hand as they walked. "I feel the same."

• • •

As the summer turned to fall and then into winter, Mirabel explored the landscapes surrounding Walnut Creek, sometimes with Janey and oftentimes alone. She loved the winter because it mirrored her moods; skies opened up and torrents of rain soaked the land for hours at a time. She rushed outside to walk alone during misty breaks. On her walks, the tiny airborne drops of water caressed the surface of her skin and brushed her cheeks with cool kisses. She awoke to winter mornings heavy with fog that obscured everything, even the treetops, in a blanket of gray, making it hard to see more than a few yards down the trail. On days when the fog cleared and the sun broke through, the air was scrubbed crystal clear. Sun drops sparkled off the dew, creating little diamonds on the tender green plants bursting through the gravel trails. Looking up, the skies were a sharp, clear blue with clarity so intense it reminded her of transparent cerulean sapphires. On these lucid days, Mirabel could see far into the distance. The Sierra Nevada appeared detached from the earth and floating in the air.

On her melancholy days, Mirabel fought her tears. Every part of her was obscured by a thick blanket of gray; thick eyelids, thick sinuses, thick heart. She was confused about what made her feel this way. *I should be happy...* Anything could set it off. For a while she assumed she was still grieving the loss of her mother, but then she realized she longed for something else. She would pull out the silver acorn, which fit perfectly in the palm of her small hand, and stroke it. As she did, she became aware that she wanted more; something unidentifiable and elusive. Now aware of her longing, her mood shifted and her dreams opened into crystal-clear visions of a magical place that was filled with music and lights dancing off verdant green fields filled with little white, shimmering flowers.

Mirabel would wake from these dreams full of joy and presence, and discovered anchors inside herself, holding her fast to something nameless. She knew that dark storms were brewing in the distance, looming over her future. Her anchors held her fast to a magical place of stillness and peace at her core, and Mirabel cautiously felt herself strong enough to hold on through the coming tempest.

Mirabel hiked the hills to ease her sadness. She found high places in which to sit and gaze off into the distance. She treasured the way the heather-colored hills transformed into green as the winter progressed. In the winter months the new, lush growth pushed up through the residue of fawn-colored grasses burned by the previous summer, desiccated by the heat and lack of rain. The weave of colors was subtle yet complex; heather and green transmuted into purple where the folds and creases on the hillsides came together. Barren, dark-purple, leafless valley oaks stood out among this variegated backdrop. In contrast, the live oaks were evergreen with gnarled tangles of branches ending in dark-green, ruched hats. These gave a feral, uncultivated, and ancient magical air to the hills.

Mirabel's favorite shift at work was the last one of the day. Her work day started at 3:00 p.m. and the coffee shop closed at 10:00 p.m. She rose early enough to get to the hills and hike before work. She bought a used bike from one of her coworkers, which allowed her to explore and find new places to hike.

Mirabel discovered buckeye trees on one of her adventures, and realized that her silver "acorn" was actually a buckeye and not an acorn at all—her original hunch about the nature of the gift had been right. Her father had been wrong. She imagined her mother was close by when near the buckeye trees.

Mirabel loved the buckeyes more than any other trees. The groves cast a spell of enchantment on her. *I can almost see fairies dancing and cavorting in these groves.* Closing her eyes, she saw images of vibrant green lawns with enchanted, tinkling flowers and the lights that hovered around them. *It feels almost like my dream world here.* She picked up the buckeye seeds and savored how the smooth, silky feel caressed her hands. It calmed her. She held them out in front of her; they had a nice, solid weight, fitting almost perfectly in her hand as she cupped it, and stroked the smooth surface with her thumb, using it like a worry stone. *These must be the trees I resonate with, like Janey said, even more than I ever resonated with the aspens.*

Hiking in the buckeye groves, Mirabel also sensed something on the edge of her awareness, like something glimpsed out the side of her eyes, but when she turned to look, there was nothing there. It reminded her of the deer from her childhood. There was a tugging and pulling in her gut, and spirals of energy swirled in the middle of her palms that tingled and penetrated to her core, moving up and down her spine, and teasing her belly and groin. *I wonder what it means? I feel different when I am in the groves.*

The two-peaked mountain she had first glimpsed from the train was called Mt. Diablo. She spent more and more time in the secret groves she found among the foothills there. She appreciated how much the mountain dominated the landscape of Walnut Creek and the other suburbs in the area. Soon Mirabel spent less and less time with her friends from the coffee shop, but she still spent a lot of time with Janey. Mirabel smiled as she thought of how persistent Janey could be and how grateful she was for it. Mirabel treasured the way her friend always brought along her old Navajo blanket when they visited the trees, and regaled her with stories about trees she had known. *She is my tree sister.*

Mirabel explored bay groves and walked among the mystery of the oaks. Stepping under the impossibly large oak branches was a passage into a quiet, expectant stillness full of ancient magical wildness. *I can see why Janey loves them so much.*

The oaks were masters of gravity. When she walked into bay groves, she inhaled the minty, earthy, fragrant mist and it compelled her to pull off a leaf and bend it to further release the scent. She brought the leaf to her nose and drew in deeply, then put it in her pocket for more sniffs later. A walk in the hills entailed moving continually from one habitat to the next; through the dark stands of bay trees, into orchards of live oak, and then into the open savannah with great valley oaks strewn here and there. The buckeye groves existed in the folds and crevasses of the hills, those canyons carved by water as it made its way down to the ocean over the eons. There among the trees, Mirabel's troubled soul felt soothed and at peace.

Chapter Two

Something kept pulling Mirabel back to the buckeye groves. She believed that the tugging in her belly was the buckeyes pulling on a cord attached to her center. One early spring morning Mirabel rode her bike to the end of a road and found a parking lot with a trailhead. The trail was a fire road that climbed a small hill and came to a crossroads. To the left the trail was gated, so Mirabel went through the gate and hiked past a driving range, then around a curve circling a hill to the left of the trail. As the driving range disappeared behind the hill, she was suddenly in the wild, looking at a grove of buckeye trees nestled between the steep hills just beyond an open meadow. Off to the left was a sharp incline covered with sage and manzanita shrubs.

Mirabel moved into the grove, pausing to feel its magic, now noticing the sensations in her palms. She continued forward into a ravine where the incline steepened, and up through a dry creek bed, scrambling over rocks and the tree limbs of random buckeyes rooted in this crease between converging hills.

After climbing up the ravine, Mirabel discovered a second grove. She worked her way up into this new group of buckeyes, sat down, and ate her lunch in the middle, surrounded by the trees. She contemplated the orange and green lichens covering the trunks and branches of the trees. It reminded her of spatter paintings she had seen in an art book; the trees were speckled with a two-color version rendered on mottled gray elephant skin.

She could see that the ravine veered up to the left, and to the right was a grassy, steep hill where she spied yet more buckeyes. As soon as she noticed this, she became aware of a stronger pull on her belly, as if the grove sought to pull her right up the hill by its own force. Mirabel wanted to follow that source of power, but it was too late to hike up the hill and still make it back home in time to get ready for work, so she reluctantly left. On the way home, something kept pulling her back. She pedaled hard against the resistance, as if riding through water instead of air.

That afternoon a strange, elderly woman came into the coffee shop. Mirabel was sure she had never seen her before, but she was somehow familiar. She had long, gray hair pulled back into a braid. The braid was wound tightly at the top by a green cord, which was woven back into her hair and tied off at the bottom, silver leaves dangling at the ends and at the top. Her dress displayed a pattern of muted greens and oranges, uncannily similar to the display of lichens Mirabel had observed on the buckeye trees earlier that day. The woman's dress was long with an uneven hem brushing the tops of her boots. Her bodice was stitched with long darts following the curve of her hips and opening into a full skirt. The neckline was uneven and decorated with orange and green embroidery in the pattern of leaves. Dark-green, combat-style boots completed the look.

When the woman came to the counter, she asked Mirabel for tea of chamomile blended with mint. When Mirabel handed her the tea, she looked Mirabel in the eye and whispered, "The Shiashialon is waiting."

Huh? Shia...who? Mirabel silently wondered. Placing her hand on her belly, drawn there by the tugging, she stood with her mouth open. Then, before she could ask about it, the woman walked over to a table near the window and sat down to drink her tea. She didn't look Mirabel's way again. Mirabel surreptitiously stole glances at her when she could.

She can get away with that strange outfit here so near to San Francisco.

Nobody else paid much attention to the woman at all. In Mirabel's gaze, she was a beacon, standing out completely from all others in the café. Everything else—the people, tables, chairs, walls, the street outside—was two-dimensional in comparison. The effect was not quite amenable to words or descriptions. Mirabel shook her head and tried to focus on cleaning the coffee station.

Eventually, the woman left, and Mirabel settled into cleaning the tables and setting up for the nine o'clock movie rush from the theatre. When she finally got to the woman's table, she noticed a little bottle had been left behind. She picked it up to look at it. The shape and size were familiar to her, so she turned it over and saw the label, which read *Hawthorne Drug.* Mirabel sat down abruptly. The bottle was a perfect replica of her bottle of glitter left to her by her mother. It seemed impossible to her that there was a second one. Briefly, she thought the woman had somehow stolen her bottle. *But...how could she have my bottle?* Then she remembered her bottle was still filled with glitter. This one was empty. Mirabel couldn't explain why this addled her so. *That woman left it here on purpose after saying that funny name,* she thought. And the name niggled the edges of her awareness, elusive but familiar.

Okay, she ruminated. *I need to be logical about this.*

She had never ever seen a Hawthorne Drugstore anywhere. She assumed it had been some small-town drugstore near

McClave, Montana. *How could this strange woman from Walnut Creek have the same bottle?* It didn't make sense.

Mirabel finally stood up and prepared for the movie crowd, but she couldn't shake the unsettling, surreal feeling of the day. The odd coincidence of events—the resistance she experienced on her ride back from the buckeye grove, the peculiar woman in her coffee shop, and then finding the Hawthorne Drug bottle—seemed a little impossible. *Weird!* She suddenly ached with indefinable longing.

Mirabel, distant and unfocused, messed up several coffee orders when the crowds started to come in. The impatient crowd had little tolerance for mistakes, and their sense of entitlement began to grate on Mirabel's nerves. The combination of the strange events and the persnickety throngs of coffee drinkers took their toll. By the end of the evening she had a throbbing headache and could hardly wait to escape the coffee shop and get home. Mirabel knew she was doing a poor job of prepping for the morning crew, but she didn't care. Finally, when everything was set up, she tucked the Hawthorne Drug bottle into her pocket and made her way home.

When Mirabel arrived home, her head still throbbed, her body ached, and she was emotionally wrung out, but the urgency to solve the puzzle overrode her tiredness. She checked her stash to make sure her bottle was still there and to verify the other was the same. She picked up her bottle and looked at it, then looked at the bottle from the woman again. The two bottles were a perfect match, except hers had glitter in it. Unsatisfied, but not knowing what else to do, Mirabel added the new bottle to her cache. She now had a silver buckeye, one bottle with glitter from her mother, and an empty twin bottle from the strange woman. After stashing her secret treasure, she skipped eating and went straight to bed. Her sleep was filled with strange dreams, and she tossed and turned all night.

Mirabel awoke the next morning with her sheets a mess, and feeling very tired. Fortunately, it was her day off. She dragged herself out of bed and made a pot of coffee, boiled some eggs, and made oatmeal. She gulped down her food without tasting it, took a shower, and dressed for a hike. Today her goal was to reach the grove of buckeyes she suspected was at the top of the hill she had discovered the day before. *It's the Mother Grove.* Since the groves likely started with buckeyes near the top of a hill, she presumed the round seed pods from the Mother Grove would fall to the ground and roll down the ravine, seeding the next generation successfully until they reached the bottom and finally seeded the first grove she had encountered.

She packed a lunch, and as an afterthought, grabbed the bottle of glitter and the silver buckeye from her secret stash and stuffed those in her pack. With her backpack fitted on her back, she went to the garage, mounted her bike, and rode to the trail.

Once at the trail, Mirabel went through the gate, and then, pumping hard, she pedaled up the hill, making her way past the driving range that bordered the trail. There was little activity at the range, and it was quieter than when she had seen it before. As she rounded the bend and came to the meadow where the first buckeye grove appeared, she startled some deer. They ran up the steep hill on the left into the manzanita and sage, pausing to look back at Mirabel before disappearing into the scrub.

Finding a suitable small tree, Mirabel locked her bike to it and walked into the first grove of buckeyes. She breathed in the stillness, and the grass under her feet flattened as she walked over it, springing back a bit after her passage, but leaving a visible trail behind her. She scrambled up through the ravine to the second grove. Here she almost bumped into another deer, but this one didn't startle. Its coat was pale fawn; unusual for black-tailed deer. It lifted its head and gazed peacefully at her for a moment, then continued to eat grass. She was so close she could almost reach out and touch it. Without understanding why, something about the deer reminded her of the strange lady who had come into the coffee shop.

"Curious!" she murmured out loud. She remembered the deer from her childhood, and thought this one looked the same. Mirabel tried to talk to her, but upon hearing her voice, the deer looked up and moved to the side to let her pass. Looking back at the deer, Mirabel had a sense it was imploring her to continue up the hill.

Mirabel climbed the hill and finally made it to where the ravine veered off to the left. She looked up the steep hill on her right. It was a hard climb, and she would have to be careful about her footing, but she was determined to make it to the Mother Grove. She kept low to the ground as she climbed, reaching out to grab trunks and branches to help hoist herself up the hill. A force, like a magnetic pull, caused her to lean toward the grove as she climbed.

Eventually, Mirabel crested the hill and found herself in a grove of ancient-looking buckeyes. They were covered with moss and lichen, and had larger trunks than any of the trees in the lower groves. Gnarled branches rose from the center in undulating waves, then bent back toward the earth. They creaked as a light wind blew through. Mirabel focused on the tug in her belly, and felt a much stronger sensation of spiraling energy in her palms than she had noticed before. She moved slowly through the trees into the grove. A large outcropping of serpentine rock stood in the center with a potbellied, moss-covered, bearded buckeye behind it, the other trees scattered around the periphery. The rocks were covered with lichen, with the gray-green of the stone peeking through. Lichen covered the tree, as well, and there were a variety of types—sage green, frilled lichens created a lacy effect over the branches, while orange, fuzzy lichens gathered in clumps. Some bearded lichens, also pale sage, draped over branches and hung down, adding an air of mystery to the tree. Mirabel walked up and ran her hands over the lichen-covered trunk, then petted the hanging lichens.

Mirabel took off her backpack and sat down cross-legged in front of the tree. She gazed in wonder around the grove. *I feel...this is my place.* She unzipped the backpack and pulled out her tin with apple slices, cheese sticks, some crackers, and water. She spread her lunch on a small cloth and ate while contemplating her resonance with this grove. Once done with her meal, she sat in silence, paying close attention to the energies swirling in her palms and tugging in her belly. She sensed the tree behind her wanted to pull her in. Then she saw movement to her right from the edges of her vision. Mirabel could have sworn it was the strange lady from the coffee shop, but when she turned to look, there was nothing there. She shook her head and started to pack up her things. There it was again, this time off to the left—a movement in muted greens and orange, and this time she thought she heard someone whisper "Shhhiashialonnnnn..." She turned to look, still seeing nothing.

I need more sleep. First I think the deer reminds me of the lady, and now I am seeing and hearing things that remind me of her. Shaking her head again, Mirabel sighed and put her tin and bottle back in her pack, then pulled out the bottle of glitter and silver buckeye and set them in front of her. Noticing that the glitter appeared to sparkle with more intensity, she picked up the bottle and started to unscrew the cap. She had been saving the glitter for an undefined special occasion. This would be the first time she had opened it. She stopped and peered through the glass at the contents. Now she was more curious as the substance looked like glitter, but it was much finer than any glitter she had seen in the craft stores. *Maybe it is really fairy dust,* she thought, laughing to herself.

With her hand poised to make the final turn to unscrew the cap, she hesitated. *Oh...I'd better leave it unopened for now. I should ask Janey what she thinks I should do with it.* She screwed it back down. She didn't see the few sprinkles of glitter that had been caught in the bottle threads gently float down onto her lap as she tightened the cap and set the bottle back on the cloth. She picked up the silver buckeye and held it in her palm, and thought how much its weight and feel reminded her of a real buckeye.

Mirabel put the bottle and silver buckeye in her pack and leaned back against the tree. Sunlight filtered through the tree branches and landed on her, penetrating her skin, warming her bones and making her drowsy. She closed her eyes and didn't notice how a sudden, gentle gust picked up the glitter from her lap and dusted the tree. Soon Mirabel fell asleep.

At first her sleep was dreamless. Then she heard her name and moved into a dream that was lucid and very real. She could feel the sensation of the tree at her back, but found herself in an unfamiliar landscape with an otherworldly quality. The Mother Grove was there, and the trees still looked like buckeye trees, but they were also different. They had the same shape, but now they gleamed white. The patches of lichen were golden and silver instead of orange and green, and they glowed, emitting an ethereal light and forming an aura that radiated outwards as the bearded lichens shimmered in their translucence. The tree leaves had dark-green fronts with shimmering silver backs. Mirabel stood under silver-gilded moonlight beaming gently down upon her and the grove. She basked in its glow for a moment before looking down at her hands. Her skin was glowing. It had a darker hue and appeared as though it was dusted with gold. The grass at her feet was shorter, denser, fern green, and sprinkled with little white flowers—a far cry from the long grasses of California winter.

Looking down, Mirabel noticed her shoes had vanished. She was barefoot, and as she pondered her lack of shoes, she noticed her clothing was different, too. She was dressed in loose pants of sheer white fabric flecked with gold. Her tunic tapered in at the waist and then opened out, ending in an uneven, lacy hem at her knees. The garment was comfortable, and more solid than it appeared. The air was cool, but she was quite comfortable; warm even. She was near the center of the grove and the flowers condensed in a pattern, creating a circle around her about 20 feet in diameter. The rocks in front of her were smaller, and looked more like jade, forming an enclosed circle at the center of the grove.

Mirabel heard soft music and realized it came from all around. When she tried to pinpoint a location, she heard one tune coming from the trees, then noticed a lower tone was coming from the rocks. There was a ringing, like tiny little bells, which she traced to the flowers. Music tones were coming from everywhere, and together they harmonized into a beautiful symphony of gentle sound with a bit of percussion, the origin of which she couldn't locate. This place enchanted her and met her longing in a fulfilling way. Mirabel knew in her heart this was home. Standing in this magical grove, completely enthralled, joy swelled within her.

As Mirabel stood there, breathing it all in, she sensed the swirling pattern in her palms and lifted her hands to look at them. She could actually see the energy forming a spiral of swiftly moving, iridescent clouds circling round in her palms. She marveled at them and wondered what it meant. Looking around again, she sighed contentedly. This place was oddly familiar and she wanted to explore.

As Mirabel moved toward the edge of the trees, a jarring, discordant sound entered into the grove. It disturbed the harmony of the place and a sensation of fear bit at her, starting at the base of her spine, working its way upwards, and creating such tension that she became immobilized. The harmony of tones around her rose in volume, as if to combat this intrusion, but the disturbing, shrill note rose and became an unbearable shriek. Once again, the harmonized song of the grove rose in volume, but was outmatched as the screech became louder and constant. This continued until Mirabel could stand it no longer. She put her hands to her ears and fell to her knees. The sounds rose to a crescendo and the grove burst into flames around her. There was no place to go except into the inner circle of rocks. Mirabel scrambled between the rocks, her heart in her throat, and cowered at the center.

Mirabel curled into a little ball, still holding her hands over her ears to escape the pain. And then suddenly the harmonized sounds fell into silence and the screech died out. A wave of relief passed through Mirabel as she looked up. All the magic and color were gone from the grove, and the landscape beyond was devastated. Cracks of gray nothingness opened in the atmosphere around her and the air felt unstable. Blue electric flashes rent the sky, crackling with energy. She broke into a wail as grief washed over her—a grief reminiscent of her melancholy days. She fell to the ground, weeping with racking sobs until her energy was sapped and she sprawled   there, immobile.

Mirabel suddenly awoke to find herself leaning against the tree in the Mother Grove where she had fallen asleep. The sun was low on the horizon. She tried to move, but found herself physically sunk into the tree. Her arms were pinned to her sides, and the tree trunk was embracing her. Terrified, Mirabel struggled, twisting back and forth until she extricated herself. She snatched her pack, fled the grove, and made her way down the steep hill. She sprinted through the ravine as fast as she could. When she got to the main trail, she almost careened headlong into a mountain biker. She stumbled and fell to the ground.

"Whoa, are you okay? You're in some big hurry there!" He quickly dismounted and rushed over to her. He helped her up and led her over to a fallen tree trunk. "You look as pale as a ghost," he said as she sat down. "Did you see a mountain lion or something? I've seen them in this area, but always from a distance. Here, let me give you some water. I have an unopened bottle here on my bike." He walked back over to the bike, came back, and handed the bottle to Mirabel. "My name is Matt. Ya know, you might want to consider bringing a friend with you. It's always safer that way. I worry about that myself sometimes, and I've heard of them attacking bikers, but I figure my helmet will help if I get attacked. Are you okay? It'd be safer if you brought a friend, do you have a friend who can come with you?"

Mirabel just nodded and took a drink. She didn't like being told what to do, but Matt's ability to talk without pause amused her and she found herself grateful for his presence. Somehow, amidst all that prattle, he calmed her. Her breathing began to slow and she gave him a timid smile.

"Thank you," she whispered and made as if to leave. She felt a little embarrassed. It was just a dream, after all, and although she couldn't understand why she had been pinned in the tree, she knew there must be some explanation. She wished Janey had been there so she could talk to her about it. She certainly wasn't going to say anything to a stranger about it—even a very friendly one.

"Why don't you let me walk back with you?"

"Oh, thank you, but no, I just had a scare. I will be okay," she said, still shaking as she stood up and began to walk over to where her bike was locked to the tree.

But Matt insisted, picking up his bike and following along behind her until he caught up with her. "Oh, is that your bike there? I thought you were on foot. Do you ride here often? I like it here. It's one of my favorite biking trails. It's so pretty in a subtle kind of way. Besides that, these hills rock as far as getting my exercise." He paused suddenly, looking at her. "You have a name?"

Mirabel, still unsettled by her experience, looked down to hide a wave of fear, trying to gain some composure as she held back her tears. She busied herself with unlocking her bike. Finally gaining some measure of control, she looked up at Matt and noticed his stunning green eyes regarding her with concern. She warmed in his gaze. Looking up at him swept some of her sorrow aside and the memory of her strange experience faded in his warm smile. He was just the medicine she needed. She smiled. Then her smile broadened.

"I'm Mirabel, Mirabel Mairead McInness. Nice to meet you, Matt."

"Mirabel." He cocked his head as her name passed his lips. "That's an unusual name. I think you are the first Mirabel I've met."

Mirabel lowered her eyes and started walking her bike down the trail. Matt followed along beside her in silence. After his introductory stream of chatter, she could sense this silence was unusual for him. They walked for a few minutes without speaking, making their way around the bend by the driving range.

"It's a quiet day at the range," Matt said, gesturing toward the fenced driving range next to the trail. "I'm always afraid I will get hit on the head when I ride by here."

Mirabel laughed and pointed at the array of golf balls alongside the trail. "Me too. All these golf balls out here are not a good sign." She looked up at him and noticed his smile went all the way to his eyes, and the skin around his eyes was wrinkled in well-worn paths, like he smiled a lot. He had a little stubble on his face, and he wore a baseball cap backwards on his head. His skin was tanned and the sun had lightened his hair, which was light brown with blond near the tips where it stuck out of his hat.

He must spend a lot of time outdoors. She had stopped walking and he stopped with her. Suddenly, she blushed and turned her gaze back to the trail again and started walking. She never looked back at the grove.

When they got to the gate, Matt offered to ride home with her to make sure she got there safely. Mirabel didn't argue. She was happy to have him with her. His presence was soothing and warmth spread through her limbs, relaxing some of the tension she always carried. When they arrived at her apartment, he walked her to the door.

"Mirabel Mairead McInness, I'd like to see you again. Are you free tomorrow night?"

"I wish! Unfortunately, I have to close at the coffee shop where I work tomorrow. I would like to see you again too, Matt. Matt…"

"Oh, Matt Gallagher, at your service," he said, bowing. "I don't mind waiting for a late date with you."

"Okay, Matt," she said, blushing again. "Maybe you can meet me at the coffee shop across from the theatre. We can take a stroll through Walnut Creek and have a late-night snack somewhere."

"See you at nine," Matt answered as he swung his leg over his bike and took off down the apartment courtyard walkway. He swung his hat in the air as a parting gesture.

Mirabel watched him leave and giggled as he weaved happily back and forth while he made his way to the street and beyond. Still chuckling, she took out her key, unlocked her door, and entered her apartment. Once inside, she opened her pack and took out the silver buckeye and bottle. Her smile faded. Buckeye and bottle in hand, Mirabel started to think about what had happened in the grove. Her heart started beating faster and the terror of her dream experience engulfed her. She decided to call Janey. *She will know what to do.*

Feeling panicky, Mirabel dialed Janey's number, her breaths coming in fast, short gasps.

Chapter Three

*J*aney sat in her plush easy chair, meditating. The chair was a special gift to herself, and she had experienced some of her most profound meditations in it. Now she nestled in and was drifting into her inner world. The sound of her cell phone startled her. Normally, she would have turned it off, but she had forgotten. She felt an urge to pick it up. "This is Janey."

"Ja-Janey, I had a dream, and it was awful and I don't know what to do."

"Mirabel?"

"Oh, yes, it's me. I was in an old buckeye grove in the foothills of Mt. Diablo and I had this dream, and...I got stuck in a tree."

"Okay, take a deep breath." Janey paused. "Good. Now take another and then tell me what happened."

Mirabel's panic was a palpable wave coming full force through the phone. Janey talked her down by getting her to focus on her breath and grounding herself.

"Remember how I taught you to focus on your breathing? Breathe in, filling your lungs and belly, and then exhale fully.

Just notice your breath; focus on the breath and allow your shoulders to drop and your jaw to relax. Good, you're doing great." Janey consciously used her softest power voice from deep in her center as she guided Mirabel.

After Mirabel calmed down, they decided to go to Janey's favorite oak tree the next day and do a protection ritual.

• • •

The next morning Janey gathered together her ritual supplies and placed them in a pack, which she set on the old, hand-woven Navajo blanket she had inherited from her grandmother, Nana. Janey loved her grandmother. Nana had been a respite from the dogmatic religion of her parents. Her mother and Nana had not gotten along too well due to her mother's adoption of her father's "faith," which had created a break in their relationship. When Janey was able to see Nana, Nana had infused her with independence and compassion, eventually allowing Janey to forge her own path away from the harsh reality of her parents' involvement with an extreme fundamentalist church. Janey held the blanket close, recalling the story Nana had told her about its origins.

"It was a gift from an old Navajo woman I met on a trip out West. She said I was a kindred spirit from the island across the sea. She said it would help me tune into the spirits of this land."

Janey treasured the blanket as much as she missed her Nana. She remembered how Nana had taught her herb lore. One summer, Janey was allowed to stay with Nana. Every day they would go out to the woods together, and Nana would show her some of the wild plants she could use for healing. Other plants were grown in the garden. Nana taught her to close her eyes, place her palms near the plant, and feel the energy of the plant before cutting it.

"Always ask permission from the elementals first," Nana said, "and be sure to thank the plants before you cut them. Leave an offering of water afterwards."

Nana also taught her how to read the tarot. She had her draw a card and meditate on it every day. Only when the day was done was Janey allowed to read about the card from the book Nana gave her.

Nana's death had prompted Janey's departure from Missouri and sent her on an adventure that led her to California. When Janey arrived, she made friends who introduced her to Wicca, an earth-based spiritual practice, and she studied and eventually became an ordained priestess. It was a path that followed the longing in her heart for the world to be imbued with magic. She always believed that, somewhere along the way, humans had lost touch with magic and it had faded from existence. In her life she had experienced the simple magics: the mystery of life as it burst forth from a seed and grew into a plant, the energies that accompanied the changing of the seasons as the great wheel of the year turned every year. She remembered the magic of her early childhood, before her mother adopted fundamentalist Christianity and tried to sever her ties to the wonder of the natural world around her. As Janey took on Wicca, she learned to attune herself to the energies, and could now sense the vibration when she cast a circle with her athame. She prayed that one day she would be shown something beyond these simple, subtle experiences.

• • •

Janey arrived in front of Mirabel's apartment punctually. Mirabel was waiting outside. She hurried to the car, opened the door, and settled herself in the passenger's seat.

Janey looked at her and smiled. "Good morning, Mirabel. I hope you slept well." She reached over and hugged her friend. "It will be all right." She drew back and looked at Mirabel. "Are you with this? I think it will help."

Mirabel nodded and sat fidgeting while Janey put the car in gear and drove. When they arrived at the park, Janey got out and opened the trunk. She pulled out a loaded backpack and her Navajo blanket. Mirabel had a small pack that she had kept in the front seat as they drove to the site.

"Do you want to put anything in my backpack?" Mirabel nodded at the pack Janey was maneuvering onto her back. "That looks heavy."

"Nope, I'm good."

Janey threw the Navajo blanket over her arm, shut the trunk, and locked the car. They started up the trail with Janey in the lead. Climbing upwards, they followed a trail through a wooded area, which eventually opened to savannah grasslands. They passed a few ponds and headed into another heavily wooded area. Entering the copse, Janey breathed in the fusion of earthy humus and minty bay, and turned to look at Mirabel, who appeared to be doing the same.

Janey remembered when she first moved to the area and had come to this park. The oak trees drew her in. They were the grandmothers of this land and reminded her of Nana. Her breathing deepened and she completely relaxed, safe and at home under their boughs. They whispered secrets to her—secrets she could not yet understand. Someday she would crack the code.

This part of the trail was much darker than the open grassland due to heavy, leaf-laden boughs of oaks and bay trees. As they walked down the trail, the trees eventually opened to let in more light. The trail they followed veered off to the left and climbed a hill with a grove of oaks and some scrub.

Janey walked up and placed her hand on the large oak at the center of the knoll. Feeling the energy of the tree enter her, she said, "Greetings, friend. We've come to honor you and ask for permission to do some ritual work under your sacred boughs." She stood in silence for some time, her hand on the trunk, until a warm tingle penetrated her hands—the signal that she had consent from the tree. She looked at Mirabel and said, "Let's set up."

Janey spread out the Navajo blanket, then emptied her pack and placed several objects around the blanket's colorful surface. Next, she asked Mirabel to sit on the blanket at the base of the tree. Mirabel sat under the large oak, legs crossed, with her back leaning against the trunk.

"I won't sink into the tree, will I?" Mirabel whispered through a forced smile.

Janey understood her friend was trying to normalize with her weak attempt at humor. She smiled and shook her head with reassurance. She sat across from Mirabel, legs crossed in front of her yoga style. Scattered on the blanket around them were the implements of ritual. The women sat in silence. Janey picked at the splotch of dark red wax that had spilled on the blanket the last time it was used. She hadn't figured out how to remove the wax, and it still bothered her that she had damaged the blanket.

Janey blushed, suddenly shy under the spotlight of Mirabel's gaze and expectation. She took a deep breath, stopped picking at the wax, and looked up at Mirabel. In this light, she could just make out a halo of indefinable shimmer that hovered around Mirabel, more discernible when her gaze was unfocused, and she resisted the impulse to caress the contours of her friend's face. A sinking, heavy feeling right below her belly button informed her of her friend's fear—a cloud that muted her shimmer. Janey yearned to understand the mystery of her friend. She looked at Mirabel's eyes, and could see the flashes of purple she had noticed the first time they met.

Mirabel tended to be edgy and nervous, and Janey could sense an immense sadness under the veneer of cheerfulness Mirabel exhibited. Janey intuited that Mirabel did not wish to burden others with her sorrow. Her friend carried such deep grief; anguish so heavy that Janey could feel it tug on her own heart when they were together. She had introduced the practice of meditation to Mirabel in an effort to soothe her.

Janey thought back to the day not long ago when she had become one with a dragon that appeared in her meditation. She was in her easy chair when a doorway opened in her mind. She remembered how a simple shift in her attention had moved her through the door, and suddenly, she faced a dragon. When it looked at her, she merged with it. An incredible surge moved through her as the dragon lifted its wings and flew. Somehow, she had set her mind aside, which allowed her to become the dragon. Merged, they flew through mysterious, dark tunnels lined with shimmering blue rings that pulsed as they went by. She was infused with energy that spread out from her core and made her fingers tingle. She could feel the life and magic within her, until her frightened mind came back in and interrupted the experience, and she tumbled out of the dragon to find herself back in her easy chair. Since that day, she stood taller, more centered in her own power than she ever had before.

Janey looked over at her friend. "Are you comfortable here? The oaks don't frighten you now, do they?"

"No, but I don't want to go back to that buckeye grove anytime soon. The oaks feel... grandmotherly. It feels safer here."

Janey didn't know the whole story of Mirabel's encounter at the buckeye grove, as Mirabel hadn't shared the specifics of the dream. That could wait. She did know how thoroughly spooked Mirabel had been by her panicked demeanor on the phone the previous night. Janey knew she had to provide a safe space for Mirabel, so they were there to cast a cloak of protection around her until she was ready to face whatever it was that haunted her.

Janey reached across and took Mirabel's hands in hers. "Mirabel, focus on your breath. Good. Now, sink inside and find the great tree trunk at the core of your being. Sense the immensity of that trunk and follow it down to where it is rooted deep in the eternity inside you."

Nestled under the oak, they sat in silence a moment. Finally, Janey gently let go of Mirabel's hands and picked up the athame at her side. The athame was a magic tool—an obsidian blade that fit in the palm of her hand, black as the fertile earth, but it shone white where the sunlight hit its shiny surface. The athame was so reflective it picked up the various green, brown, and blue hues of the world around them. This, along with the sharp edges that cut through space, was the nature of its power and why she had chosen it.

She stood up and walked around the blanket in a clockwise circle, holding the athame out, chanting under her breath, "Spirit of the oak, spirits of this land, sanctity of our hearts, goddess of the deep, we ask for your presence here to lend us a hand." She chanted four times as she walked each of the four quarters of the circle, using the athame to pierce the air and cut out a circle of space around them. Next, she stepped into the center and cut another circle from earth to sky and back to earth again, this time chanting, "Spirits of the sky, spirits of the earth, sanctity of our hearts, goddess of the center, we ask for your presence here to lend us a hand."

Janey's skin tingled. She could sense the sphere of energy around them.

Mirabel opened her eyes and sucked in a sharp intake of air.

What was that about? Janey wondered, observing her friend.

Mirabel looked at her hands, turning them over to look at her palms. She started to breathe fast and hard. Janey heard her sharp breaths and placed a calming hand on her shoulder, reminding her, "Close your eyes and take deep, slow breaths. Concentrate on the tree trunk inside you."

Mirabel started to feel calmer.

Janey nodded. "Are you ready to continue?" She sat back down again, picked up a small box decorated with dragonflies, and opened the lid. She told Mirabel, "Imagine wrapping your fear with a cord and place it in this box."

Mirabel made the wrapping motions with her hands as instructed.

Janey said, "Envision your fear like a red, spiky ball. Cover the spikes up with the cord and render them smooth and prickless." Janey held up the box, bowing her head toward it. "Now, place the bundle in the box." She shut the lid and closed the latch once Mirabel had pulled her hands away. Janey handed the box to Mirabel, along with a small lock and key, and said, "Lock the box and place it on the blanket."

Now it was time to create a protective cloak for Mirabel. Janey lit a candle and placed it in the center of the blanket between them. She grabbed a bowl of seawater from one edge of the blanket and brought it next to the candle. She picked up a shell with dried sage leaves in it and placed that in the center with the candle and bowl. Janey picked up the athame again and placed it in the bowl of seawater. She dipped her finger into the cool water, and used it to draw a pentacle on Mirabel's forehead.

"You have such a delicate touch. That feels good," Mirabel sighed.

Janey picked up the sage, passed it through the candle flame, took the athame out of the water, and passed it through the sage smoke. Mirabel responded by breathing in deeply. As the sharp, spicy scent enveloped them, Janey saw Mirabel's shoulders relax, and the tension in her own belly released.

Janey passed the athame through the candle flame. She told Mirabel, "Since this athame itself represents earth, it now holds the energy of all the elements: air, water, fire and earth." Using the athame, Janey drew a cloak around Mirabel, intoning over and over again, "Air, earth, fire, and water, combine your powers, protect this woman. Air, earth, fire, and water, combine your powers, protect this woman." Once the cloak was drawn, she raised it to the sky and declared, "So mote it be."

Mirabel looked up and Janey smiled down at her. The ritual had calmed Mirabel remarkably. When Janey cast the circle, Mirabel had seen blue flames and felt the energy in her palms. Initially it had frightened her, because it reminded her of her dream in the buckeye grove. But she trusted Janey implicitly, and she relaxed, definitely safer inside her skin now.

"The protection cloak is created. Now repeat after me to lock it in." Janey sat down in front of Mirabel and chanted three times, allowing Mirabel to repeat her words between each invocation. "With this cloak, I am protected. I am protected within this cloak. Hold me fast, protected by the powers of air, earth, water, and fire."

Once the invocation was done, Janey took Mirabel's hands and they sat in silence, absorbing the ritual and each other. In Janey's loving hands on this blanket under the oak, Mirabel felt secure. A soft calmness permeated her being, allowing her to relax further. The present enveloped her like a subtle blanket, and she heard the rustle of the oak leaves above her head along with the repetitive *tsick-a-der-der* of an oak titmouse, followed by a chorus of soft *tsip tsip* calls from the busy flock of bushtits flitting around the branches of the oak. The scent of sage lingered until a breeze wafted across her, caressing her cheeks and picking up tendrils of hair, tickling her forehead.

Mirabel was suddenly filled with peace—something so rarely experienced in her life. She started to cry silent tears. They tracked down her cheeks, dropping and christening her blouse and lap. Unlike the shuddering bouts of weeping that overcame her fairly often throughout her life, these tears were sweet. She opened into a new awareness inside herself, to a name she couldn't quite remember, but she heard it in her mind. *Shi-ahhh...* it started and tapered off, and then again, *Shi-ahhh...* She melted into the soft embrace of a silent presence that reached toward her from the bottom of her being, and she lingered in this sublime awareness even as she could still hear and feel all the sensations of her surroundings under the oak tree. Her deepest self and her environs were bound together in a profound dance of life that flowed through and around her being.

Mirabel had never before lingered in such profound stillness. Reluctantly, she opened her eyes when Janey gently whispered her name.

"Mirabel, Mirabel, open your eyes."

Mirabel gazed into Janey's gentle brown eyes. Her gaze caressed her with love and compassion, and she swelled with immense gratitude for her friend. She released a silent prayer of thanks to the universe for Janey's presence in her life.

Janey said, "I hate to say it, you look so peaceful, but it's time to wrap this up." She squeezed Mirabel's hands before letting go of them.

Mirabel sat still while Janey picked up the athame and opened the sphere she had created around them, thanking the spirits she had called in as she turned counter clockwise. Next, she blew out the candle flame, poured the seawater under the oak, and scattered the now cold ashes of sage over the wet earth. She packed up her tools and implements, stowed them in her pack, and handed the decorated dragonfly box to Mirabel, telling her, "Be sure to keep this in a safe place."

Together they walked back down the trail. Janey turned to Mirabel and said, "Someday you will have to tell me the whole story of your dream under the buckeye, but not today."

Mirabel, now enveloped in warm relief, gazed warily toward a dark and heavy future.

Chapter Four

Mirabel's invisible cloak gave her a sense of being wrapped in a protective shell that warded off any negative energy. She was finally able to let loose and enjoy herself. She put the dragonfly box with the rest of her secret cache, and the crystal fairy was given the new job of guarding it. After rearranging her cache, she proceeded to ignore it. After the ritual with Janey, and in anticipation of her date with Matt, Mirabel put on a whole new attitude. She actually felt... *happy*.

That evening Matt arrived at the coffee shop half an hour early, and hung out at a table by the door. Mirabel did her closing routine and looked his way every once in a while, stealing glances and smiling shyly at him. She shivered inwardly when she looked at him, as she could see he watched her with an awestruck look, and it pulled at her heartstrings. His presence sent delicious little tremors through her limbs.

Oh boy, I am in trouble already and I barely know him!

He seemed so innocent and so full of goodwill. It made her feel safe and warm despite the shivers, which were definitely not unpleasant. This was the first time in her life she had experienced these sensations, and it was delightfully overwhelming.

After she closed the shop, they strolled around downtown Walnut Creek and found an open restaurant close to the old section of town. The restaurant had a covered patio and they chose to sit outside and enjoy the evening air while they ate a light meal. The heat lamps in the patio made it comfortable to sit outside in the cool weather.

"How much do you ride the trails around here?" Mirabel asked.

"I get out as often as I can, when I can get away from the shop."

"Shop?"

"Yeah, I have a bike shop called Shell Ridge Bike Shop and Sports Bar. We sell and repair bikes and the bikers can hang out at the bar next door."

"How did you end up in that business?"

"Well, I kind of fell into it. I thought I was going to be a surfer, but that didn't work out. I moved to California after I finished school, with plans to live in Santa Cruz. Once I arrived I found out how expensive it was and ended up here."

"That's funny. I was going to live in San Francisco and ran into the same issue. That's how I ended up here. But that still doesn't explain the bike shop."

Matt smiled. "As luck had it, I found a job at the bike shop. You see, I never became a surfer and picked up mountain biking instead. The shop was where I met Doug."

"Who's Doug?"

"Doug was like a second dad to me—actually, more like my dad than my dad, if you know what I mean. He took me under his wing. I trained with him, won some local races, and I did some modeling for the shop. He always said it was my local fame from winning the bike races here that made the shop what it was. That wasn't true. He was what made the shop what it is."

"What do you mean Doug *was*...isn't he still around?"

Matt's face lost its smile and he shook his head.

"Oh, I'm sorry, I didn't mean to pry."

"No, it's okay. It just still hurts sometimes. He was such a great guy. I guess you could say I loved him. He died a few years ago. Pancreatic cancer."

"I'm so sorry. I can tell he meant a lot to you."

"Yeah, he did. He gave me everything. I moved in to help take care of him before they moved him to hospice. It was horrible to watch him deteriorate. I have him to thank for everything. He didn't have children of his own. That's how I inherited the shop and his house. I'd give it all back in a minute if it meant he would still be alive."

Mirabel was at a loss for words, but she could see Matt's grief. She reached over and took his hand. "Seems like he was lucky to have had you, too."

"He did a lot for all the bikers in the area. They loved the concept Doug came up with. Come to the shop, buy your bike parts, and fix your own bike. Of course, people could always have the shop fix it as well, but a lot of the bikers are into do-it-yourself, and Doug recognized that and turned it into a profitable business. He put the sports bar next door, so the place became a destination. He mentored me and I learned the ropes from him."

"I'd like to see it sometime."

"Of course, but you'll have to put up with the gang and all the shop talk. Are you sure you want to subject yourself to that?"

"Yes, I do. Anyway, maybe we can go for a ride sometime and then stop for something to eat."

"That would be fun. So, you said you were going to live in San Francisco but it was too expensive. Where are you from?"

"Montana."

"Montana? What brought you here?"

"The winters are harsh. I wanted a nicer climate. I like winter here much better," she told him. "It gets so cold in Montana. Winter here is like spring there, only better."

"What was it like growing up there?"

"I never fit in. I think I was meant to be here," she responded, leaving out the details about being teased and feeling desolate and lonely all the time.

He gazed at her warmly and smiled. She liked being the recipient of that green-eyed admiration. He was easygoing, charming, and funny. They joked about stray golf balls, pretend mountain lions, and arrogant mountain bikers.

They decided to take another stroll after eating and Mirabel took Matt by the cupcake store, which unfortunately was closed. They peered in the window together at the enticing line-up of cupcakes, and Mirabel let out a sigh of longing.

"I could get a brick and break the window," Matt laughed.

Together they expanded upon a tale of breaking in, getting caught, and landing in jail with frosting smeared across their faces and hands.

Eventually, it got late and even the coffee shops and bars closed. Matt walked Mirabel to her apartment instead of driving her. They both wanted to prolong the evening. He left her at her apartment door, but not before cupping her chin in his hand, looking into her eyes, then bending down to kiss her shyly, tenderly brushing his lips against hers, careful not to force himself on her, but waiting until her lips parted slightly as she arched herself toward him, asking for it. Mirabel was grateful for his tenderness and deference. Before he left, they agreed to see each other again.

Mirabel swayed her way through her apartment in a happy swoon. Typically reticent and shy, now her body filled with giddy liveliness. She called Janey, warbling about her evening.

On the other end of the conversation, Janey listened as her heart sank. Matt sounded like a great guy, but she couldn't help feeling like she had missed her chance somehow. *Maybe I should have let her know how I feel?* Sometimes it was so hard being attracted to the same sex, especially when the inclinations of your beloved weren't clear. Janey was afraid to scare her friend off by jumping in too soon. Now it was already too late.

"That's wonderful," she lied as Mirabel told her about the date, and waxed ecstatic about Matt's green eyes.

"Oh, Janey, I want you to meet him. He loves nature, like us."

Janey reluctantly agreed that she was going to have to meet him. After she hung up the phone, she sighed. *Well, I can't very well hate him. He did help her and he sounds sweet.* Still, she felt remarkably jealous and didn't like it. Jealousy wasn't the type of emotion a compassionate person should harbor. *I'm going to have to do some kind of letting-go ritual. I'll look for the right candle tomorrow at work.* Janey sat in her easy chair and tried to meditate, finally giving up and allowing her tears to break free. *I want her in my life no matter what, even if I just have to be a friend.* Dejected, she crawled into bed and snuggled with Tarsi, her cat and dedicated companion.

● ● ●

The next few weeks for Mirabel were a whirlwind of spending time with Matt, working at the coffee shop, and taking walks with Janey. Her friend seemed kind of distant and preoccupied. Mirabel asked her if everything was okay, but Janey just shrugged it off.

"I've been doing a lot of readings, and it kinda takes it out of you," she said.

Since Matt often stopped by to get a cup of coffee, hang out at the coffee shop, and ogle at her, Mirabel had become the brunt of ribbing from all her friends at work. The girls oohed and ahhed about how cute he was, and he had a knack for making all the baristas—male or female—feel comfortable and at ease.

Mirabel and Matt biked all his favorite East Bay bike trails. One day they made a special trip to Point Reyes National Seashore, which Mirabel fell in love with from the moment they arrived. The mix of Douglas fir-covered coastal mountains and the open savannah-like grasslands was wonderful. The ocean and estuary made it romantic and timeless. Depending

45

on where you were in the park, the air could be steeped in fog and mist or clear and sunny. Looking toward the east from the coast, the blue sky in the distance created a surreal border, imbuing the atmosphere with mystery. As the day aged, the fog broke up and the sun pushed through along the beaches, brightening and clarifying the ridges and tree lines. They spent the day hiking from the visitor center over the coastal range and down to the beach, where they poked around in tide pools and soaked in the sea air. Toward the end of the day, they drove to the Drakes Estuary and bought oysters from the Drakes Bay Oyster Company. They brought them home and roasted them on the grill at Matt's place, and ate them with barbeque sauce and red wine.

They were sitting on the couch together holding hands when Mirabel felt Matt bend to look at her. She turned to gaze up into his incredible green eyes. She just wanted to melt into him as he shyly leaned over to kiss her. The touch of his lips on hers was warm and soft as he tenderly parted her lips and pressed his tongue forward, then pulled her tongue into his mouth, gently sucking and igniting a sudden fire in her groin. Any will she had to wait longer was lost in that moment. He picked her up and carried her off to the bedroom. He removed her clothes, one garment at a time, kissing every corner of her body as he discarded each piece. He did this with such tender passion that each kiss brought with it the dual sensation of warmth and tingle to that particular body part, but also had the effect of building the sweet pulsing tension between her legs, so that when his mouth finally moved there to her most vulnerable, tender place, her entire body exploded in waves of ecstasy. When he finally entered her, she was open and ready and they moved together, pouring themselves into each other and filling the empty places with joy and pleasure. They alternated between holding and caressing each other, and making love late into the hours of the night. Eventually, they fell asleep in each other's arms, their desire satiated and their bodies exhausted.

Mirabel woke up late the next morning to the smell of bacon and the sound of a very out-of-tune Matt singing in the kitchen.

"Way down yonder in the yankitee yank, a bullfrog jumped from bank to bank, just because he had nothing better for to doo, oooh, ooh, ooh, ooh."

Laughing, she threw on his T-shirt and joined him in the kitchen to find him creating an omelet with sautéed onions, dill, and Havarti cheese. He had sliced oranges, bacon laid out on the plates, and English muffins in the toaster. He handed her a cup of her favorite Earl Gray tea. He flipped her omelet, let it cook a few more seconds, then turned the perfect omelet onto her plate and handed it to her with a big, goofy smile. Next, he cracked a couple more eggs, whisked them, and started his own omelet. He turned and asked her, "Can you manage the muffins for me?"

While she guarded the toaster, he finished his omelet, returning to a repeat belting of his bullfrog song and winking at her. After all preparations were complete, they sat down to a sumptuous breakfast. Mirabel could not think of a more ideal way to start the day than over an omelet and tea with Mr. Matt Gallagher, extraordinary lover and cook.

• • •

While Mirabel's life continued in a rhythm of work and time spent separately with Matt or Janey, she became frustrated with her inability to get them all together in one place. For some reason she had a hard time arranging for Janey and Matt to meet. It seemed that Janey always had something to do and couldn't make it. But she knew Matt was anxious to meet her, as Mirabel had frequently lauded her virtues to him.

When Mirabel was alone, her thoughts would eventually turn to that day in the buckeye grove. She would shudder with fear, and grief would claw at her heels. When this happened, she would push the memory aside and busy herself with cleaning or creating. She found a bead shop in downtown

Walnut Creek and started collecting beads. She loved to sit at the kitchen table and pour the beads over her hands, letting them dribble into a glass bowl and listening to the pleasant clinking of glass hitting glass, until the last one left her hand and she grabbed another handful, repeating the gesture. It calmed her and she reveled in all the rich colors and patterns on the lamp-work glass beads. She used these to create earrings, necklaces, and bracelets for herself, Janey, and the other girls at the shop.

Mirabel also developed an obsession with fairies and started collecting more fairy figurines, creating little fairy altars all around her apartment. Matt would joke about her enchanted fairyland when he came over. The beads and fairies were a convenient distraction when Mirabel was alone. Having Matt in her life allowed her to pretend that nothing had ever happened in the buckeye grove, and that her former sadness was just a passing phase. Every once in a while, a tremor of fear, or the creep of sadness would invade her being, but she quickly suppressed it, pretending all was perfect.

The only thing that is not perfect is that Matt and Janey haven't met.

Tired of trying to coordinate a meeting between her two friends, Mirabel finally took Matt into Mystic Dolphin and forced the meeting. Janey appeared surprised, but Mirabel could tell Matt liked Janey immediately. When they arrived, Janey was between tarot readings and there was another associate taking care of customers, so Janey suggested they go have coffee together. Mirabel relaxed. She had begun to wonder if Janey was avoiding meeting him.

For her part, Janey finally had to give in when Mirabel brought Matt into the store. She had in fact been avoiding it. She knew that once she met him, she would be unable to escape the truth of their relationship. Up to this point, she had done numerous rituals and affirmations, trying to let go of her desire for Mirabel, but none of them ever held. She always caved when she saw Mirabel. She loved her and wanted more. She couldn't help it. Still, she was surprised to find that she liked Matt, and it was obvious he adored Mirabel as much as she did. And he was funny. Despite her jealousy, she enjoyed being in his company. He seemed genuinely curious about her spiritual inclinations, her work at Mystic Dolphin, and asked a lot of questions about tarot and magic.

"How do you do a tarot reading?"

"Well, I always ask the client to put their energy into the cards before I draw them, and then I read them," she responded, not knowing how deep to go.

"But how do you know what they mean?"

"It's a combination of a couple of things. It helps to know the meaning of the cards, but it's also an intuitive thing. The cards tell a different story for each client."

"What is that intuitive thing like? Where does it come from?"

She thought it was an intelligent question, not one a skeptic would likely ask. He seemed interested, not disparaging, and now he had earned her respect. "I am a kinesthetic intuitive. I feel something in my gut and then I can see the story in the cards."

"How did you learn that?"

"It actually took me a long time to understand it. I have to translate my gut feelings, and that wasn't always easy. I learned to meditate and somehow that helped. It opened me up and made me less anxious about doing it right. I don't always have a strong hit with a client, but it's gotten pretty consistent."

"Wow, that's fascinating. Will you do a reading for me sometime?"

"Well, I usually don't do readings for friends. They are too close and it makes it harder to see things because I am already biased," she lied. She didn't want to see what was in the cards for Matt. "I know I just met you, but," she looked over at Mirabel, "to be honest, it's a bit of a conflict for me to do a reading for you since Mirabel is my best friend. I am afraid I am going to have to pass."

He looked disappointed, but he accepted her response graciously. "That makes sense. I don't want to get between the two of you. Mirabel talks about you all the time, and I can see why she adores you."

You already have gotten between us, but you'll never know about that. Janey smiled warmly at him. He was a genuinely nice man and she couldn't hold it against him. She completely understood why he was so besotted with Mirabel. *He's the lucky one.*

After Mirabel had forced the meeting, Janey started hanging out with them more and they developed an easy camaraderie. Knowing Matt actually made it easier for Janey, rather than harder. The three of them enjoyed hikes together, and Matt asked Janey to teach him about the energies. Often they would stop at special trees and she would guide his hands on the trunks, instructing him on how to sense the energy. Despite his interest, he liked to tease her about her "witchy ways," and she put up with it because she knew he respected her and was just being mischievous. It was part of his charm.

Mirabel was happy to have them all together at last. She watched her friend and her lover as Janey placed his hands on the trees and instructed Matt on the properties of magic and the vagaries of energy. *Almost perfect,* she thought, mystified by what was missing.

To fill in what was missing, Mirabel started a new quest. It started when she checked out the new library across from Mystic Dolphin. She decided to look up mythology to find out more about fairies. That quest soon developed into an obsession that extended beyond fairies. Matt bought her a laptop so she could do more searching online, and she began to study different mythological creatures in her free time alone. She loved the stories of Pegasus, the winged horse from Greek mythology. *What a majestic being.* She wanted to see one, and dreamed about riding the majestic creature.

Another creature fascinated her, and also gave her the chills. She ran across it after typing "mythological creatures" into Google. It was called the manticore. She looked it up on

Wikipedia. *The manticore is a legendary creature similar to the Egyptian Sphinx. It has the body of a red lion, and a human head with three rows of sharp teeth. The tail is like a scorpion. It was known as the man-eater,* it read.

The man-eater, eh? I wouldn't want to run into one of those.

She read more. The myth of the manticore was Persian in origin, also called *martichora* by the Indians.

Mirabel thought, *these creatures have to have some origin in truth. Why does this all feel so familiar to me?*

Something kept drawing her back to the myths of the past. The more she read the more she felt like she belonged in another world—another time.

Chapter Five

Summer rolled in on the heels of spring and Matt and Mirabel went on an excursion to Briones Regional Park, where she and Janey had performed the protection ritual. The park bordered the suburbs in the Walnut Creek area, and the highest peak in the park offered panoramic views— canyons dense with bay, oak, and maple trees all between large, open tracts of grassy hills. Mirabel explained how she and Janey had gone there once and performed a ritual under an oak tree on Janey's Navajo blanket. Matt pantomimed mock disdain at the mention of ritual. Mirabel enjoyed how he liked to tease Janey about her "woo-woo witchy" ways. She knew he loved Janey for being such a good friend to her, and she could tell he trusted Janey and felt at ease in her presence.

Mirabel didn't tell him about the details of the protection ritual. She hadn't shared with Matt what happened in the buckeye grove, preferring to push the experience into the deep recesses of her mind. He didn't press for more information, figuring it was a "female" thing that he didn't need to know about.

Matt and Mirabel rode their bikes up the trail at the end of Old Briones Road. The climb was tough, but they were both strong, determined riders, and enjoyed the exercise. At the top of the hill they made their way up to a bench overlooking some old cow ponds situated next to a heavily wooded area. There they laid out a cloth and ate a light lunch. The sun added warmth on this early fall day, making it pleasant and comfortable to be outside. The grass was already dried out from the summer heat. After lunch, they romped around, teasing each other and rolling in the crunchy, dry grass. Afterwards, Mirabel had burrs and foxtails all over her clothing. As she sat on the bench picking them out, Matt called to her.

"Mirabel, come look what I found!"

Matt stood near a grand old oak just inside the cow gate that separated the wooded area from the open grassland. He was looking into a hole in the trunk. Mirabel walked over and peeked in. Inside she found a figurine of a fairy. Hanging on the tip of the fairy's wing was an amethyst and white-gold ring. Mirabel put her hands to her mouth in surprise as Matt reached in to grab the ring, then went down on one knee.

"Mirabel Mairead McInness, I love you. Will you marry me?"

Mirabel squealed and threw her head back, then laughed aloud. She looked at Matt and said, "Matt Gallagher, you are full of surprises and tricks!" Cocking her head to one side, she added, "And of course I will marry you!"

He placed the ring on her finger, then stood up and circled his arms around her waist, picked her up, and spun her around. When he set her down, she asked, "How did you know I don't like diamonds?"

"I didn't, but the purple of the amethyst matches something in your lovely eyes. I couldn't resist getting an amethyst instead of a diamond. And, I thought if you didn't agree to marry me, it would be easier for you to keep the ring as a token of my undying love for you without feeling like you would be obligated to give it back. Now I am doubly glad that I didn't get a diamond. That would have been a disaster!"

Mirabel and Matt lingered until the sun started to set, then packed up and rode back down the hill to the parking lot where they had left the car.

Matt was giddy. *She said yes!* He couldn't believe his good fortune. Before he met Mirabel, Matt would marvel at how he had landed in a lifestyle so perfect for him. The only thing that was missing was love. But now he had Mirabel and she had just agreed to marry him. She had awed him from the moment she almost ran into him that day on the trail. There was something otherworldly about Mirabel that was hard to describe. She was so earthy, but she glowed. That she loved and collected fairies fit her perfectly. *She's like a fairy herself.* He laughed, a little discomfited with this thought, but when he was around her, he couldn't help himself. There was also something fragile about her, like a spider web—fragile to the human hand sweeping the gossamer silk away, but in the context of the world of insects and small prey, full of tensile, flexible strength. He was not sure about the context of her strength, but he could sense something. She exuded mystery and her fragile strength was one of the reasons he had fallen hopelessly in love with her.

This paradoxical fragility made Matt want to hold her in his arms and protect her. He was aware of her sadness, which sat just under the surface, and it terrified him. He could sense that it bore the potential to tear her from his life. She inspired his protective nature. He longed to be her hero. He wanted to ward off the dark secrets that lay under the surface. He didn't know how, but he made it his mission to protect her through whatever she had to face. In the meantime, he would do his best to make her happy, to bring whatever joy he could into her life. His love for her was the marrow of his bones, the tissue that created the blood that surged through him, feeding his heart and igniting his desire. She became the purpose of his life. Everything else was extraneous. As long as she wanted to pretend that he was what she needed, he would be the stage for her fantasy, and one day when she finally had to face her fate, he would do everything he could to support and protect her, even if he had to let her go. But he would never stop loving her.

Once he had met her friend Janey, he often found himself wondering what part she played in this tale. He knew Janey loved Mirabel too, and he was grateful for the support she gave her. He knew Janey's love and compassion for Mirabel ultimately helped him. *Janey has her own kind of magic, and that magic helps Mirabel.* As far as he could tell, his life had always been promised to Mirabel, to be whatever she needed and to let go when she needed.

Nevertheless, these promises were easy to forget in the midst of the fantasy. They lay under the surface and need not intrude upon his day-to-day happiness. In the newness of their love, Matt and Mirabel were happy—their bodies satiated with lovemaking, their minds engaged in shared interests, and time filled with bike riding, hikes with Janey, work, and now, wedding plans.

Janey convinced them to do a hand-fasting rather than a traditional marriage, and the ceremony was held in late October when the weather became more pleasant. The days were still warm and the evenings cool. They wed outdoors amidst a cadre of bikers, coffee shop baristas, and Mystic Dolphin employees who hiked up the hill at Briones. Janey, being an ordained priestess, officiated. They said their vows at sunset on a hill that overlooked the eastern portion of the bay in the distance, where the San Joaquin and Sacramento rivers merged. They were surrounded by open savannah and deep bay and oak forests behind them. A sprinkling of maple trees added a splash of yellow, orange, and red coloring to the backdrop.

The setting was as perfect as it could be. Janey tied their right hands together and they shared their vows. After vows were exchanged, all the guests formed a tunnel, holding hands high above their heads in pairs with enough space between to allow Mirabel and Matt to squeeze through with their hands still tied together. The guests hooted, hollered, and called out suggestive remarks with broad, knowing smiles as Matt and Mirabel moved through the phalanx. Janey waited at the end and welcomed them into their new life, then untied their hands, after which they were showered with flowers by the whole troupe. Next, the somewhat raucous wedding party made their way to the Shell Ridge Bike Shop and Sports Bar and partied late into the evening. Matt and Mirabel crept out at midnight and drove to the Lafayette Park Hotel in Lafayette, a town neighboring Walnut Creek. They had reserved a luxurious suite with a hot tub and champagne for the occasion. The next morning they drove up to Mendocino and spent a glorious weekend kayaking the ocean coves, hiking in the mornings, and making love in the lazy afternoons. They had a perfect honeymoon. Mirabel wondered what she had done to deserve such a lovely and easy interlude.

Chapter Six

After the honeymoon, Matt and Mirabel came home to Walnut Creek and started to build their life. Although she didn't need to work anymore, as Matt's income from the bike shop provided for them nicely, Mirabel kept her job at the coffee shop. She enjoyed her friends there, and Matt was busy during the day. She knew she needed to fill her time. For Mirabel, time spent alone was not good. It frightened her. As time passed, Mirabel's joy in her life with Matt began to fade. She dove deeper into her studies of ancient mythology, which stoked her longing and made her feel more like something was missing. Sometimes foreboding completely swept her happiness away, leaving her terrified and full of doubt. More than anything she wanted to extend the illusion that she could live this way indefinitely. Janey's magical, protective cloak was wearing thin, but Mirabel clung with ardor to the belief that her life with Matt was perfect; that her purpose was to build a life with him. Mirabel decided to put all her efforts into getting pregnant, sure that this would finally bring her the happiness that was so elusive.

A child is what I need. I can be the mother I always dreamed of having. It must be why I am feeling so sad again, because I haven't had a child to make up for what I missed.

Matt wanted children as much as Mirabel, so was quite happy to perform his duties toward this goal. Of course, it wasn't a duty, but a pleasure. Making love became the one place where Mirabel lost herself in the joy of the moment, and of course, Matt could never resist an opportunity to worship at the altar of Mirabel. One suggestive look from her swept him into a river of desire. They dove into enthusiastic and varied trysts for months, making love in secret coves in the hills, once or twice in Matt's office, and several times took themselves away to Inverness or Tahoe for the weekend. But every month, Mirabel's menses came like clockwork and soon this began to color Mirabel's moods. The inability to get pregnant frustrated and depressed Mirabel, and some days Matt would come home to find Mirabel exhausted and listless. Her mood began to impact their happiness, as well as their lovemaking.

Matt worried about Mirabel, and called upon Janey for help. So that Mirabel wouldn't over hear their conversation, he called from the shop. "Janey, I am really worried about Mirabel. She's depressed and distant, and I don't know what to do. I'm at a loss. It's been months since we've been trying to get pregnant. Each time her period starts, she is almost inconsolable."

"I know. I'm glad you called. I am worried about her too. Has she ever talked with you about her childhood?"

"Just stuff about growing up on the ranch. Her father got drunk a lot after her mom died. I think she was lonely. Do you think it's normal for her to be so distraught?"

"I don't know. I don't think so. There is something more, but I can't put my finger on it. The day you met her, she had a weird experience by a buckeye tree up on Lime Ridge. Did she ever tell you about that?"

"No, she didn't. I thought she just saw a mountain lion or heard something that scared her. What happened?"

"She said she got stuck in a tree after a dream, but I don't know the whole story. She never told me the dream. She won't talk about it. I did a ritual with her to create a protective, magical cloak, and that seemed to work for a while. Maybe we should do it again."

"Do you think it will help? I'm afraid she is going to break."

"Maybe. I can't make any promises. It did seem to help last time. Maybe I can toss a little fertility ritual in, too."

"You know that whatever you can do I will be grateful for. I know she trusts you and I'm glad you are her friend."

"We will have to work together to make this happen."

• • •

Janey invited Mirabel to hang out at Mystic Dolphin when she wasn't working or spending time with Matt. Janey was worried about Mirabel. She could sense the protective cloak was cracking and that a deep, relentless sorrow was creeping in. Mirabel often seemed tired and frayed around the edges, although she covered it well when with others. One day, during a lull in customers, Janey decided to convince Mirabel that perhaps they should renew the cloak.

"Mirabel, why don't we go back to the oak tree and do another ritual. Your cloak could probably use some renewing... and maybe we can cast a fertility spell?"

"Oh, Janey, thanks, but I will be fine. Besides, Matt and I are thinking of trying in vitro fertilization. And...no offense, but I am not sure I believe in the cloak anymore."

Janey raised an eyebrow. "Mirabel, it can't hurt. Maybe this could be one last-ditch effort before you consign your life and womb over to doctors. The cloak did seem to work last time, and remember? You felt so free afterwards. Why don't we try it one more time?"

"Wasn't the cloak to protect me from what happened that one time in the buckeye grove? I never go there anymore. And besides, I think I must have dreamed it all. It was silly."

"Well, like I said, it can't hurt. Besides, it might be fun. We can pack a lunch. It'll be just us girls out in nature…good for the soul!"

"Okay," Mirabel finally agreed.

Janey sighed, relieved. She believed her friend needed the cloak more than ever now, and she simply didn't know what else to do.

• • •

Janey had been insistent about redoing the cloak ritual. Both Matt and Janey doted over Mirabel a lot lately, overwhelming her at times. Mirabel finally agreed to do the ritual to please her friend and to get her off her back. Truthfully, she didn't want to be reminded of the incident in the buckeye grove. She wanted to believe it was a stupid dream, but a part of her knew it wasn't. She feared messing with the status quo. She didn't want to risk her fraying hold on happiness. But Janey could be pretty convincing sometimes. Mirabel wondered whether Janey had used her magic arts to influence her. They made a date for the ritual when they were both free the following week.

Chapter Seven

or the ritual this time, Janey asked Mirabel to bring something sacred with her. She said Mirabel needed to be more invested in this ritual than the last. *Whatever that means.* Mirabel went to dig out her stash from behind the books on the bookshelf that Matt had given to her for her things: the dragonfly box, which contained her fears; the silver buckeye; the two Hawthorne Drug bottles; and her original crystal fairy, which was a gift from Janey. Mirabel had hidden her items on the shelf when she moved in, finding a secret place behind her tarot books, a collection that had grown along with her relationship with Janey and time spent browsing at Mystic Dolphin. Matt was never intrusive, so she wasn't really hiding them from him as much as she wanted to ward off her past...and, unconsciously, her destiny. So she placed them there, hidden from her view and subsequently her awareness. There the items waited, biding their time until she was ready to acknowledge their importance in her life.

She reluctantly pulled the books from the shelf and set the crystal fairy aside for the moment, as she would not need her for this ritual. She eyed the dragonfly box, bottles, and buckeye. Her fears, her past, and her future fate were all contained there within. She didn't know how inextricably they were interlinked. She had put them there together—she thought, as a matter of convenience—storing them away, out of sight and out of mind. Now she drew them toward her. Gingerly lifting the box and items, she wrapped them in a scarf and placed it in her backpack.

Janey has a way of drawing me out, Mirabel thought as she prepared for their outing. Matt kept her safe and Janey kept her grounded, but Janey also demanded a certain adherence to authenticity, even when it hurt. Janey's deep-brown, wise eyes drew aside the veils of illusion and asked Mirabel to face herself. This both terrified her and attracted her. The tie that cinched it was Janey's love.

• • •

From a distance, the benevolent beings known as "the Weavers" watched over them. They knew Mirabel preferred to escape her fate, but Janey lovingly led her toward it. Neither Janey nor Mirabel were conscious of the Weavers. The pattern had already been decided long before the weaving began, and neither Janey nor Mirabel could change the warp. Together, Janey and Mirabel unknowingly plied the weft, pushing the pattern in place as surely as the beater bar on the loom would firm up and solidify the pattern.

The Weavers watched and the Creator slept; she had been sleeping for eons. But there was another who plucked at the warp, listening for the tones and timbres, looking for patterns and signs just like those with special gifts who read tea leaves, the lines on palms, or cards as set down from the mysterious mistress from far beyond. This one was the woman of the grove—the woman Mirabel had encountered in the coffee shop so many, many months ago. The very act of pulling out the bottles and the silver buckeye from behind the books on the shelf had called her forth again, unbeknownst to Mirabel, but already foreseen by those who watched and understood her fate in their benevolent but unchanging eyes. They too were rendered impotent to change the course of Mirabel's destiny, for to do so would forfeit the balance of the whole, and this they could not do. But for them, it did not come without the price of understanding Mirabel's anguish, and it caused them deep sorrow.

In compassion, they tenderly whispered prayers, which dropped down into the world like an effervescent dew, sprinkling the waters of compassion upon Mirabel, unseen by all but them. Still, though the dew was unseen, it was not unfelt by those who worked at keeping their hearts open and their spirits aware, like Janey. She transformed their dew into compassion. Eventually, this sacred dew would cool the raw fear and heartbreak that Mirabel would face in her coming journey. Though unable to change her fate, this at least they could do, and they did it with rapture.

Janey and Mirabel walked the trail to the oak tree. Once again, Janey spread out her Navajo blanket and together they laid out the implements of ritual around them. This time the Hawthorne Drug bottles and silver buckeye went into the center, where Janey asked Mirabel to place what she had brought. Janey's eyes widened in surprise when she saw what Mirabel had.

"Mirabel," she said, "those are amazing. Where did you get them?"

Mirabel looked at her and said, "They are my inheritance from my mother."

"Can I touch them?" Janey asked.

Mirabel nodded in assent.

Janey gently picked up the silver buckeye, turning it around in her hand and admiring it. She looked at Mirabel. "This is so unusual—so curious that it is shaped like a buckeye and that you are so attracted, if now frightened, of buckeye trees."

As she expressed this thought, she was suddenly struck immobile, as if nailed to the ground, her typical physical signal that something powerful was afoot. She gazed long into

Mirabel's eyes, now more worried about her friend than ever. She couldn't shake a sense of foreboding creeping through her limbs. At last, she placed the buckeye back in the center and picked up the Hawthorne Drug bottle that was full of glitter.

"Did this come from your mother, as well?" she asked. "Such a strange bottle. Hawthorne Drug. Hmm, never heard of that one before." She didn't mention to Mirabel that it was also familiar to her for some reason. The glass bottle had a purple cast and the glass was warped, like it was old. From the front and back, it appeared almost round. From the side it was narrow and had a flat bottom to allow it to stand. The name *Hawthorne Drug* adorned the label in scrolled writing, which appeared to be handwritten. But then Janey looked at the empty bottle from the woman at the coffee shop, and the label was exactly the same, making her question her analysis. The label had no other information on it, no address, and nothing about what was contained within.

"Did these both come from your mother?"

Mirabel shook her head. "It was the strangest thing. The day before I went to the buckeye grove where I had the dream, this strange woman came into the coffee shop. She ordered tea, said something strange, and then went to sit by the window. After she left I found this on her table. I brought it home with me to compare it with mine, and have had them both ever since."

Janey's sense of awe grew with every passing moment, such that she began to feel completely out of her element. She looked at Mirabel and said, "Tell me about the lady."

Mirabel told her about the woman's strange clothing and how she stood out so strongly to Mirabel, but also how no one else appeared to pay any attention to her at all.

"How odd!"

"Yes," Mirabel went on, "and then when she ordered her tea, she said the strangest thing to me. She said Shia... something...was waiting."

"Huh?" Janey responded.

"I know," said Mirabel. "That was my reaction too."

"Did you ask her who Shia—whatever—is?" Janey asked.

"No, I didn't get a chance. We were having a rush and she walked away before I could ask her. But the word was somehow familiar, even though I can't remember exactly what she said."

"Mirabel, did you ever think that this had anything to do with your experience in the grove?" Janey said, prying a little deeper.

"Well…no, not really. I tried not to think of it at all, but now that you mention it, when I was near the grove, I had an encounter with a deer that strangely reminded me of her; and then when I sat down, I kept seeing things out of the corners of my eyes that reminded me of her. At the time, I simply chalked it up to my imagination, and then afterwards, I just wanted to get out of there and forgot all about it. At first, the dream was nice…and then it became horrible. It was like everything I loved burst into flames and then it was all gone. And when I woke up, I was stuck in the tree. How does something like that happen? I don't understand it!"

Janey held Mirabel in her steady gaze, feeling more and more out of her depth. For once, she was at a loss for words. Mirabel started to breathe faster and harder, panic creeping in.

"Janey," she said, sucking in a couple of short breaths. "Janey, what does it mean?" Grabbing Janey's hand, she said, "It…it scares me. I-I-I can't…I don't want to think about it." She began shaking and put her hands to her face. Tears welled up and dropped into her palms.

"Mirabel, look at me. Take a deep breath. That is in the past. Now we are here, under this sacred oak. Bring yourself to the present. We are safe here. Remember how much better you felt last time after we did this?"

Mirabel nodded and took a long, deep breath.

Janey reached out and took her hands. "Look at me, let's ground together. Breathe in and out slowly. Let your shoulders relax and feel the earth holding you safe. Now close your eyes and find yourself inside that great tree. Feel your roots sink deep down into the earth and watch them as they anchor themselves, wrapping three times around the earth's core. Allow yourself to feel the strength that runs from these roots attached to the Great Mother Earth. That strength runs all the way back up into your physical body sitting here under this great sister oak."

Janey could see that Mirabel's panic was starting to fade as she focused on Janey's words. Once they were grounded, Janey began the ritual, following the same format she had used the last time. Once again, Mirabel wrapped up her fears and put them in the dragonfly box. This time, however, Janey added a new twist; she included a fertility rite into the ritual before creating a new cloak for Mirabel. She handed Mirabel a pregnant goddess figurine and asked Mirabel to repeat after her.

"Great Mother, may fertility grow in me. Let me conceive that I bring a new life into this world. Bless my womb with a new life." Janey looked at Mirabel and asked her to pick up the silver buckeye in the other hand, and said, "Now repeat after me again. Great Mother, as I hold my mother's gift in my hands, help me to continue my line, mother to daughter, daughter to new child. Bless my womb with a new life."

Mirabel followed Janey's instructions and repeated after her. As she spoke the words, she caressed the buckeye, stroking it with her thumb. A subtle warmth emanated from it, sending energy into her palms. She opened her palm and traced the surface with her finger, and suddenly something in her groin woke up. "Oh!" she said with a start as a tingle made its way from her vulva toward her womb. Overcome with desire, she opened her mouth and squirmed, trying to keep her sensations hidden from Janey. A secret pleasure grew inside her and she wished Matt were present to share it.

In the meantime, Janey busied herself with picking up a bag that had three separate packages in it filled with teas, which she handed to Mirabel. "These are the best herbs to promote conception. Drink three cups of tea a day, one of each. You can add peppermint for more flavor if you like. Now, hold these teas in your hands and repeat after me. Great Mother, bless these herbs so that fertility may grow in me, bless my life with a child of my heart. So mote it be."

Mirabel repeated after her. Next, Janey drew another cloak and asked Mirabel to lie down on the blanket while she sprinkled ocean water over her. She told Mirabel to just let go, to relax and focus on all her sensations, to clear her mind and let the spells begin their work. "I will be here right beside you doing the same thing."

They lay side by side for some time. The sounds of nature around them filled Mirabel's ears. The leaves of the oak rustled above her and she could hear the *tsip, tsip, tsip* of a flock of bushtits. Every once in a while an airplane would fly overhead, filling the sky with a drone. She didn't let the intrusion of human sounds annoy or distract her; they were just part of the whole of her sensation. For the first time in a while, she sighed, at peace.

Unseen by Janey and Mirabel, a lone doe had watched the proceedings from a distance. Lying there in the grove, relaxed and peaceful, Mirabel fell asleep and dreamed of a beautiful lake filled with strange flowers, and strangely sensual stirrings in her loins that soon bloomed into ecstasy as the doe watched on. When Janey eventually got up and touched Mirabel's arm, the doe turned and walked away, disappearing into the woods unnoticed.

Mirabel, afraid she had made noises in her sleep, blushed, now a little sheepish. She shyly looked up at Janey and said, "I'm afraid I fell asleep…I didn't snore," she paused, "or anything, did I?"

"No, you didn't snore or anything," Janey laughed. "Enjoying a little dream tryst, were we? Well, I guess my ritual worked to open up something in that…you know…area of your body."

Mirabel giggled, suddenly not shy anymore, but didn't give Janey any details.

Janey considered the ritual a success. She had noted Mirabel's little surprised "oh" when she was holding the buckeye, and had intuited that Mirabel had had a pretty racy dream. *I am glad I could give her a little pleasure.* She wanted to linger, but it was getting late and would be dark soon, making it difficult to get back to the car safely.

"Mirabel, we should wrap this up," Janey announced. She then completed the ritual, calling out to the four directions to thank them, and released the circle.

Together they packed up their things to go and made their way back down to the car.

Chapter Eight

Later that evening when Mirabel arrived back home, Matt was waiting for her anxiously. When she came through the door, he hopped up, took her things, and pulled her into a hug. After several moments, he drew away and looked into her face. Mirabel smiled and Matt relaxed. Mirabel seemed more at ease and happy than he had seen her in a while.

She touched his cheek and said, "Wanna go make a baby?"

Matt grinned. *How can I resist?* He took her hand and led her to the bedroom.

Mirabel tore off her clothes and started unbuttoning Matt's pants.

"Are you in a hurry?"

Mirabel giggled and pushed him onto the bed and crawled on top of him. Straddling his body, she teased him until he couldn't take it anymore, then finally guided him into her. Afterwards, they spent hours tracing the contours of each other's bodies and held each other close. Matt marveled at the smooth texture of her skin, like luxurious silk against his body. Drawing in the heady scent of her hair, he smiled, silently saying another prayer of gratitude for her presence in his life. Mirabel snuggled in further.

"I hope Janey's spell works. I want a little girl," Mirabel said.

"I am glad you have Janey. I've never known anyone quite like her. She's a good friend for both of us. I'd like a little girl, too."

• • •

Once Matt arrived at work the next day, he called Janey.

"This is Janey," she answered.

"It's Matt. I think whatever you did worked. How can I thank you? You are a godsend!"

"Glad to hear it. I could tell Mirabel was in much better spirits afterwards. I am happy to hear it appears to have stuck with her."

"What can I do for you? You have given us so much. I don't even know how to begin to repay you."

"No repayment necessary. You know I love Mirabel and would do anything for her. Keep an eye on her, though. Let me know if anything changes."

"Okay, will do, but all seems better for now." Matt hung up the phone. He had hopes. High hopes.

• • •

Mirabel religiously drank the herbal teas that Janey had given her, and as spring approached she felt healthy and hopeful. It wasn't long before the time for her period came and went with no sign of blood. Mirabel went to the drugstore not long after she missed her period and bought a pregnancy test. That night when Matt arrived home from the bike shop, he found the table set with their best china and a beautiful bouquet of flowers. A bottle of red wine was already open for him and a bottle of sparkling water for Mirabel sat next to it.

Mirabel came out to place wine glasses on the table, an apron tied around her waist and flour in her hair. She put her finger to Matt's mouth and said, "Wait..." Before he could say anything, she ran off to the bathroom to retrieve the test. She came back into the dining room with a broad smile and a skip in her step, and handed the pregnancy test to Matt.

He looked at it, then at her, and said, "Does this mean?"

"Yes," she said. "Yes! We're going to have a baby."

Matt picked her up and swung her around, put her down, and then suddenly sat down. "A baby. A baby? I'm going to be a father?" Struck with the unknown, he stammered, "I don't know how to be a father."

Mirabel came over, sat in his lap, and took his face in her hands. "Matt Gallagher, you will make the most wonderful father in the world and I wouldn't want to have a baby with anyone else."

They celebrated with a nice dinner that Mirabel had fixed for the occasion. They cuddled together on the couch afterwards, talked about setting up a nursery, and started to make plans for the baby.

"Matt, I've been thinking, wouldn't it be great to have a garden? I want my baby to have healthy, fresh foods."

"Sure. I can get some help."

The following week, Matt hired a couple of day laborers to come to the house and create a garden patch in the backyard. Mirabel pointed and directed as they cleared the sod and tilled the earth, and built planter boxes and filled them with garden soil. Mirabel planted lettuce, beets, and carrot seeds. The workers rototilled an area for tomatoes, and Matt helped her plant the tomatoes and erect cages around them. She put in squash and zucchini on the other side of the tomatoes where the workers had prepared the dirt for them.

After the workers left, Mirabel turned to Matt. She bounced as she clapped her hands and ran to give him a hug. "I'm so excited. I can't wait for tomatoes."

Mirabel kept busy and had little time to think about her experience in the buckeye grove. She existed in a bubble of progesterone satisfaction. She watched the tomatoes grow, put on fruit, and begin to ripen. *Like me.* She rubbed her tummy. "Hi, little one. I can't wait for you to see your garden."

• • •

Late summer arrived and the vines were laden with tomatoes. Mirabel decided to try her hand at canning, and contracted Matt to assist. Mirabel planned for tomatoes going into stews, spaghetti, soups, and casseroles over the winter months. She wanted fresh jars of tomatoes from the garden, as they would make flavorful dinners through the winter, making the time they spent packing and canning tomatoes in the late summer heat worth the effort. Mirabel deemed it was even more important to have the healthy food from the garden and to save it for the coming year for their growing family. She planned and divided the workload between them.

Mirabel stood over Matt as he peeled the last batch of tomatoes from the water bath. She impatiently tapped the tongs she used to pick up the jars and rocked on her feet. Matt picked up a small tomato, playfully aimed it at her, and threw it. Mirabel stood there for a moment in disbelief, eyes raised and mouth open, tomato juice dripping down her face.

"Oops," Matt said, grinning. "That was meant for your apron."

She picked up a tomato from the bath and smooshed it in his hair. The tomato burst, its juices rolling over his scalp and dripping onto his shirt.

"Oh yeah?" he said as he grabbed another tomato and pushed it on the top of her head.

"That was a perfectly fine specimen of a tomato you just wasted, Mr. Gallagher." She picked up the last tomato from the cooling bath and crushed it into his chest.

"And you are a perfectly fine specimen of a woman." He laughed, picking her up and carrying her off to the bedroom.

They both stripped down and got into the shower, washing each other's hair and lingering under the warm downpour, caressing each other's bodies. Mirabel looked down as he traced the outline of her protruding belly and gently placed his hands along the sides. She could feel the rolling movement of a little butt or foot as it pushed along the interior of her womb against his hand.

"Did you feel that?" He looked up at Mirabel, eyes wide and glistening as they filled with moisture.

"Yes, our little miracle," she said as she laid her hands over his.

• • •

Janey came by one day and Mirabel took her on a tour of the garden. Janey could see how proud Mirabel felt about her efforts, and indeed, she did seem to have a magical green thumb. Janey, delighted and surprised by how vibrant and healthy the plants were, said, "Well Mirabel, it seems you have a magic touch with plants. This goes beyond a green thumb. And look at you! You positively glow!"

Mirabel smiled broadly in response and placed her hands on her growing belly.

"May I?" Janey asked, gesturing as if to touch Mirabel's belly.

Mirabel nodded, lifted her top, and Janey placed her hands on Mirabel's bulge. Janey could feel the flutter of movement under her skin. She grinned, thrilled to feel the life growing and moving inside her friend. She looked at Mirabel's belly. Since Mirabel was so tiny, her baby bulge looked even bigger, and Janey had noticed that she was starting to waddle when she walked.

"I think this diet of fresh vegetables is doing you well. Have you been drinking the pregnancy tea I gave you?"

"Of course!" Mirabel looked at her friend. "I don't know what I would have done without you. You are my best friend and I have so much to thank you for."

"No thanks needed, Mirabel. I just want you to be happy. Anything I may have done was a pleasure."

Even though Janey was happy for Mirabel, she regretted losing the opportunity to make the relationship more before Matt came along. She loved Mirabel wholeheartedly, but she had tired of being jealous of Matt. He was such a kind, loving man. She would never want to separate them. She resigned herself to being a best friend, and she could love Mirabel freely in her own way.

"Do you want to go look at the nursery?" Mirabel asked.

"Of course, I'd love to."

Mirabel led Janey to the nursery. She had designed a fairy theme in colors of yellow and blue with touches of purple and pink. On one wall was a mural of a tree festooned with glowing fairies and fairies peeking out of the grass at the foot of the tree. Colorful butterfly decals fluttered across the ceiling. A mobile of sparkling, crystal fairies hung from the ceiling near the window, catching the sunlight and causing a kaleidoscope of colors to cascade across the painted surface.

"Ooooh, that's so magical," Janey said.

"I thought you would like that. It only happens once a day when the sun comes in at that particular angle."

A pale wooden crib was set against the wall opposite the mural and a matching changing table with drawers sat close by. Plush butterflies and animals sat scattered about the room.

"This is lovely, Mirabel. What a lucky child to sleep in here. I wish my room was half as nice!"

Together they made their way back toward the kitchen and Mirabel made tea. When Janey finally left after lingering over tea with a content Mirabel, she was relieved that things appeared to be going so well. She said a prayer under her breath, appealing to her gods for Mirabel's continued well-being.

Chapter Nine

October rolled around and now Mirabel was eight months pregnant. Her belly was large and extended, and she was starting to become uncomfortable. She still had at least a month to go, but she was anxious for the birth and the arrival of the little one. A new neighbor had moved in next door, but Mirabel had yet to see the new occupant. Unbeknownst to her, the neighbor was watching Mirabel...and waiting.

Mirabel received a letter from the Fergus County Sheriff's Office in Lewiston, Montana. The office served a wide region, including the almost nonexistent town of McClave, where she had grown up. She sat down abruptly as she started to read. Her father had died, it said, and there was a box at the office being held for her. The sheriff expressed his condolences and relayed the difficulty they had in locating her. He wrote that the box had been sitting in the office for many months already, as her father had passed in the spring. The letter went on to detail that her father had not been found for some time; that one of the locals had gone out to the shack to check on him since no one had seen him for a while. Mirabel remembered it had been his habit to go into Lewiston at least once a week, because she would go with him and sell her knitting to the local general store. The letter said they had collected any possessions salvageable from the cabin, removed the body, and buried him at the local cemetery. The old cabin had then been burned down. The letter ended with another set of condolences and inquired about what they should do with the box of items.

Mirabel called Matt, weeping. "Matt, can you come home, please?"

"What's wrong honey, is the baby…are you okay?"

"It's my dad. I got a letter. He died."

When Matt arrived, he found Mirabel sitting on the kitchen floor weeping with guilt and remorse. She handed the letter to him and he read it. When he finished, he picked her up off the floor and held her.

"I never really loved my father, but I shouldn't have left him the way I did," Mirabel said. "He must have drunk himself to death. I never knew my mother. All I knew of her was from what he told me about her death. He made sure I was clothed and fed and that I went to school, while he spent his days out with the sheep and drank himself to sleep every night."

"Mirabel, I'm so sorry. There are some people you just can't help. You had every right to leave and get out of there. He made his own choices."

Mirabel burrowed in Matt's arms for a while and eventually looked up at him. "What should I do about the box?"

"My suggestion is that you contact them and ask to have the box shipped here. It doesn't seem a good time to travel and it sounds like there is nothing left for you there, anyway."

Mirabel agreed. Her body was over-ripe and everything felt uncomfortable; sitting, sleeping, walking—all were equally awkward. She was weary of being so big and feeling so unwieldy. She couldn't imagine traveling to Montana in this shape.

The next day Mirabel called the Fergus County Sheriff's Office and asked them to send the box to their address. The sheriff said he would get it in the mail immediately. Mirabel spent the next few days holed up in the house, pacing when she couldn't sit any longer, lying down and trying to nap when she got tired of sitting, and fussing with the stuffed animals in the nursery when she couldn't sleep. The physical discomfort of late pregnancy made an unholy alliance with her impatience and sense of remorse. Even though she never loved her father, she grieved his loss and regretted that lack of closure to their relationship. *I just never felt like I belonged to him.* Yet, he had been her primary companion in her childhood and the only link she had to her mother. She wondered what she would find in the box. What odds and ends could they have gathered from the humble home of her father?

Finally, the day arrived when she found a box left at their doorstep. She called Matt at the store after the mailman left. She dreaded opening it by herself, and asked if he could come home to be with her.

"Oh, honey, can you wait till I get home? Unfortunately, I have an important meeting with the bank this afternoon I can't miss. I'm sorry, I don't want you to be alone. Why don't you call Janey?"

Mirabel fell silent, phone in hand, trying to figure out what to do.

"I can tell you aren't going to wait till I get there and I'd rather you not be alone," Matt suggested. "I wish there was a way for me to be there," he added.

Mirabel hung up and called Janey to see if she could stop by.

"Mirabel, what's up? Are you okay?"

"I am sorry to bug you, Janey, but I got bad news the other day. I received a letter about my father. He...he...passed last spring and I didn't even know."

"Oh, Mirabel. I am so sorry. Why didn't you call me? I would have come over," Janey responded.

"Oh, I know, I should have called but I didn't know what to do, and Matt came home and, well, I didn't really love my father and I didn't want to bug you."

"Bug me! Are you kidding? Don't you know how much I care about you? You *never* bug me! And, even if you didn't love your father, it is still a loss."

"Janey, sometimes I feel like this relationship is so one-sided. You always help me. What do I do for you?"

"You brighten my life, Mirabel. You are like magic. The room shines when you enter. When you smile, I can't help but feel joy. When I help you, I feel like...well, I don't know, like I am connected to something larger than myself, larger than you. I don't know how to explain it."

"Oh," Mirabel said. "I, I didn't know..." She trailed off, suddenly shy. "Well," she said after a pause, "there's more. My father left behind a few things, not much, and I received a package today and I just don't want to open it by myself. I already called Matt and he has an important meeting he can't miss. Can you come by and be with me while I open the box?"

"Of course! My shift ends here in half an hour. Can you wait forty-five minutes?"

"Okay. I can wait," Mirabel sighed. "I have been waiting days already, what is another forty-five minutes?"

Mirabel put the phone down. Her life was wrapped around waiting. She decided to start some tea and busied herself tidying up until Janey arrived. Forty-five minutes passed, then an hour, and Janey had yet to show up. More time passed and Mirabel looked at her clock. It had been an hour and fifteen minutes. Mirabel was pacing back and forth, wondering what to do, when her phone rang.

"I am so sorry," Janey said. "We had a rush just about the time I was supposed to leave and I had to stay and help the new girl. I am on my way."

After fifteen impatient minutes, Janey finally arrived. Mirabel greeted her at the door and led her to the kitchen. She got a cup of tea for Janey and reheated her own, and they sat across from each other at the table. The unopened package sat in the middle between them.

"It's not very big," Janey said.

"I know," Mirabel remarked, staring at the box and chewing her lower lip. "We never had much. Apparently, my father died and no one found him for quite some time. They gathered these few things before burning down the shed."

"Oh, Mirabel, that's awful! Were they able to discern the cause of death?"

"No, the body was too far gone to be sure, but when I talked to the sheriff, he said the report indicated he probably died of acute liver disease and that he probably drank himself into a stupor and just never woke up." She paused. "My father was an alcoholic. He never recovered from my mother's death. Heck, he may have been an alcoholic before that. Who knows? It's not like we spoke a lot. He only talked about her after he hit the bottle."

Janey reached over and grabbed Mirabel's hand. "I am so sorry. I am sorry that he died and I am sorry that you had to grow up in that atmosphere. It must have been hard."

"It was, but I solaced myself by spending my time out in nature. I had a great imagination. I used to imagine that I was a fairy princess and that I ruled Fairyland with a kind heart and that I was kidnapped, but one day I would return to Fairyland. I spent my childhood wandering the streams near my home when I wasn't in school. I went to school in Judith Gap, Montana—a small town nearby. I hated school."

"Why?" Janey asked.

"The kids teased me relentlessly. I didn't fit in. They said I looked strange and called me names like Pixie Poop and Venus Fly Trap. Even the parents didn't like me. I made a friend once, in the fifth grade. It's not like there were a lot of kids, but a new girl came to school and she invited me over to her house. Her mother took one look at me and then pulled her aside. I never knew what she said to my friend, but I had to leave right after they spoke. When we went into Lewiston, people always seemed to be afraid to look at me, but then I could see them steal glances from the sides of their eyes. They dealt fine with my father, but it was clear they were uncomfortable around me."

"Oh, I don't understand how people can be so cruel. Sometimes when someone shines, like you do, other people get jealous and mean. Folks don't like what they don't understand. You might not know how beautiful you are, but it is not hard to see how special you are. Sometimes small-town folks can be so insulated and myopic."

"Well, enough of that." Mirabel waved at the air in front of her, as if waving away her past. "Shall we open the box?"

"Absolutely! I can't wait to see what's inside."

Mirabel stood up, pulled a box cutter from a drawer in the kitchen desk, and started to cut the taped seams. Inside a larger box they found another old, faded box, also taped down. The seams and corners of the lid were fragile and starting to tear away from the top. Mirabel gently lifted the lid and peered inside. On top of some folded papers was a dog whistle. Mirabel picked up the whistle and showed it to Janey.

"This was my dad's favorite whistle. He used it to train the ranchers' dogs for herding sheep."

Next, she pulled out the papers and set them on top of another stack of papers on the table, intending to look at them later. Underneath the papers were a few pictures, and that was all there was; not much to tell the story of her father's life. She began to look through the pictures. There were old sepia pictures and some old photo portraits, the kind with color added. She thought they must be old pictures of her father's family. The very last picture was a Kodachrome image of a young woman with a baby in her arms. Mirabel instinctively knew she was the baby pictured. She was tiny, with delicate features. Then her eyes traveled to the woman holding her and she was taken aback. This must be her mother, but she didn't look anything like Mirabel imagined. The woman was large and plain with a kindly face. This was the first picture Mirabel had seen of her mother, or of herself as a baby. She had always imagined that her mother was beautiful, graceful, and small, like her. Seeing the picture shattered the image she had always carried in her mind and she was shocked by the reality. As a child, she had frequently asked her father if he had a picture of her mother, but he always told her there were none and not to ask about it again. Still, she kept asking. The last time he had gotten so angry that she became afraid to ask again. Now, finally, the picture of her mother she had longed for all her life was there in her hands. She hoped at last to have a sense of who she was, but this only deepened the mystery of her origins.

How can I be so different from my parents?

Something didn't add up. While caught up in the shock of her mother's appearance, Mirabel hadn't noticed the woman standing behind her mother, but now she directed her gaze there. Her jaw dropped as she looked at the familiar face. It was the woman from the coffee shop. In the photo, the woman leaned over her mother's shoulder, smiling down at the infant Mirabel. Mirabel abruptly sat down, stunned and somewhat bewildered.

"Mirabel?" Janey said, placing her hand on Mirabel's arm.

Mirabel silently handed her the picture. Janey took it from her and looked at it, then up at Mirabel. "What am I looking at? Is the baby you?"

Mirabel could only nod her head.

"Is that your mother holding you?"

"Yes, I guess it is," Mirabel whispered. "But I've never seen a picture of her before, and...well, she doesn't look like I imagined."

"Well, I don't think that is unusual, Mirabel. We all make images in our heads that often don't line up with reality."

"It's just disconcerting. I just don't feel...well, like I belonged to her, or to my father for that matter. They are so different than me. But that is not the strangest thing." She pointed. "See the woman standing over my mother? That is the same woman I told you about from the coffee shop, and she doesn't look much younger in that picture than she did when I saw her."

"Are you sure? How can that be? Maybe they just look alike."

Mirabel shook her head. "No, Janey, it's her. I am sure of it! I feel like I don't know anything about my life, except for what I have here. And you and Matt, of course. Who am I? Who is that woman and why did she follow me all the way to California? If she knew who I was, why didn't she introduce herself and let me know that she knew my mother? It's just too strange. I don't understand. I feel all weird about it."

Janey suddenly had that out-of-her-depth feeling again, just like the time when Mirabel first told her about the woman. *It's so strange.* She studied the picture. The woman didn't look evil or anything. In fact, the affection she showed as she gazed at the infant in the picture was plain to see. Janey couldn't understand why she wouldn't have introduced herself to Mirabel, or tried to contact her again.

Janey looked up as Mirabel stood and started to clear the packing materials and box from the table in a flurry of nervous activity. Janey followed her after she picked up the stack of papers from the table and carried them into the office, where she put them into a basket. Janey then trailed Mirabel back out to the kitchen and placed her hand on Mirabel's shoulder, gently turning Mirabel to face her. "What can I do, how can I help you? You're all flummoxed and jittery."

"I don't know. I don't know anything. Who am I?" Mirabel lamented.

"We will figure out a way to solve the mystery, but I have to think about how. Do you suppose that there are people in Montana who might remember your mother? Have you thought about going back?"

"Well, I talked to Matt about it when I got the letter. We decided it wasn't necessary for me to go, so we just had them send the box here." Touching her belly, she sighed. "Besides, I am not exactly in any condition to travel. I hate it, but it will have to wait until the baby is born and is old enough to travel."

"Well, I think that is wise, Mirabel, although I know you hate to wait. I would be impatient, too. But look at it this way. It's pretty much been a mystery all your life. It can wait a few more months, no?"

Mirabel frowned and said, "It has to, I guess."

"Well, I think it is important that you don't think about it too much for now. You have enough to deal with already. You just found out your father died and you have a baby on the way. You look tired and uncomfortable. I think what you need is rest. I can give you some teas and herbs to help with stress— some that won't harm the baby. Can I drop them by tomorrow after work?"

Mirabel nodded. They both had forgotten about the folded papers Mirabel had put in the basket in the office.

"Now I think you should go lie down." Janey led Mirabel into the bedroom and covered her with a throw. She tenderly swept Mirabel's hair from her forehead and waited there until Mirabel appeared to be sleeping. Janey stayed until Matt came home.

"I'd let her sleep," she said when Matt entered the room. "It's been a harrowing day for her."

Janey followed Matt to the kitchen, where she showed him the picture and relayed the afternoon's events. Matt shook his head, at a loss for words as she told him about their conversation.

"I worry about her, Janey. She's so fragile sometimes, so mysterious."

"I know how you feel," Janey said. She turned her head, afraid to let Matt see the deep well of feelings that arose as she thought of her friend. They sat at the table for a while in uncomfortable silence before Janey finally gathered her things to go. "Take care of her. Watch over her. She needs to know she belongs with someone," Janey said as she left.

Part II

The Awakening

Chapter Ten

The next morning Mirabel woke up, made breakfast, and saw Matt off to work. She decided to spend the day curled up with a good book to help stave off her impatience. At about 10 a.m. she went outside to catch some rare winter sunshine in the garden space. Even though it was winter, they had put a crop of broccoli in; a good California winter crop. She wandered among the plants. Some nice heads had formed and Mirabel found that a few were ready for picking, so she started making plans for dinner.

She went back to the kitchen to get a knife, and was on her way back out to the garden when the baby hiccupped hard. It wasn't the first time the baby had had hiccups, but these were unusually strong. She stood still for a few moments, rubbing her tummy and murmuring softly to the child. After a minute the hiccups stopped, and Mirabel moved toward the broccoli, cut a few heads off, and took them into the kitchen where she rinsed them and placed them in a colander to drain.

Mirabel returned to the sofa and picked up her book. Typically, the baby moved a lot during these quiet moments.

This time, however, the baby was still. Mirabel's brow wrinkled with concern. *I worry too much.* She went back to reading.

As the day progressed, she continued to sense no movement, and by noon Mirabel had become quite concerned. She called her midwife, Sandy, who told her she would come over right away. Next Mirabel called Matt.

"Is it possible you can come home? I am worried about the baby." Mirabel requested.

"What's going on? Did something happen?"

"I'm not sure. The baby had hiccups this morning and hasn't moved since then. At first I just thought the baby was sleeping, but then I started to worry because the baby always moves when I am resting. I called the midwife and she is on her way over. Oh Matt, I'm scared."

"Mirabel, I am coming right home. It will be okay. Please don't worry so much," Matt tried to reassure her.

Matt hung up the phone. His heart raced and he ran his hands through his hair. *What if something goes wrong?* He looked at the picture on his desk. Mirabel smiled back at him, holding the fairy he had given to her when he proposed and showing off her ring. *She's been so happy.* He took a deep breath and squared his shoulders. *I can't let her know I worry so much. I must be strong.* He gathered his keys, let his staff know he would be gone for the rest of the day, and left.

When Matt arrived home, Sandy had just pulled in. He helped her carry her bag and they approached the house. Mirabel waited at the window. Matt could see the fear on her face when they entered. He walked over and gave her a hug, then turned to Sandy and asked if she needed anything.

"No, I have everything I need," Sandy replied. "Mirabel, why don't we go to the bedroom so I can do an exam."

On their way to the room, Matt heard her ask Mirabel if she had felt any movement since they spoke. Mirabel shook her head and looked anxiously back at him as he trailed them into the bedroom. Sandy gestured for Mirabel to lie on the bed and he quickly stepped in to help prop her up on some pillows.

Sandy took out a stethoscope and asked Mirabel to bare her belly. Mirabel complied. Sandy placed the stethoscope on Mirabel's abdomen and kept moving it around. Matt noticed the growing look of concern on her face, and her silence terrified him. Mirabel looked at Matt and he took her hand. They clung to each other, and he did his best to put on a confident, caring face.

"Mirabel, Matt," Sandy finally broke her silence. "I am going to have to pass this on to a doctor. I recommend that you go to the emergency room right away. I am sorry, but I can't find a heartbeat and I want to make sure you are in good medical hands. It's possible I could be wrong. Matt, can you help Mirabel to the car? I will follow you to the hospital."

Mirabel became silent as fear closed in around her. She looked at the midwife with pleading eyes. Then she touched her stomach, closed her eyes, and whispered, "My baby, please be okay."

Matt and Mirabel drove to the hospital in silence, unable to voice the fear that now held them.

As Sandy pulled her car out to follow, the neighbor next door watched them and began to make preparations. She had been observing Mirabel in the garden, and saw the midwife come, followed by Matt soon after. She knew it was time. She left the house, put a note and a cashier's check in the mailbox, and walked away toward the woods.

After the initial triage interview, a nurse quickly whisked Mirabel, now in a wheelchair, off to a room, and Matt followed. Once in the room, another nurse came in and took her temperature and blood pressure. She asked Mirabel to change into a gown and told them to wait for the doctor. Matt helped Mirabel undress and put on the gown. Fortunately, they didn't have to wait long. The doctor arrived and asked Mirabel some questions, then spoke with Sandy. He listened for the baby's heartbeat and ordered an ultrasound. Matt held Mirabel's hand while Sandy sat by her other side. He stood by, powerless, as he watched the tears course down Mirabel's face, her eyes pleading for anything other than the apparent reality.

We need Janey, Matt thought. Thinking this gave him some sense of control.

"Mirabel," Matt said, "I'm going to go call Janey and ask her to come, but I need to step out to make the call. I promise I will be right back."

Mirabel nodded.

Matt looked over at Sandy and understanding his non-verbal request, she turned to Mirabel, took her hand and said, "I'll stay right here with you."

Matt made his way to the entrance of the hospital, pulled out his cell phone, and gave Janey a call. Janey's voicemail picked up. "Janey, can you come to John Muir Hospital as soon as possible? Something is wrong with the baby. And Mirabel—well...we both need your support." Matt's voice trembled as he struggled to contain the grief welling up inside him, but he was determined to keep it together as long as he could for Mirabel's sake. He believed he needed to be strong for her. Inside, he didn't want to give in to the reality that the baby was most likely gone. He added, "Janey, we are in the emergency ward. I will leave word with the triage nurse to let you come in." He turned off his phone, stopped to let the nurse know a friend would be coming, then made his way quickly back to the room where they were keeping Mirabel.

"Mirabel, I left a message for Janey. She didn't answer, but I know she will come as soon as she can."

Mirabel nodded and sat there silently. He watched as shock set in. An ultrasound technician came in to take Mirabel off to the lab. Matt looked over at Sandy for an indication of what to do, and she nodded her head for Matt to follow.

The tech held up her hand and said, "No, I will need to take her alone. The doctor will be joining us and there is not enough room in the lab for all of us." She settled Mirabel back into the wheelchair.

Matt squeezed Mirabel's hand. "I will be right here waiting for you," he said, then reluctantly released it as he watched the tech roll Mirabel away.

Matt waited with Sandy, each minute a torturous stretch filled with every worst-case scenario he could think of.

"Matt," Sandy finally interrupted his internal monologue. "This kind of thing happens sometimes. Not all pregnancies end well. I know this is devastating for you and Mirabel, but you both are young…"

Matt lashed out, "No! I don't know if we will have a second chance. Mirabel…her state of mind is so fragile sometimes, I am afraid she will not recover. Don't tell me we can try again and that it will all be better in the long run, because it won't!" He squeezed his eyes shut, trying to hold back the tears. He put his head in his hands, no longer able to hold back the rush of emotion. "Oh God, oh God. This can't be happening. Everything was going so well. Why is this happening?"

Sandy came over, put her hands on his shoulders, and murmured, "Matt, I'm sorry. I didn't mean to suggest…well, I was just trying to help."

He shuddered, and then sobs progressed from his gut to his chest. Sandy stood by as a silent presence until they subsided.

Matt sighed. "Can you try Janey again?" He handed her his phone. "Mirabel will need her… and so do I."

Sandy left him there and went outside to make the call, but just as she started to punch in the numbers, the phone rang and she answered.

"Matt?" Janey said.

"No, this is Sandy, the midwife. Matt just asked me to try and call you again."

"Oh. Sandy, what is happening? It doesn't sound good."

"No, it doesn't look good," Sandy said. "Mirabel called early this afternoon worried, so I went to the house. After I got there, I couldn't find a heartbeat. The doctor here in the emergency room couldn't, either. Mirabel is getting an ultrasound right now. Can you come? They need you. Matt is breaking down and Mirabel is in shock."

"Oh my God. Oh no. I will be there as soon as I can."

Sandy hung up and went back to the room. Matt was slumped in the chair, still waiting.

"I reached her," she said. "She is coming right over."

Matt nodded, relieved that Janey was on her way.

"Can I get you something?" Sandy asked him. "Some water or something?"

Matt shook his head. Sandy had been through this kind of thing before and she knew there was nothing she could do to make the pain go away. She also knew from here on out it was primarily in the hospital's hands, but she could still be of use if they induced labor and she could try to comfort Matt until Janey came or Mirabel got back. So they sat there together, in silent vigil.

After the ultrasound tech brought Mirabel back to the room where Matt waited, Matt helped Mirabel onto the bed. The doctor followed them in. Matt stood next to Mirabel and his eyes bored into the doctor, imploring him for good news. Mirabel already knew the truth, but still held out for some small shred of hope.

"I am sorry," the doctor said. "It looks like the baby is no longer alive. This happens sometimes. We are not sure why. In cases like this the child needs to be removed."

"Removed? What does that mean?" Matt said, his voice breaking.

"We will need to induce labor and birth. You will need to decide if you want to have an autopsy done on the child. I know this is a hard decision to make." He went on to explain the risks and procedures for induced labor. Finally he said, "I will let you consult with each other to decide about an autopsy and will return as soon as I can."

Mirabel watched the doctor leave, all hopes removed. Her shock moved into grief. She turned to Matt and began to cry.

"Noooo...oh, my baby. No. This can't be happening. No, no, no, no, no..." And then she broke down as the sobs tore through her.

Matt stood by her, tears streaming down his face. Sandy stood at her other side, holding her hand.

Janey burst through the door and ran to Mirabel's side as Sandy stepped aside to make room. Janey embraced Mirabel and the two of them cried together. Mirabel felt the well of Janey's warmth and dove into it, all of her grief flowing into the compassionate container that her friend had become.

Eventually, Sandy broke the tender spell. "Mirabel, Matt...I know this is hard, but you have some decisions to make."

Janey, still holding Mirabel, turned toward Sandy and said, "For God's sake, let them have some time. How can they make any decisions at a time like this?"

Just then the doctor came back in. "Mirabel and Matt, have you made a decision?"

"I can't, I don't know..." Mirabel looked at him and wailed, "How can I decide on such a thing?" Suddenly angry, she yelled at him. "My baby is gone and now I have to decide if you are going to cut it open or not?"

"Ms. McInness," the doctor said, "I understand this is hard. But time is critical for your health and we need to proceed with inducing labor. I'd rather you make the decision before we get started."

Mirabel was grateful as Janey looked at the doctor and calmly said, "Give us a few minutes."

"Okay," the doctor sighed. "I'll be back in a few minutes."

Janey turned back and looked directly into Mirabel's eyes. Looking back into that extraordinary calm made Mirabel stop and consider. Janey then said quietly, "Mirabel, I am so sorry, but the doctor is right. The sooner this part is done, the better for you. I wish you didn't have to make this decision. It all depends on whether you want to know what happened to the baby or not."

"I don't care what happens to me. How can I care? My baby is gone!" Mirabel started to weep again as she spoke.

Matt came over and gently grasped Mirabel's shoulders. "I care! I care about you. I can't bear to have something bad happen to you, too. Please Mirabel, I'd like to know why this happened, but I also hate to think of anyone doing anything to the baby, and I will understand if you decide not to do an autopsy."

Mirabel looked up at Matt. "No, I don't want anyone cutting my baby. Oh God, Matt…" She broke off as sobs overwhelmed her again.

Matt nodded at her and went out to find the doctor to let him know their decision. Janey stayed with her, holding her and murmuring soothing words.

The nurses came in and prepared Mirabel to go to a delivery room. The emergency room doctor had called in an obstetrician to do the job and she would arrive within the hour. They placed Mirabel in a wheelchair and rolled her off while Matt, Janey, and Sandy followed, a forlorn procession through the halls of the hospital and up the elevator, only stopping when they finally made their way into the maternity ward and settled into a room.

A delivery nurse came in and explained to Mirabel that she was going to insert a catheter and start a Pitocin drip to induce labor. The drip would also include some other medicines to soften her cervix and prepare her body for labor. Before she set up, she turned and asked why Janey and Sandy were there. Sandy explained she was the midwife and that Janey was there for support. The nurse said they would normally only allow Matt in the room, but since Sandy was a midwife, she could stay. Janey would have to wait in the waiting room. Mirabel pleaded with the nurse to let Janey stay, but to no avail. The nurse was firm.

Janey frowned, angry at the nurse, but it seemed there was nothing she could do. Before she left she gave Mirabel one last embrace, then pulled Matt out into the hall. "Since I can't be in there with you, I might as well be useful. Can I go back to the house and gather some things for Mirabel?"

"Yes," Matt said. "That would be good. I don't think either Mirabel or I can think of what is needed right now. Can you manage? I trust you will gather the right things. And Janey," he paused, "thank you for coming."

Jancy reached up and pulled Matt into a hug. "Matt, I am so sorry." She held him and he set his sorrow free, body trembling as he allowed the grief expression. Finally, he stepped back, wiped his eyes, and said, "I need to go be with Mirabel. Janey, I have to keep it together for her. I don't want her to see me like this."

Janey gently touched his cheek and said, "I know you will be strong for her, but it is good for her to see your grief, too. Grief shared is better than grief alone."

Matt nodded and went back into the room. Janey stood there for a moment. *He looks so helpless.* Her heart broke for him.

Janey went to the house to gather necessities as the Pitocin started its work on Mirabel, causing contractions that slowly built over time. When Janey got back to the hospital, she handed Mirabel's things off to the nurse at the station and asked how things were going. The nurse explained that it would take time for the contractions to build and for Mirabel's body to respond and go into full labor.

Janey went to the waiting room and stared blankly at the walls.

A woman sat down next to her, and with a deep, musical voice layered with a complexity of timbres, said, "Janey, you've been a good friend to her, dear."

Janey, startled out of her thoughts, turned to look at the woman attached to the voice. She saw an elderly woman with long gray hair, which was tied in a braid by a green cord with dangling leaves on the ends. At first, Janey's impression was of an elderly woman, but as she took her in, Janey noticed her beautiful skin, soft with nary a wrinkle in it. Her eyes widened with recognition and she said, "You!"

Chapter Eleven

"Yes, dear," the woman said.

"Who...who are you?"

"Magdalena. I am called Magdalena."

Suddenly mad, Janey exclaimed, "Why are you following Mirabel? I saw you in a picture with her mother. I know you saw her at the coffee shop over a year ago. Why didn't you introduce yourself there, and why show up now, all sudden like? You scare her and she doesn't need any more stress right now." Tears of anger and worry squeezed out the sides of her eyes, and her face took on an uncharacteristic red tint.

"Yes, dear. I know, and I am afraid that is outside my control. I am not here to see her right now, but to see you."

"Me? Why would you want to see me?"

"I will explain. Would you be willing to walk with me?"

"Why should I go with you? I don't know who you are and you never said anything to Mirabel when you had a chance."

"I am her Watcher. I know that you cannot possibly know what that means, but I mean Mirabel no harm. I have watched her from a distance all these years, only revealing myself once when it was called for, or visiting her in other forms. I know this is all quite strange for you and I will explain, but not here. I need you to come with me to a more private location."

Other forms? Janey stared, dumbfounded for a minute, and then found her voice again. "But what about Mirabel and Matt? I can't leave them now." She paused. "Besides, how do I know I can trust you? You were in a picture with her when she was a baby, for God's sake, and you've never revealed yourself till now. This is just far too weird!"

"I know, dear, but Mirabel and the child are in danger and they need your help. I need your help."

"Danger? As far as I know the child is already gone and Mirabel—well, she is very distraught to say the least, and she needs me here," Janey spat. She bristled. "I am not running off with some strange woman just because I saw you in that picture or because you tell me I have been a good friend to Mirabel."

"I understand, dear, but I cannot tell you more inside this place of human healing arts. It is too public. I propose we take a walk around the grounds outside and I will explain a few things to you about Mirabel. There is time. The baby won't come for many hours."

Janey, now wondering about the phrase "human healing arts," and torn by the conflicting desire to go with Magdalena and also to stay near to Matt and Mirabel, finally relented. She had that expansive, riveting sensation in her gut and craved to hear what the woman would tell her, and she was tired of waiting alone in the waiting room with only her own thoughts and prayers to keep her company while a tragedy continued to do its damage to her friends in the delivery room.

I hope she will shed some light on all the mysteries surrounding Mirabel.

"Okay, but I need to let Matt know that I will not be here. It wouldn't be good if he comes out to get me and I am gone."

"That will do, dear, but don't tell him about my presence right now if you don't mind. Just tell him you are going for a walk to help clear your mind. That will make some sense to him."

Janey went to the nurses' station to leave a message for Matt and Mirabel, then walked back to Magdalena and said, "Okay, let's go…and by the way, I am not your dear, so please stop calling me that."

Magdalena nodded her head, then led Janey toward the stairs next to the elevator. Smiling, she said, "I prefer to use my own legs to go down."

Janey didn't argue. Once down the stairs they found the nearest exit and Magdalena led her to a secret trail behind the hospital.

Magdalena said, "Janey, I know you do not trust me yet, but you must swear to whatever deities you worship not to share this with a single soul in this world."

"What do you mean, in *this* world?"

"Janey, I think you know that Mirabel is not quite what she seems." Magdalena paused. "No?"

Janey, already feeling out of her depth with this woman, and now a little awed, could not deny what she said and only nodded.

Magdalena started to share the story of Mirabel's origins to Janey. She had to prod Janey to keep moving, because as Janey listened, she kept stopping, too stunned to respond as she began to understand exactly how far out of her depth she was. What Magdalena was telling her was far beyond anything she could have imagined. Nothing in her past compared with the creeping, bewildered awe she now experienced. This magic was much bigger than the little magic of her practice.

Magdalena said, "Mirabel is not of this world, and neither am I. Our world and your world are connected through special trees. What you call magic is what we call ethereal. Your magic comes from our world through these trees, but has not been so apparent in these past years."

Janey trembled, suddenly more alert. Her longing for more magic had finally been answered, quite unexpectedly.

"Both our worlds are in grave danger," Magdalena said, stopping and looking directly into Janey's eyes.

Janey's excitement turned to dismay as Magdalena turned, began walking and continued her tale. That magic she had just discovered was at risk of being snatched away before she could even touch it. In fact, it was in peril of being irretrievably lost. But then Magdalena started talking about the part that Mirabel had to play in all this. Mirabel's fate was tied to the fate of both worlds and she would find no peace in this one. Suddenly, Janey understood something about Mirabel that had never made sense before—her magic and her sorrow.

Magdalena turned to Janey again and said, "Now that you know the truth, I need your help."

Janey looked at her and nodded. She would do anything for Mirabel, and anything to save the magic.

Magdalena took Janey's hand. "Mirabel and Matt trust you implicitly. There is a letter in the package that came with her father's things. When the package arrived, it was not yet time for the letter to be read. It would have created an air of forgetfulness when she touched it. I will send you a sign when it is time for the letter to be read. Another Hawthorne Drug Bottle will appear, and then I will need you to make sure she finds the letter, and that she reads it. Once she has read it, I need you to convince her to go back to the buckeye grove where this stage in her journey began. But beware, she may resist!"

"Mirabel is afraid of that grove. I am not sure I will be able to get her to go there, and she will be devastated about the baby. I am worried she won't recover," Janey replied.

To that Magdalena answered, "She has been under a spell made to block her memory, put there to protect her, but the unfortunate effect of this spell is that it creates an indefinable feeling of loss and sorrow. She trusts you, and your love for her will help break the spell."

"I will do what I can, but I don't understand anything about this," Janey said, shaking her head.

"Once upon a time, long ago, there was a tribe of people on your world that came out of the desert. We do not know where they came from, or what had happened to them, but they came out of the desert with a sickness in their spirits. They brought with them beliefs about harsh, jealous gods and used these stories and fear to control the people they conquered. They hated the Shiashialon, the people of Ynys-Avalone, and convinced others that worshipping trees was blasphemy. They blamed women as the cause of all evil in the world. Over time, they spread their sickness across the region. This sickness severed all who succumbed to disconnection from the Shiashialon."

"The Shiashialon...who is that?"

"She is the Creator of both our worlds and the source of love."

Janey suddenly shivered with recognition. . *The Shiashialon. That name...it's like a sigh. It's like I have known her all my life.*

Magdalena continued. "Soon men feared, then sought to control the magic that flowed into this world from ours and they began to cut down and destroy the trees—the portal trees that gave access to our world. They kept some trees, but controlled access to them. For many years distant parts of this world were protected, but over time, the sickness spread to all corners. All but a few links between our worlds were cut down and destroyed. Some of my people crossed over and sacrificed themselves to save the remaining trees and put protection spells on them, which prevented men from noticing the trees. But we came too late. The women who crossed could not return, and they had to hide among your people. Many shamans and healers of your world knew the truth and provided sanctuary for them. But now, those who knew the truth, both villains and protectors, are gone. All the remaining links are threatened by greed, hubris, and a lack of awareness, which is the result of this sickness. Our mutual stories have been made into fairytales and myths, and not many believe anymore. Those who do are ridiculed and sidelined. There are those who unconsciously wish, out of fear and disconnection, to destroy the magic that seeps into this world from ours. They desire to sever the links forever. Severing the final links will eventually leave your world as barren as ours is now."

Janey abruptly sat down on the trail. Looking down, she shook her head back and forth.

"Janey, I know this must be overwhelming, but you must pull yourself together for Mirabel. I know you love her. There is more I need to tell you. Make sure she brings the bottle of pollen and the silver buckeye with her," Magdalena said as she pulled Janey to her feet.

"Pollen?"

"Yes, the bottle that says Hawthorne Drug is filled with the magical pollen of the Shialon Tree."

"The Shialon Tree?"

"Yes, it has been called the Tree of Life, the World Tree...there are many legends of this tree on your world. It is the original tree, the mother of all trees. It was also the child of the Shiashialon after The Weavers. The pollen of the tree opens the gateways between our worlds. The magical trees that hold the gateways will open if sprinkled with the pollen from the One Tree—The Shialon Tree."

Janey touched her heart. Her love of trees had always been with her, and now it made more sense. On a deep level, she knew her love of trees was tied to an unconscious awareness of this tree. She didn't know how she knew this, but she just did. *The Shialon Tree.* She liked the name Mirabel's people had given it.

Magdalena watched her with knowing eyes and nodded when Janey looked at her. As they began to walk back toward the hospital, she gave Janey instructions to pass along to Mirabel after she read the letter, what to do with the bottle of pollen, and the importance of the silver buckeye. Finally, she said, "Janey, I know that you and Matt always sensed there was more to Mirabel than was apparent, and I am glad for your skill at seeing into people. As the magic has drained away from this world, we have rarely found allies here. I will share one more thing with you and leave it up to you whether to tell Matt or not. I cannot read whether it will make things easier or harder for him. He is not the father of the child. He cannot be. The women of our world give birth parthenogenetically; they don't need male seed. The reason for this is the purity of it; it kept the magic in our world strong and our population stable. They do this when the time comes and their bodies ripen on their own, when needed. Our children are not born often and all are gifted. It is harder for pregnancies to occur when our people are away from our world, but your spells and her dreams helped. There is also the prophecy from long ago..." Magdalena trailed off, looking off into the distance.

"Magdalena?" Janey said after a long silence.

"Yes?" Magdalena brought her focus back to Janey. "The buckeyes in the grove where Mirabel had her dream are Mirabel's strongest medicine here, but all trees are good for her. All trees originated from the Shialon Tree. I think your love, which is true and pure, helped awaken Mirabel's dreams, her body to ripen and hope to sprout within her. Matt's love for her also helped. We have you and him to thank for making what was once barren fertile, and for giving our world a fighting chance." Magdalena bowed to her. "Thank you."

Janey's eyes welled with tears—tears that were a mix of joy and sorrow; joy for confirming the truth about magic, and sorrow for what was to come.

As they reached the hospital grounds, Magdalena looked deep into Janey's eyes and said, "Janey, trust your dragon. That experience was real, as your heart is true. Your gifts will unfold and if Mirabel succeeds, the magic you long for will grow with each coming season."

Janey gazed back, mesmerized by Magdalena's deep-purple eyes filled with glints of light. Joy radiated from her center as the realization sunk in. *Maia is alive!* Then she thought about not being able to tell Mirabel and Matt and her stomach churned. *How will I manage to keep that from them?*

Magdalena interrupted her thoughts. "Now I must go. I don't have much time and you need to go back. Janey, be strong!"

Janey watched as Magdalena began to walk away. She turned and gave one last instruction. "When the child goes missing, please act as dismayed as the rest."

Janey stood there for a moment. The leaves in Magdalena's braid fluttered in the wind and the uneven hem of her skirt floated around her green combat boots, somehow not quite attached to gravity. As Janey watched, she just disappeared—completely faded into the background somehow. Janey was left there standing alone, wondering how Magdalena knew so much about her.

Caught for a moment in the wonder of it all, she almost forgot the tragedy that was unfolding in the hospital. She had more hope now than she had prior to meeting Magdalena. She knew there was much at stake and a high possibility for failure, so she steeled herself for the coming difficulties and vowed that she would be strong, for Mirabel and her world, and also for her own. Inside she held a shining flame of hope for the possibility of finally experiencing the magic she had longed for all her life. She now knew her instincts about it had been true.

Slowly, Janey turned and made her way back to the waiting room. She checked in with the nurse at the station to find out how things were going. The nurse said she would let her know as soon as she heard anything. Janey sat down, overwhelmed with the happenings of the day. She sat there reviewing her conversation with Magdalena until she had worn it into the ground, and finally rooted around for a magazine to distract her from her thoughts. She located a *Good Housekeeping* magazine and tried to focus on an article about decorating walls. After reading and re-reading the first paragraph three times, she put it down. She found it impossible to concentrate. Her mind kept drifting back to her encounter with Magdalena. *What in my life has prepared me for this?* She was grateful for the alternative path she had chosen, to break with the Christian religion of her upbringing. At least this had made her open to possibilities. But she never, ever, in her wildest imagination, would have guessed that she herself would enter into such a fantastic tale.

As Janey's thoughts turned to Mirabel, her heart twisted inside her chest and she wanted to cry. *Poor Mirabel, it just isn't fair.* An image of Matt came to mind. Surprisingly, she felt even worse for him. He was losing his baby and would soon lose Mirabel, too. *Actually, we will both lose Mirabel.* In that realization, she suddenly felt closer to him than she ever thought she could. The weight of it settled on her shoulders and she knew she needed some release, so she headed for the bathroom, found a stall, and broke down, weeping until no more tears would come. In the calm after her cry, she made a silent prayer for them all. Picking herself up, she made her way back to the waiting room and sat in a chair, staring out the window, waiting and anticipating the coming events.

Chapter Twelve

In the delivery room, Mirabel's contractions were coming closer and closer together. The obstetrician had finally arrived and Mirabel had a devoted staff attending to her, along with Matt and Sandy. Weighed down with the heaviness of disappointment and grief, somehow Mirabel found the strength to endure the intense, painful contractions of labor induced on a body not quite prepared for it. She had only bitterness and barrenness to look forward to at the end of it. Finally, deep into the next morning, the doctor announced her cervix was open enough for her to start pushing the baby out. Matt stood resolutely at her side, and Sandy encouraged her to breathe and use the strength of her breath to push the baby out.

Soon the deed was done. The stillborn baby was birthed, and the nurse took the limp child and gently cleaned it up and swathed it in a blanket while the obstetrician attended to Mirabel. Once the placenta passed and Mirabel was cleaned up, they sat her up and placed the baby in her arms to allow her and Matt to say their goodbyes. The nurse helped them clip a lock of hair and let them know they had taken hand and footprints while the doctor finished up with Mirabel.

A quiet, reverent sorrow took over the delivery room as Mirabel looked down at the tiny girl child. She had a delicate little face reminiscent of her own. Her eyes were closed but framed with long, lush lashes and she had a tiny little rosebud mouth. Mirabel lifted her dainty little hand in hers and noticed that her fingers were long and graceful. She looked up at Matt with wonder and said, "She could have been an artist."

Mirabel was surprised at how calm she felt as she gazed at the child. Her grief percolated just under the surface and she knew it would erupt again, but here, holding the baby, the silence held and soothed her and she was able to experience the miracle in the little lifeless body. Something inside her quickened as she held the child, but the feeling was ephemeral and she didn't have the energy to chase the meaning behind it. And so she sat there, propped up on pillows which also supported the tiny body in her arms, with Matt and Sandy standing by her side, contained within a momentary bubble of peace and contentment.

Matt looked down at his stillborn child and saw himself chasing a small version of Mirabel through fields of flowers, squeals of laughter ringing in the air. His tears flowed as he grieved what would never be. Mirabel was right; the child was beautiful, unearthly, and he couldn't fathom why the universe would not allow her to live. Afraid to break the spell, he whispered, "Can I hold her?"

Mirabel tenderly handed the child to Matt and he brought her to his chest, holding her close to his heart and rocking her gently. She felt fragile and almost ethereal in his arms. *She is precious.* His heart broke again. He wasn't sure how much more it could break before it shattered into irreparable pieces. As it was, each broken piece felt raw and exposed. The veils that shielded his vulnerability had fallen, and there was nothing left to do but stand there next to Mirabel and cradle the inert being in his arms.

Sandy finally broke the spell and asked if she should go get Janey. Mirabel silently nodded, keeping her eyes on Matt and the baby.

Janey came to the door and looked in to see Matt gently placing the child back into Mirabel's waiting arms. She slowly walked into the room, hyper aware of the quiet presence lingering in the atmosphere.

Mirabel looked up at her as she approached and said in a trembling voice, "Janey, would you like to see our child?"

Janey nodded, came to Mirabel's side, and looked down upon the beautiful baby. With a shadow of a smile on her lips, she said, "Mirabel, Matt, she is precious. Do you have a name for her?"

Mirabel said, "We decided if we had a girl that we would call her Maia Jane. Maia, like the Greek goddess; and Jane, after you."

Janey gazed down at tiny Maia Jane and fervently wished that she could tell Matt and Mirabel the truth. To hold back and deny them hope was the hardest thing she had ever done, and she almost broke down and told them right then and there. But she kept her promise to Magdalena. Knowing that she would eventually be able to tell them when the time was right kept her strong. Gesturing at Maia Jane, she asked Mirabel, "Can I hold her?"

"Janey, do you think you could bless her?" Mirabel asked.

"Of course," Janey replied. She tenderly took Maia Jane into her arms and regarded her thoughtfully; then, turning to each of the four directions, asked for the guardians and spirits of each to bestow blessings on Maia Jane for the journey to come. She purposely left her language vague, knowing that her understanding of the journey she spoke of would be quite different from Matt and Mirabel's. The spirits she called would follow. She drew a pentacle on Maia Jane's forehead and said a silent prayer for protection. She placed the baby back into Mirabel's arms and said, "Little one, may you always be blessed, wherever your little soul wanders."

The nurse had been standing back and watching all this. She stepped in when things appeared to be coming to some kind of close. She murmured, "I am so sorry for your loss. May I take the child now and have her prepared for services? I know how hard this must be for you."

Mirabel clutched the child to her breast and wept, thinking, *Maia, Maia Jane, I wish you could stay with us. I'm so sorry, my little Maia Jane.* She bent her head, kissed the baby's forehead, and said quietly, "I love you."

Janey clutched the bedrail, holding herself back from breaking her promise to Magdalena as she watched Mirabel reluctantly hand Maia over to the nurse. The nurse gently promised she would take good care of her as she received the child. Matt stood on the other side of the bed with his head hung low, and Mirabel quietly wept as the nurse carried little Maia Jane off.

Janey, still holding her tongue, came over to hold and rock Mirabel while Sandy helped Matt into a chair and stood by him. Janey and Sandy held vigil with the grieving parents until exhaustion took over and it was apparent that Mirabel needed the respite that only sleep could provide.

Sandy finally broke the silence. "Matt, Mirabel, I must leave, but please call me if you need anything." Nodding her head at Janey, she quietly gathered her things and left.

Janey still held Mirabel and could feel her deflate in her embrace when Mirabel whispered, "I would like to have Maia cremated and I want to keep the urn with us." She looked over at Matt and he nodded. She turned back to Janey and said, "Do you think you could help Matt with the details? After the cremation, I'd like to have a small service under the trees at our place in Briones and would like you to preside. Can you do this?"

"Oh Mirabel, I am so sad about all this," Janey replied. She fidgeted, trying to find a way to say something that wasn't a lie, as she was not a good liar. "I want to do whatever I can. You and Matt are so important to me."

"I am tired now, so tired," Mirabel sighed, looking out the window. After a long pause, she added, "I am not sure I will be able to sleep, but maybe the nurse will be able to help out with that." She pressed the call button for the nurse and the nurse came in almost immediately.

Matt stood up. "Can you get her something to help her sleep?"

The nurse nodded and stepped out.

Janey was quiet, holding her peace. Keeping her secret was excruciating. She thought the less she said at this point, the better. She knew that Magdalena was probably doing her magic right now and whisking Maia off to a safe place, and more than anything she wanted to take Mirabel in her arms and tell her it was all okay. She worried about her friend.

Janey stood aside when the nurse came back and adjusted Mirabel's bed. The IV was still attached and they were giving her fluids to keep her hydrated. The nurse added something to help Mirabel rest. Janey and Matt stood by until Mirabel drifted off to sleep. Janey walked over to Matt and embraced him. They stood there for quite some time before finally moving apart. Together, they left the room.

As they left Mirabel, now asleep, Matt dug deep into himself to find the strength to take care of the unpleasant business of preparing for a funeral service and filling out papers. He had learned his own particular way of coping with grief back when his mentor Doug had died of cancer. Now he used that knowledge to give him the fortitude to take care of business when all he really wanted to do was crawl into bed with Mirabel, hold her, and never let go. Ultimately, he thought Mirabel was the more fragile partner so it was his duty to take care of the details.

Chapter Thirteen

Janey and Matt searched out the hospital staff to help them make arrangements for a cremation. The nurse called an on-site advocate who had been assigned to them, who took them into a private room. They had paperwork that needed to be filled out, and while they were working on that, she called down to the morgue to get the records information about the baby. Matt was focused on filling out the papers, but stopped when he heard the advocate say into the phone, "Are you sure?" She had a look of grave concern on her face as she stepped out of the room. Matt looked over toward Janey and then back at the door.

Janey thought wryly, *Okay, here comes my chance for an Academy Award.*

Outside the office the advocate said sternly into the phone, "How could you lose the baby? I have the father right here with me. What should I tell him?"

Matt and Janey, overhearing this, looked at each other. Janey already knew what was coming next, but kept a puzzled look on her face and put her hand on Matt's shoulder. She hated keeping the truth from him, but she had given her word to Magdalena.

The advocate finally walked back into the room visibly upset. She looked at Matt apologetically. "I am afraid the baby's body has been misplaced. I am sure she will show up soon. They are looking for her right now."

Matt looked at her blankly for a few moments. "The body was misplaced? What do you mean *misplaced*? How can you misplace a baby?"

"I am sure they will find her," the advocate said. "She could have been put in the wrong section of the morgue. They are looking everywhere right now."

"What am I going to tell Mirabel?" Matt looked at Janey for support, then turned toward the advocate and fumed, "You tell them to find her. I can't tell my wife the baby was *misplaced!* How can this happen?"

"I understand. I know this is frustrating." The advocate reached over to reassure Matt. "We will just have to wait until they complete their search. I am sure they will find her."

"Matt," Janey murmured, "I agree, this is unacceptable, but we can't do anything until they find her. Why don't we go get something to eat, or some coffee or something? You are tired and need some food. It's been a long, terrible day."

Matt sat for a moment, looking confused and troubled before he finally nodded at Janey. He turned toward the advocate again. "Will you come find us in the cafeteria as soon as they find her?"

• • •

Janey led Matt to the cafeteria, got him settled at a table, and went to order some food. Matt sat with his hands on his head. He was nearly at his limit with the events of the day already, and now this. He didn't know if he could take any more. *What did we ever do to deserve this?* He raged at the universe, torn by grief and dismay at the same time. All he could do was hold his head and stare at the table. There seemed to be nothing to do but wait. He certainly wasn't hungry, but what else could he do while they waited for news? *At least Mirabel is asleep.*

Janey came back to the table with a bowl of soup, some bread, and a cup of tea. "Matt, I know you probably don't feel like eating, but you need your strength. Soup will do you some good. Come on—eat."

Matt picked up the spoon and stared down into the soup, then began stirring it absently. "Matt, eat some soup," Janey repeated.

He scooped some into his spoon and put it in his mouth. The smell of food and the warmth stirred his appetite and he silently spooned up the rest of the soup and ate the bread.

"Good. I know this is hard, but you need to take care of yourself. You are doing amazingly well considering."

Matt looked into her brown eyes and her concern and love flowed into his broken heart. It helped. Janey couldn't magically erase the day, but at least he had Janey's support, and wasn't alone in his concern for Mirabel. He had an ally. They sat there together in shared silence, waiting. After a while, the advocate found them still at the table.

"Mr. Gallagher," she said, "can you come to the administrator's office with me?"

"Did they find the baby?" Matt looked up, hopeful.

"The hospital administrator will explain. Please follow me."

Matt glanced at Janey and she nodded her head for him to follow. "Okay, but I want Janey to come with me."

"Okay," the advocate responded.

When they arrived, the administrator motioned for them to sit down. Once they had settled into their chairs, she said, "Mr. Gallagher, I am sorry to have to inform you of this, but it appears that the baby's body has been taken. We have contacted the police and they are on their way over. They will probably want to speak with you. I am so sorry. I know this is difficult, especially after losing the baby. The hospital will do everything in its power to help resolve this."

Matt sat there, speechless.

"How could this happen?" Janey lied.

"I don't know," the administrator replied. "This is the first time something like this has ever happened at this hospital. We have checked our security cameras and the police will do a thorough investigation. I don't know what else to tell you. This is outside my experience."

"Oh God, Mirabel!" Matt exclaimed. "This is too much. How can I tell her the baby is missing?"

"Matt," Janey said softly, "let her sleep for now. She needs her rest; some peaceful rest. We can tackle this when the time comes."

The phone rang and the administrator picked it up. "Yes, please send him up." She looked at Matt and said, "The investigator is on his way up to my office."

The investigator knocked on the door and came into the office. Putting his hand out, he said, "Inspector Williams, nice to meet you Mr. Gallagher. I am sorry about your loss. I need to ask some questions." He turned to Janey. "Miss?"

"Ms.," she emphasized. "Ms. Janey McGann."

"Mzzzz McGann. May I ask what your role is here?"

"I'm a friend. I am here to support Mirabel and Matt." She deliberately spoke calmly, but inwardly she bristled.

"I need to question you both separately."

The investigator tried to be as compassionate as his nature would allow, but it was an interrogation nevertheless. He took over the administrator's office. Then he separated Matt and Janey. He asked Matt all kinds of questions about his friends, family, whether he had any enemies, and who knew they were at the hospital.

Next it was Janey's turn. She stepped into the office, nervous and unsure whether she would crack under the interrogation. The investigator's suspicion got under her skin, and made her feel exposed, afraid. The investigator tried hard to crack her. She knew he couldn't put a finger on it, but she could tell he knew something was off. Finally, he had to give up because her story was locked up tight—she had been in the room with witnesses when the baby went missing. She knew he wasn't the type to give up easily, but he finally relented.

Once the questioning was over, the inspector gave them both his card and said he would be in touch. He also asked them to call him right away if they thought of anything he needed to know. Before he left, he asked to speak with Mirabel, but Matt insisted that he let her sleep through the night and come back in the morning. The inspector reluctantly agreed, saying he had hospital staff and the doctor to speak with, and could do that first. But he let Matt know he would be back by 8:00 a.m. the following morning to speak with her.

Matt and Janey were both exhausted. Matt had made arrangements to have a roller bed brought into Mirabel's room so he could stay with her, and he told Janey she might as well go home and try to get some sleep, too.

Janey gave Matt a hug and said, "I will be back first thing in the morning."

Chapter Fourteen

When Janey got home, she made some chamomile tea and settled into her plush chair to meditate before going to bed. She smiled tentatively, glad to be home with Tarsi, who had greeted her, tail held high, when Janey entered. Now Tarsi was curled up in her lap, warmth radiating out from her slender body. Janey was grateful for Tarsi's devotion and love. She stroked Tarsi's soft fur and murmured endearing words, and Tarsi looked up at her, eyes narrowing softly in the way cats do, communicating her unconditional love.

Janey started to cry soft tears that held all the grief, wonder, hope, and sadness of the day. The tears streamed down her face and landed on her sweater. She took a deep breath, letting out a long sigh as she exhaled, closed her eyes, and sank into her center, surrendering to all the sensations in her universe—the vibration of Tarsi's soft purr rumbling through the blanket and penetrating into her legs, the soft hum of the refrigerator in the background, and the plush softness of the chair enveloping her. This was her time to reconnect with her divine source. Janey sank down and dozed off.

Janey woke up with a start as her head fell forward. She picked up Tarsi and placed her on the floor, then made her way to the bedroom. She made sure to set the alarm for 6:00 a.m., as she wanted to be at the hospital by 7:30, before the inspector arrived to question Mirabel. She thought about how Mirabel might respond to the news of the baby's disappearance as she slipped into bed. Tarsi, purring, pawed at the blankets and Janey lifted them for the cat to crawl under and curl up by her side.

She slept fitfully, waking up frequently and tossing and turning through the night. Every time she woke up, images of flames and screaming women haunted her. At one point, she turned and looked at the clock around 4:00 a.m., and then lost track. The alarm finally startled her awake at 6:00 a.m., and she got up and got ready to go back to the hospital.

When she arrived, Matt sat in the chair next to the bed and Mirabel toyed with her breakfast. Matt looked at her and nodded. From this Janey knew he had waited for her to arrive before telling Mirabel the news.

Janey sat down on the opposite side of the bed from Matt and turned to Mirabel. "Did you sleep well, Mirabel?"

Mirabel nodded. "Yes, whatever they gave me helped, but I wish I hadn't woken up. As long as I was asleep I didn't remember that Maia Jane was gone. It's so hard to be here, longing for a living child in my arms with a happy Matt by my side." Tears were welling in her eyes and she looked at Janey. "How am I supposed to get through the day now?" Shudders took her body.

Janey placed her hand on Mirabel's thigh and looked up at Matt.

Matt finally spoke up and said, "Mirabel, I don't know how to tell you this and I don't want to, but I have to." His voice cracked. "Mirabel, the hospital can't find Maia Jane's body."

Mirabel looked up at him, suddenly still, and said, "Wha...what do you mean?"

"Janey and I were filling out papers late yesterday when we found out. We...we didn't want to disturb your sleep. You needed your rest, and it seemed there wasn't anything we could do but wait. The hospital looked everywhere and when they couldn't find her, they called the police. The inspector is coming at eight. He wants to ask you some questions."

Mirabel just sat there. She turned to look at Janey for confirmation. Janey nodded, but didn't say anything.

What can she say? She can't bring my baby back, Mirabel thought.

They all remained silent while Mirabel struggled to absorb the news. Tragedy piled on top of tragedy, and an overwhelming weight of grief bore down on her, strangling her voice and numbing her mind. No one spoke, and an unhappy silence prevailed until a nurse entered the room and removed Mirabel's breakfast and checked her vitals.

At 8:00 a.m. the inspector knocked on the door.

Matt raised his head and said, "Come in."

The inspector walked to Mirabel's bedside and handed her a card. "Ms. McInness, I am Inspector Williams. I am sorry for your loss and I hate to intrude, but I need to ask you some questions. I want you to know we will do our best to track down the child's body."

Mirabel took the card and stared at it distractedly, then looked out the window. If she looked at him, she would have to acknowledge that her baby's death was real and she just wanted to pretend that she was somewhere else—anywhere but there.

"Ms. McInness, I know this is hard, but if we are going to find the baby, I will need your cooperation. Can I sit down and ask you some questions?"

Mirabel swallowed and kept looking out the window as the inspector sat down and pulled out his notebook.

"Do you know anyone that would want to hurt you or your family?"

Mirabel shook her head.

"Can you tell me all the people who knew you were coming to the hospital?"

Matt interrupted, "Inspector Williams, I already told you that last night."

"Yes, but I need to ask her, just in case it might be different."

Mirabel, still looking out the window, said, "Only Sandy, my midwife. I called Matt and Sandy, that's all."

The inspector made a note in his book. "How many people knew you were pregnant and near term?"

Mirabel said, "I don't know. Matt, Sandy, Janey, the lady at the grocery store, people at Matt's shop, people at Mystic Dolphin." Finally, she turned and looked at the inspector and pleaded, "Why would anyone want to take my baby, Inspector?"

The inspector looked at Matt, momentarily at a loss. Finally, he answered, "Ms. McInness, I wish I could answer that question for you, but that is not my job. My job is to try to locate your baby so that you and your husband can put her to rest. Can you tell me, did you notice anything strange before you went to the hospital, anything that could help lead us to what might have happened?"

Mirabel shook her head and stared out the window again. The inspector appeared to realize he wasn't going to get much here, and would have to rely on the information he had gleaned from his interrogation of Matt and Janey and the hospital staff yesterday. He said his goodbyes and left to pursue other avenues.

Mirabel asked Matt, "Can you call the nurse? I just want to sleep."

Matt complied and the nurse came in.

Mirabel said, "Can you give me something to help me sleep?"

"I will need to check with the doctor first. Let me go call her," the nurse replied.

Mirabel stared out the window again and Matt and Janey looked at each other. Neither of them had any idea how to help Mirabel, who was slipping into despondency. Matt looked like he wished he could just go to sleep, too. Janey struggled against her frustration, burdened by having to wait to offer some kind of hope. She wished she could run off and find Magdalena to ask her how she was supposed to manage this. She was pulled apart by concern for Mirabel and the tension of keeping the very secret that might help her. She longed to burst out and tell Mirabel that Maia Jane was safe with Magdalena. Clenching her hands, she held her tongue.

They all remained there in silence; Mirabel looking out the window; Matt sitting by her side, head hung low; and Janey fidgeting, until the nurse came in and gave Mirabel a pill to help her sleep. Eventually, Mirabel drifted off and Matt told Janey to go on home. He said he would call her if anything changed. She didn't know what else to do, so she went home to Tarsi.

• • •

After a day, they released Mirabel from the hospital. The inspector kept in touch, but didn't have any news about the baby. The disappearance remained a mystery and made its way into the unsolved mysteries files. Inspector Williams expressed his regrets, but he had other more pressing cases to follow up on and let the ball drop on this one.

At home now, Mirabel sank further into depression. Matt tried to get her interested in the garden, hiking—anything to bring her out of her gloom, but without much success. He was struggling too, trying to understand why his life lay shattered in pieces all around him. He had no idea how to put it all back together again.

Janey kept her vigil and waited for the signal that would guide her to revealing the letter that sat unnoticed in the basket in Matt and Mirabel's office.

Chapter Fifteen

orning light came in through the curtains in her bedroom and woke Janey. She got up and started to get ready for work. Since meeting Magdalena, something had shifted and the tarot readings she did for clients had become more precise and powerful. Her schedule was busier than ever as a result. The owner at Mystic Dolphin was thrilled and wanted her to schedule more time, and Janey readily agreed. It was good to keep busy while she waited for her sign from Magdalena. But she was impatient nonetheless. *How long will I have to wait? I hate seeing Matt and Mirabel so unhappy.* She had no one else to talk to about her secret, so she went to the trees. As soon as she completed her readings for the day, she would take her Navajo blanket and hike up to the tree where she had done the cloak ritual with Mirabel.

One day, as she sat on her blanket under the tree, she pressed her back against the trunk and closed her eyes. A wren warbled in the woods behind her and she could hear the "kee eeee-arr" of a red-tailed hawk far above her. She felt heat along her body, starting where her back connected to the tree. The energy pushed into her belly and swirled in a spiral deep in her center, then moved outward, down her legs, and into her hands. The whispering of the tree, ever so subtle at first, grew louder. She sighed. *I wish I could understand.* Her inner gaze opened and she became aware of doorways. She trembled, excited, but knew her excitement could override the experience, so she breathed deeply, touching the calm at her center. The tree whispered inside her. It said, "Shiaaah..."

She sensed the tree was calling, like it was calling to its maker, and her heart twisted a little. *The tree is sad.* A tear fell from the corner of her eye and rolled down her cheek. She picked it up with her tongue, tasting the salt. She turned and gently touched the tree *I love you. I will do what is within my power, I promise.*

The next day Janey got up, took a shower, meditated, and got dressed slowly and with intention. Eating breakfast was a new experience. She could feel the flavors as they spread across her tongue. She noticed that different areas on her tongue received flavors, some more or less intensely. She chewed thoughtfully. *I am awakening.*

She placed her dishes in the sink. When she opened the door to leave, she intuitively looked down. Lying there at her doorstep was a Hawthorne Drug bottle with a trace of glittery substance at the bottom. Her heart danced in her chest as she reached down and picked up the bottle. *Yes.* It was time. In response, gates opened inside her and energy flooded into her body. She took a deep breath and went back inside and called the store. Caroline, the store owner, picked up and Janey said as calmly as she could, "I am sorry, Caroline, I won't be able to make it today. Can you find someone to cover for me?"

Caroline said, "Janey, this puts me in a bit of a spot. Are you sick?"

"No, but I have to take care of something and I need to do it today." Janey hung up the phone. She thought about calling Matt and Mirabel, but decided to just show up at their doorstep unannounced because she didn't know if she could hold her silence until she got there. There was a risk that Matt might be at the bike shop, but she decided to deal with that when she got there.

Janey arrived at the Gallagher house and was relieved to see that Matt's car was still in the driveway. She paused before getting out and closed her eyes, finding her center and feeling the stillness there. Then she opened the car door and picked up the Hawthorne Drug bottle from the passenger's seat. She walked to the front door and rang the bell.

Matt answered and looked surprised, but she could tell he was relieved to see her. "Janey. We weren't expecting you, but it's good to see you. Come in. Mirabel is in the bedroom resting, but I'll go get her. It will be good for her to talk to you."

Janey put her hand on Matt's arm. "Matt, how is she doing?"

Matt answered, "I wish I could say that she is coming around, but she is just going through the motions every day. She doesn't even cry anymore. Most of the time she just sits and stares out the window."

"I have come because...well...there might be something to change things. Can you go get her? It's important."

Matt gave her a puzzled look, then walked down the hall to the bedroom while Janey went to the living room and waited.

Matt came out, followed by Mirabel. Mirabel shuffled into the living room and asked without curiosity, "Janey? What are you doing here? Don't you have to be at work?"

Janey said, "I took the day off. I have something important to tell you. You'd better sit down first."

Mirabel, a mildly perplexed look on her face, said, "Okay." She sat in the easy chair next to the window.

"Do you remember the day the box arrived from your father? I've been thinking about it, and if you remember, there were some papers in the box. I don't think you ever looked at them."

"What?" Mirabel now looked thoroughly confused. "Why would you be thinking about that after all this time..." She paused. "And everything?"

"Well, I was thinking it might be important and it has to do with why I am here today." She looked back and forth between them, unsure of where to start. She feared telling them the truth now, after she had betrayed them to their grief for all this time. "Mirabel, Matt, I don't even know how to start and...well, I guess I have to apologize, because I know how hard everything has been since Maia Jane." She took a breath. "I know it seems impossible, but there is hope."

"Hope for what? Janey, you're speaking in riddles. Maia Jane is gone. There is no hope. What does this have to do with the papers from my father?"

"Mirabel, Matt...I know you might not forgive me. I, well...I haven't been exactly honest with you. I never wanted you to hurt, but I made a promise and I had good reason to keep it until now."

Matt and Mirabel stared at Janey, confusion written all over their faces.

Janey continued. "I got a sign today, a sign that let me know it was time to reveal the secrets I have been keeping. I want you to know that I hated keeping this secret from you. It went against everything in my nature." She hesitated. She would just have to blurt it out. "I know where Maia Jane is and she is safe for now."

Matt suddenly stood up "What? What do you mean you know where she is? All the anguish..." He stared at her. "Janey, where is she...and how could you?" He was pacing, obviously agitated.

Mirabel sat there looking stunned.

Janey reached down and pulled out the bottle. She unscrewed the cap while Matt paced around, and threw the glittery substance into the room when Matt had his back turned. Mirabel watched, a look of surprise on her face. Then she shook her head as if shaking something off. Mirabel's eyes met Janey's. Janey could see a new light in those eyes, as if something had cleared.

Mirabel turned to Matt and said, "Matt, wait, sit down. Let's listen to what Janey has to say."

Janey said, "I saw the strange woman from the coffee shop in the hospital the day Maia Jane was born. Remember? They sent me out to the waiting room. She suddenly appeared next to me and convinced me to come outside with her. Oh Mirabel, she told me incredible things; things about you, things about Maia Jane. But she made me promise not to say anything to you until I got a sign from her. She said, 'When a Hawthorne Drug bottle appears, it is time for secrets to be revealed.' That is why I am here today. The bottle appeared today." Janey handed it over. "Here, you can see it."

Matt turned to Janey and grabbed the bottle. "That sounds crazy. I don't understand. What could be so important that you would keep such a secret from us? You said you know where Maia Jane is? Where is she, and why would anyone take our dead baby?" He stopped. "And you knew about it? How could you? I thought you were our friend."

His voice cracked as he said this. Janey could see he was at a breaking point.

"Because there is hope that Maia Jane can still live, but that hope would have been lost had I told you before. The lady— her name is Magdalena—told me. Timing was everything. She needed to take Maia to safety before the spell could be broken."

"Spell? What are you talking about, a spell? I think you've gone stark raving mad. You aren't making any sense at all. I mean, I know you believe in magic and stuff, but Janey, this is going a little too far. Maia Jane is dead and we never got a chance to have closure with that, and now you come prancing back in here telling us you've kept secrets from us about where she is and claiming she can still live. Janey, I am sorry, but you should just leave. How can you do this to Mirabel? I thought you cared about her."

Mirabel held up her hands and shouted, "Janey is right. I can feel it. Something has changed. I feel it in my soul. Please sit down and let Janey finish. Can you just sit down and listen, please?"

Matt looked over at Mirabel, shaking his head, but he abruptly sat down. He wasn't a match for the two of them.

Janey looked at Matt, and in her softest voice said, "Matt, I am sorry, the last thing I ever wanted to do was hurt you. I know this is hard to believe. If I hadn't seen Magdalena with my own two eyes...but there was something about her that made me believe. Matt, she gave me hope. There is hope."

Mirabel said, "Janey, please finish your story."

Janey took a deep breath. "She told me that you aren't from this world and when she said it, suddenly everything about you made sense to me: the sparkle I see around you sometimes, the purple in your eyes." Looking at Matt, she said, "Matt, don't tell me you never noticed that." Turning back to Mirabel, she continued, "The way I am drawn to you; and yes, Matt, I know you feel that too, I see it in your face when you look at her. It was the same for me with Magdalena. I felt drawn to her and there was even more purple in her eyes. So strange, and yet so compelling—like some special kind of magic. Mirabel, you have that too, a special kind of magic. I suspect this is why you always felt so...well... not at home here. And Mirabel, it explains why you are so attracted to the buckeye groves. She told me they are portals to your world."

Mirabel looked at Janey and nodded, knowing that she was hearing the truth. And as the truth settled on her, she suddenly felt more grounded than she ever had in her life. But one thing screamed out to her in all this that she had to know about. Janey said there was hope for Maia Jane. Life poured back into Mirabel, waking her from the numb purgatory she had been in. No, even more than that; now she knew she had been in a sort of purgatory all her life. This surge of life coursing through her brought with it a glow.

Matt looked at her. He looked stunned and unable to say anything.

She looked back at Janey and whispered, full of hope, "Maia...tell me about Maia."

"She told me that children born in your world can remain dormant," Janey continued. "That they often are born and stay that way until a special ceremony is performed. She didn't tell me everything about the ceremony. She said the letter would explain more. That's why I am here today, to prompt you to read the letter. The letter was in the box from your father. It is a letter from your mother—the mother you never knew. Mirabel, you remember the picture of the woman holding you as a baby in her arms? You knew when you looked at the picture that she wasn't your mother. You were right; those people weren't related to you. You were hidden there with them, by Magdalena, with a spell to keep you unaware." Janey started to cry. "I never wanted to keep a secret from you, never! But Magdalena told me the child would die if she didn't get her away from the hospital and wrapped in a special bundle from your world. And the timing had to be right to wake you from the spell. It was so hard to see you in the hospital so devastated. I wanted so badly to tell you. It was the hardest thing I have ever done in my life to keep that secret." Her tears flowed freely now, weeks of tension releasing and falling to the ground.

Mirabel sat forward in her chair eagerly, absorbing everything Janey said, knowing the truth and now feeling a sense of joy.

Janey wiped her eyes and continued, "She also told me there is danger. Magdalena told me we must act with haste once the secret has been revealed. You have been safe up until now, but the release of the spell and your awareness puts you in grave danger, too. Mirabel, go find the letter and read it."

Mirabel got up to find the letter, but first she went over to Matt, looking down at him with concern and love. "Matt, are you okay? I know this must be hard to take in."

Matt looked up at her, awe written on his face, and he just nodded. She took his hands and looked at him for a moment before dropping them and heading into the office. Janey and Matt sat in silence, waiting for Mirabel to return. In a few moments she came back in, remarking, "I found it. It's funny how I forgot about it after taking it out of the box."

"There was a spell," Janey said.

Mirabel opened the letter. As she looked down at it, at first the writing was unfamiliar, but it transformed into English as she began to read the contents out loud for Janey and Matt to hear. They both sat silent, listening intently.

> *Dearest Mirabel,*
>
> *I write now knowing that you will never see me, as I will be long gone from this world soon after you are born. I will give you over to the hands of my Watcher, Magdalena, whom I trust will care for you and keep you safe. More than anything I wish I could be with you, but at times we must make sacrifices, and this is one of those times. My precious little Mirabel, we are not of this world, but of necessity I will give birth to you in this world. At this time, I am barred from returning back to our own.*
>
> *Ours is a tragic story. Our world, Ynys-Avalone, was once beautiful and so full of life and magic. I wish that you could have been born there and experienced it for yourself. It is a world of ethereal music and beauty. Once upon a time, people from this human world and our world could cross over into each other's. The truth behind the many ancient myths and legends comes from the experience of those who crossed over.*
>
> *Our world is the twin to this world. When the Silent One, the Shiashialon, our divine mother, gave birth, she gave birth to two worlds. This one she called Gaia and the other she called Ynys-Avalone. They were always connected, deeply intertwined. Both worlds carried a special gift of the Shiashialon, and the two freely shared their own gifts with the other. The gifts flowed between them, strengthening and balancing each world. And so the destiny of each was tied to the other. Gaia's gift is firmament:*

the stability and solidity of its forms and processes. Ynys-Avalone's gift is magic: the ethereal, creative forces of manifestation and change. Gaia feeds Ynys-Avalone with a certain stability, and Ynys-Avalone feeds Gaia with ethereal magic that keeps it from becoming too static and mundane.

The two worlds are connected through special trees whose roots cross the boundaries between the two. These trees are portals for both worlds. Not all trees on both worlds are so connected, and they are scattered loosely across the land. Only trees that came from the seed of the Mother Tree hold this magic and come in many forms: oak, yew, rowan, fig, cedar, and buckeye, among others.

For many eons the people of Gaia understood this, and the women in particular came to worship at these trees, leaving offerings and love. This kept the trees strong and healthy. They also prayed for our kind to cross over and give birth to healers who could shake up the inertia that caused diseases of mind, body, and systems. Gaia's people gave us many names: the fae, nymphs, goddesses, spirits, angels, oracles. People from Gaia traveled to our world to help us build structures for our people to live in comfortably. There was much travel and sharing between the worlds, and our connection to the Creator, the Shiashialon, was strong. Both worlds were filled with her love. But a sickness crept into this world which originated from desert people. This caused the Shiashialon to grieve and retreat.

Eventually, she slept, and while she slept the people of this world became even more disconnected, and that changed things further. Since our world holds the original tree, we were closer to the Shiashialon. On Gaia, the disconnection caused a longing, which led men to develop the idea of ownership to fill the emptiness they felt. Eventually, they became fixed in static heaviness as they began to accumulate wealth and grasp for more. They began to fear change, and feared the nature of magic at the same time they coveted our adeptness with it. They became jealous of our powers. And so, they began to take control of the access between the two worlds. Over time they created gods in the image of themselves and forgot about the Shiashialon, or altered her story, making her seem subservient to their new gods. They raped our women and captured our children. They held elaborate ceremonies to make the people believe that the children born of us came from their gods. Worst of all, they began to cut down the trees and use them to build great temples for their gods, or fortresses and palaces. Women who were found to worship at the trees were punished, and this forced them to turn away from us in fear.

Slowly, the links between our worlds were destroyed and the magic that flowed between the worlds decreased to a mere trickle. Gaia became more static and more violent as the people got stuck in thought forms that held them hostage. The impact on Ynys-Avalone was devastating, too. Without material substance to hold it together, a dissonance made its way into the harmony of its music, the heart of its magic. This caused many sacred places on our world to erupt into flames, or to dissipate and float into the ether. Volatility reigned in many places on our world and it became dangerous to travel. We feared we would disappear if we left the stable areas, and in fact, many of the people and creatures living in the unstable areas disappeared forever. However, there are pockets in our world which remain stable due to the places where the magic trees are still safe. Most people of Gaia have long forgotten their sacred connection to us, but there are still some places that hold it. It is my hope that it will remain so.

As I sit here by the stump of the last magic tree in Gaia's Scotland, many women here have been tortured and all the sacred trees in this land have been cut down to make a pyre upon which to burn them. My access to Ynys-Avalone has been cut off. I came across in hopes of bringing renewal and healing to this world in order to begin to reverse the damage. Unfortunately, I failed to understand how the continued destruction of the trees over time has created a deep-seated fear of change in these people, and they spread this sickness across the lands here. Now I will have to sacrifice my life in order to pour the life of our land into you so that you can live. And even so, Magdalena may keep you in stasis. With all the turmoil in this world, it will be safest if

Magdalena waits to awaken you until such a time that she deems will hold more hope.

Mirabel, your memories will also be tied to mine, but once Magdalena brings you out of stasis she will cast a forgetting spell on you until it is time for you to understand. We may be separated by my death and by many, many years, but it is the fate of our kind that the spirit and memories of all our foremothers remain present in our children and their children. It is thus that we are immortal. Mirabel, now that you are reading this letter, it is time for you to remember.

Your hope and our hope will come in the form of a child. Your body can only ripen in this world when it is touched by the dreams of the flowers of Lake Pergosia. There are some in this world that have ancient links to our own, and the touch of a woman who remembers magic and the worship of trees will help. I can only hope that this will become possible by the grace of the Silent One. There is a legend on our world that says a time will come when there is great destruction across our land. It says that a healer born on Gaia will cross back over and traverse the Nygel Plain to find the one original tree of the two worlds. Her child must be placed within the trunk of this tree. It is said that this must happen when the worlds cross a cosmic threshold that aligns them with the center of the universe. After transferring her life force into the child, this healer will pass into the tree and drop into the void where she will awaken the Shiashialon from her slumber.

Mirabel, when I left our world, the Nygel Plain was already disintegrating. Your journey will be a dangerous one, and you will have your child with you as you travel. It grieves me to leave this task to you, who are yet unborn, but my strength fails me and Magdalena must stand at a threshold somewhere across this world, away from the violence here in Scotland. She can only leave for short periods of time and will have to take you back there. I will call her soon, as your birth is near. Already you have gone into stasis, as I no longer feel movement.

My precious little Mirabel, you are the hope of our worlds. If all ties between the two worlds are severed, they will both perish.

Trust Magdalena. She will guide you. To call her, hold the silver fruit in your hands and call her name.

Know that you have all the love of my heart, and how I wish I could lay my eyes upon your face. I send a magical prayer for you and for the journey ahead. Magdalena will take you away to another part of this world where the magic trees still exist. I leave you with the pollen from the Shialon Tree. This magical pollen will help you cross over when you are among those trees. I also leave you with the silver fruit of this tree from our world. Its purpose will be revealed in time.

With much love,
Your mother, Melusine

Memories poured into Mirabel, and she began to remember life in her world through the memories of all those who came before her. She was suddenly at home in her skin in a way she never had been before. All her longing and grief over the years now came together, tempered by the strength of her foremothers, their love, the magic of her world, and the vibrant timbre of life force that was hers. She straightened, strong, able, and informed by great purpose. She still felt frightened by what was to come, but now she had hope and possibilities that had been absent before this day. And Maia Jane! Her heart swelled when she thought of her, her child, and the hope of all beings on both worlds. She would do anything to save Maia Jane, and this gave her the courage she knew she needed for the coming journey. Tears streamed down Mirabel's delicate face, and those tears were mirrored on Janey's.

Matt sat, his head hung low. Not only did there seem to be no place in this story for him, but he knew now that Mirabel would soon leave him. His life had now completely fallen apart, yet his heart ached for Mirabel and her coming journey. The only joy he could find in this story was the fact that Maia Jane was still alive. Smart enough to read the between the lines, he knew that she wasn't the child of his body, but he still loved her; she was the child of his heart. He held out hope that

132

Mirabel would succeed in her journey and that someday he might meet Maia Jane again. He held unbearable grief and loss on one side, and the fear of total destruction of both worlds on the other. Part of him still couldn't grasp how this world wasn't quite what he thought it was. What in his life had prepared him to hold this terrible burden in his heart and mind?

Mirabel walked over and knelt in front of Matt. "Matt, I don't know what I would have done without you. You brought a measure of joy, sanity, and love into my life here that helped me survive. Don't ever think you aren't important to me. And Matt, I need you still. Maia Jane needs you. Just knowing you gives me courage. Without that courage, I can't make this journey. Matt Gallagher, I love you. I will always love you. Don't ever forget that."

Matt looked up at her. Mirabel gestured for him to rise from the chair and when he stood, she put her arms around him and held him close for a long time. Finally, she pulled away and said, "Matt, I must prepare to go."

They all stood looking at each other. They didn't know where to start.

Mirabel finally said, "I am going to need a backpack, and a sling for the baby."

Janey said, "Mirabel, you should call on Magdalena. Remember what your mother wrote? Hold the silver fruit and call her name."

Mirabel went to the bookshelf and pulled out the books. She stuck her hand to the back and pulled out the dragonfly box Janey had given her, the Hawthorne Drug bottles, and the silver fruit of the tree. She brought these things to the center of the room and cleared a place to sit on the floor, cross-legged. She put the silver buckeye in her hand, holding it up in front of her, and clasped her other hand over it. Next, she closed her eyes, took a deep breath, and called out, "Magdalena." Nothing happened. She called again, "Magdalena." Still nothing. Then her memory filled her and she said, "Magdalena, by the spirit of my mother, Melusine, I call you. It is time for my journey."

She blew onto the silver fruit and it rang out with a pure, single tone that filled the room.

After the tone dissipated, everything in the room became quiet. Matt and Janey looked on, caught up in the stillness. Mirabel saw the energy swirl around her, and a spiraling cloud of sparkling energy enveloped her. A space opened up in front of her. She saw Magdalena's face and heard her voice in her mind.

"My dear Mirabel, welcome to your heritage. I have been waiting and watching for this moment for many, many years. I was your mother's Watcher, and now I am yours. I hear your call and know it is time. Do not worry about what to bring on the journey, except for the silver fruit and the bottle of pollen. I have everything prepared and I have little Maia Jane safe with me. Meet me by the buckeye grove where you had your first dream of your home. Meet me there at dusk. You may bring Janey and Matt with you, but they can only come as far as the grove. They cannot go beyond. The journey is yours to take—yours and Maia Jane's."

Her face faded as the swirl of energy closed in again, and then it too subsided, leaving Mirabel sitting in silence in the middle of the room. She looked over at Matt, then at Janey. They both shook their heads, as if waking up from a trance.

"Did you call her?" Matt asked.

Mirabel said, "Yes, I know what to do. I need not worry about bringing anything with me except for the bottle of pollen and the silver fruit."

Part III

The Journey

Chapter Sixteen

Early afternoon arrived, and Mirabel knew she had to meet Magdalena at the grove at dusk. She told Matt and Janey what Magdalena had said, and they all waited together in the living room, each caught up in their own thoughts. Finally, Mirabel got up and began wandering through the house, trailing her hands along all the familiar contours of her home, knowing that she would never see it again. She went into the nursery, a room that Maia Jane would never see. She looked around at the magical space, with all the fairies and sparkle, and realized that she had unconsciously tried to create a mirror of her own world in this space for her and Maia. She could see how these fairies were icons of the spirits and magic of her world, which at one time had passed into this world more regularly.

Every plant, flower, and creature on her world had a glowing spirit. Its shining, magical life force could be seen by her people, and by a select few from Gaia. It created in humans an altered state of consciousness; took them out of their earth trance. The magic of the firmament induced a trance in its denizens, making things seem more solid than they were in actuality. Of course, the tearing down of the trees had made it even harder for humans to enter this altered state. The human mind on Gaia, without access to the magic of her world, existed in a constant state of attachment to static forms. The doorways in the human mind were now rusted shut after so many years, and now very little magic seeped through.

Janey has her own kind of magic, which makes her mind more pliable somehow.

There was some connection between the two of them, but that remained a mystery. Mirabel certainly understood Janey's longing for magic. Janey's mind was open to it, and Mirabel could see that Janey felt cheated of the experience of the ethereal.

You just can't force magic. Magic is subtle and connected to life itself, and technology has no subtlety.

As the portal trees died, so came the extinction of the creatures, the corruption of the waters, and the contamination of the air. Mirabel knew there wasn't much time left before both worlds were irreparable. Deep in her train of thought, she suddenly found the strength and courage she never knew she had. Yes, she was terrified, but she was prepared to walk through that terror; to walk through whatever she might meet on her world.

She glanced around the room one last time and said out loud, "Maia Jane, I promise you a future the magic in this room represents, whatever it takes."

Mirabel went to her bedroom and found her hiking gear. She undressed and pulled on her pants with all the pockets, then several layers of athletic-type shirts. Next, she pulled on her lightweight hiking boots. She didn't know whether they would be appropriate, but they were all she had, and had been comfortable gear when she and Matt had hiked or biked the California landscape. Before she left the room, she turned and looked at the bed. Tears trickled down her face as she remembered all the beautiful love that had been expressed in that bed—all that she and Matt had shared over their time together. She said a silent prayer that he would one day find a similar happiness again. She was profoundly grateful for his tenderness, and now that she had all the memories, she knew that he was much like the men of long ago, before the trouble started—gentle, caring stewards for the land, creatures, and the women and children. Now she knew why she had been so deeply attracted to him.

Mirabel tried to see into the future. How would her journey and her success impact the outcome? Unable to see into this mystery, she would have to wait to understand. Without her journey and her sacrifice, the outcome was clear—devastation all around. Her shoulders dropped, heavy as the understanding of the gravity of her task sank in.

The afternoon was waning. Mirabel walked back to the entrance to the living room and silently observed Janey and Matt. Matt wept openly and Janey, crying alongside, held him close. They clung to each other for comfort, and this heartened Mirabel. Her task became more bearable knowing that the two people she loved most in the world would have each other for validation and comfort. They could share the secret that no one else in their world would know for quite some time.

She stood and looked at them for a few minutes, remembering all the times they had spent together; seeing herself with Janey under the oak tree, their first conversation at Mystic Dolphin, and Janey blessing the motionless Maia Jane. She thought of the hikes and bike rides with Matt, their wedding, the wonderful honeymoon, and how he made her laugh with his bullfrog song, always sung deliberately off key. She had this brief, precious moment to watch them and engrave these memories in her soul. Finally, unable to absorb any more, she walked into the room and quietly murmured, "Matt, Janey, it's time to go."

Janey stood up while Matt wiped his eyes with the back of his sleeve and looked at Mirabel. His glance said it all. She read his desperation. He had lost his child, only to lose it again, along with her. She broke the silence with the only thing she could say. "Matt, can you drive?"

Matt nodded and Mirabel gathered her jacket.

Janey, wanting to do something useful, went into the kitchen and filled Mirabel's reusable bottle with water, brought it back out, and looked deep into Mirabel's eyes as she handed it over.

Mirabel took it from her. "Janey, thanks. I might need this."

Janey nodded.

They left the house, locked it behind them, and climbed into Matt's truck. In silence they drove to the parking lot at the open space closest to the buckeye groves. Matt parked and they piled out, made their way to the gate, and started walking up the trail, heads down. Matt trailed Mirabel and Janey brought up the rear. They traversed by the driving range and came round the bend without a word.

Mirabel left the trail and followed a deer path through the grass into the lower buckeye grove. Her love of the groves filled her heart and she could feel the magic of the trees permeate her skin. She paused and turned to Matt and Janey.

"I think it is okay for you to follow me up to the Mother Grove. We have to walk up through the ravine to the second grove, and then hike the steep hill on the right to get there."

Janey looked around. Her eyes widened. She could feel the magic, too. Now she knew why Mirabel had been so drawn to these trees. Their gnarled branches were covered with lichen. The grove looked like an orchard, with rocks strewn here and there. If she hadn't come under such sad circumstances, she knew she would have felt ecstatic. The magic was palpable and energized her. Her fingertips tingled and she sensed heightened sensations in her palms. Briefly, she closed her eyes and tapped into her center. Strength flowed from deep inside and it was connected to the trees...and to something deeper. It whispered "Shiasheee..."

Janey watched Matt look over at Mirabel and nod. She could tell he didn't feel the magic. His heart was broken and the nearness of Mirabel's departure weighed him down. The way he carried himself made his feelings plain. Since his demeanor was normally cheerful, seeing him so broken caused her heart to twist. She glanced over at Mirabel. She had transformed. Janey could see a faint shimmer. It must have appeared when they entered the grove, because she didn't remember noticing it on the way up there. Her heart quickened. *How did I enter into this amazing story?*

The change that had taken place in her life since meeting Magdalena was hard for her to fathom, even now, after she'd had time to absorb it. Suddenly, she was in a fairytale. It didn't matter that she had longed for such things all her life. Now she *knew* magic was real, and she breathed it in.

Mirabel interrupted her thoughts. "We should move on. It's getting late."

Janey fell in step behind Matt. They made their way up into the second grove and paused again.

Mirabel's skin tingled. The closer they got to the Mother Grove, the more she felt shifts occurring inside her. Not only did her skin tingle, but her steps were lighter, as if she could float. She stopped, held her palms out in front of her, and investigated the intense force now moving in them. A distinct spiral pattern was beginning to glow softly under her skin. Suddenly, feeling shy about it, she quickly put her hands back down at her sides and waited for Janey and Matt to catch up. Then, pointing up, she said, "This is the hard part. Now we have to climb this steep hill to get to the Mother Grove. Follow me."

Mirabel grabbed a small shrub and hoisted herself up onto the deer trail, working her way up the steep incline until she found herself entering the Mother Grove once again. It had been more than two years since she had run out of that grove in a panic, and in all that time she had never returned. Her senses stepped up another level. The tingle on her skin increased and the spirals on her palms glowed intensely. Now she could feel power emanating from them.

As Mirabel stepped fully into the grove, she saw Magdalena sitting on the rocks cradling a bundle. Mirabel paused and inhaled a deep intake of breath. Magdalena looked up at her and they gazed at each other silently. Now that all of her foremother's memories were part of her, Mirabel knew Magdalena. But the experience was unique. She was thrilled at meeting her for the first time. The encounter at the café so long ago had been brief, and she had been unconscious of her truth at that time. But here, now, for the first time, Mirabel was face to face with one of her own kind. It magnified the feeling of coming home that she had experienced after reading her mother's letter.

Mirabel was also aware of how long Magdalena had waited for this moment, and a deep love welled up inside her, pressing against her breast and filling her center. Magdalena had spent centuries of exile on earth, watching over Mirabel and waiting from a distance. The love Mirabel felt from her mother's memories mingled with her own. Magnetized by these feelings, she walked purposefully toward Magdalena. A new grace flowed into her gait, giving her small size a new stature. She had become more. She was stepping into her legacy.

Magdalena stood and waited as Mirabel approached, holding out the small bundle that had the baby in stasis wrapped up safely inside. Mirabel stopped before her. Without lifting her eyes from Magdalena's, she received the bundle, little Maia Jane, into her arms. The baby had been thoroughly wrapped in cloth so that no part of her was visible. Mirabel received her child and clutched her closely to her breast, overwhelmed with all that she felt and understood.

Magdalena reached up and caressed Mirabel's face. *"Sho lone' mea cunaris Mira'belis, failte ti mathairin.* Child of my heart, Mirabel, welcome to your heritage."

Mirabel reached over with one arm, still holding the bundle in the other, and wound it around Magdalena's waist, laying her head on Magdalena's shoulder.

"Magdalena," she said. *"Mea Liouradion."* These words had come to her suddenly. It meant "My Watcher" in the language of her home, but also more than that. It carried deep affection, love, and most of all, honor for the role of the Watcher, which was ultimately one of sacrifice and unwavering loyalty.

Mirabel pulled away and tenderly placed her hand on Magdalena's cheek. She didn't need to say anything. Magdalena accepted all the gratitude and love in the gesture and nodded her head.

Janey stood at the edge of the grove with Matt, watching this interchange. Matt looked stunned and awed by the transformation in Mirabel. Mirabel had grown somehow, without getting bigger. She was enveloped in grace, and a radiance surrounded both her and Magdalena. Together, Janey and Matt stood rooted to the ground. Janey took his hand. She could feel that, somehow, a sense of peace had seeped into his tattered heart.

Janey moved as though she had stepped into a different Janey—one that didn't feel the constant tug of longing—and this felt strange. She was fully present and calm, accepting the scene in front of her and her part in it as the most natural thing in the world. This new reality had fallen into her life like gentle snowflakes, laying down a blanket of snow in incremental layers until the world was wholly transformed and strange, and suddenly you were surprised at how different it had become. Her hungry eyes scanned the grove. She felt inexorably drawn to the tree behind the rocks where Magdalena stood. The tree pulled her toward it with a sensation that showed up in her belly. As she started to walk toward the tree, Magdalena left Mirabel and stood in front of Janey before she could go any farther.

"Janey," she said, "I know what you are feeling, but you must resist it for now. A time may come one day for you to enter, but not now."

Janey looked at her and frowned. She wanted to touch the tree so badly, but Magdalena shook her head.

Matt walked over to Mirabel and looked down at the bundle. "Is it..."

Mirabel nodded her head.

"Can I see her?"

Magdalena took Janey's hand and brought her over next to Matt so that they all stood around Mirabel.

"You must not unwrap her," Magdalena said to Mirabel. "Your hands are activated by proximity to the tree, and touching her might awaken her. You don't want that to happen right now."

Matt looked at Magdalena. "Can I hold her?"

"I see no harm in that. Perhaps you can hold her while I prepare Mirabel to pass through." She handed the bundle to Matt, who held her with quiet reverence while she continued. "Can you do that? Do not unwrap her. It would cause her great harm. It will be best if you stand or sit at the periphery of the grove. Janey, why don't you go wait with Matt?"

Janey looked back at the tree longingly, then turned to follow Matt to find a place to sit, away from the tree and rocks at the center of the grove. He settled on the ground under an oak on the periphery, and she sat down next to him. They both looked on in silence. Janey had to fight the impulse that pulled her toward the tree. Somehow, Magdalena's presence always created some kind of internal war; but she was not angry, just bemused. Magdalena's last words to her, *"A time may come one day for you to enter..."* looped over and over in her mind, giving her hope and strength along with impatient anticipation. *Someday...* But then Magdalena started to instruct Mirabel, and Janey became caught up in the scene before her.

• • •

Mirabel stood before Magdalena, ready for instruction. She focused all her attention on Magdalena, afraid to miss anything her Watcher said. Failure would cost the life of not only her child, but everything on both worlds.

"Did you bring the pollen and the silver fruit?" Magdalena started.

"Yes, I have them in my pants pockets."

"Please take out the bottle of pollen and give it to me. I am going to draw a circle with the pollen around the tree and rocks to protect the others. Then I will hand the pollen to you. Once you enter the circle with Maia Jane, you must sprinkle some at the tree's root. Not much is needed, and you should save some. Quickly screw the cap back on and put the bottle back in your pocket. A portal will open and you must walk through immediately. I will remain in the circle to close the portal behind you. You will find supplies for your journey on the other side. Do you understand what you need to do once you get to the other side?"

"I think so. I must make my way to the Nygel Plain and follow the path to the Shialon Tree."

"Yes. The journey will not be easy. Keep your wits about you. There are specters in the plain. They are dangerous, and will eat your soul if they capture you. They will try to spook you off the trail and lead you to your death. Do not completely trust your eyesight. Do you feel a slight tug toward this tree in your belly?"

Mirabel nodded.

"You will feel a stronger tug toward the Shialon Tree on the other side. That is your guide. Always follow the direction of that tug no matter what, even if it seems like you will walk off a cliff or walk right into danger. The specters can fool your vision, but they cannot fool your inner sense. Do you understand?"

"Yes," Mirabel answered.

"When you must rest, sleep on the trail. There will be a cloth in your supplies which will protect you. Cover yourself and Maia completely when you sleep. There is also a snug to hold the child. Never put Maia down! Always keep her in the snug next to your body. The snug is made of special, protective cloth that will keep her hidden from the prying eyes of the disappeared."

"The *disappeared?*"

"Yes. Many of our people were swept up into unstable areas and desire to cross back over, but they can't, and don't understand they are lost. They live in an ever-changing dream world. They will attempt to reach across the gap to touch Maia Jane because some part of them will understand that she is the savior. Although she is in stasis, her life force is strong, and will call to them energetically. You mustn't let them confuse you. The cloth will help disguise her. Their voices will compel you. You will be drawn to them as you are to me, because they are your own kind and the full beauty of their voices will fill you with a desire to be with them. Your voice will change when you pass over, as the full power of who we are is attuned to our world and not this one. But if you leave the path, you will become as lost as they are. No matter how much they plead or how much you want to connect, you must turn away. It will be hard. Do you understand?"

Mirabel nodded again, but began to feel less confident than she had been earlier. As she listened to what Magdalena had to say, she wondered if she had the strength to follow through. Briefly, she looked over at Matt and Janey, and saw the bundle in Matt's arms. The thought of Maia Jane girded her heart for the journey.

"Now, go say your goodbyes. I know this may be the hardest thing you ever do." Magdalena touched Mirabel's face again. "Alas, this life you tried to build just wasn't meant to be. I know that your heart aches for Matt and your friend. Please try to keep it brief."

Mirabel swallowed the lump in her throat, determined to hold back her tears. She nodded at Magdalena and turned to walk toward Matt and Janey. She stopped in front of Janey first, took her hands, and looked into her face. "Janey, you have been the truest friend anyone could ever know, and I love you. I wish we had more time to spend under the trees, making magic together; to become old ladies together and watch Maia grow."

Janey threw her arms around her. "Oh Mirabel, I will miss you so much. I will never forget you, never! And I will pray every day for you. I know that you will succeed. I wish I could give you something for strength, but I can see the power in you. I believe in you. You are amazing and I love you."

Whispering in Janey's ear, Mirabel said, "Janey, help Matt. He will need you and your special magic to help him. With you, someday his wounds may heal. I couldn't leave him in the hands of a better friend than you." She pulled away and looked Janey in the face.

Janey nodded, bowed her head, and backed away.

Mirabel went over to Matt and gently lifted the bundle from his arms as he held it out to her. She turned toward Janey and said, "Can you hold Maia for a moment, Janey?"

Janey took the bundle and cradled her, waiting.

Mirabel took Matt's face in her hands. "Matt, I love you. You are my heart's desire. You have been a loving, loyal husband and I don't know what I ever did to deserve you. I wish we could spend the rest of our lives together raising Maia Jane, and retire in Mendocino by the coast, like we always wanted."

She pulled him toward her, wrapped her arms around him, and kissed him hard. All of her love, her sorrow, her longing, and the joy and memories they shared went into that kiss. Matt wrapped his arms tightly around her and they clung to each other, desperate to imprint on each other everything they felt for one another. Finally, Mirabel pulled back and looked Matt in the eyes.

He shook his head and started to say, "I will never stop..."

Mirabel put her finger on his lips. After one last long look into his eyes, Mirabel pulled away and took Maia back from Janey.

Matt reached out to touch the bundle one last time and said, "Maia..." His voice cracked and nothing more came out.

Mirabel turned and walked toward the grove. Janey took Matt's hand and they watched Mirabel step across the boundary Magdalena had created while they said their goodbyes. Blue light shimmered in a translucent web of lace, swirling and transforming whenever the viewer's eye lit. It wasn't solid, because Mirabel stepped right through and they could see her on the other side.

Janey's senses came fully alive. The exhilaration reminded her of how she felt when she was one with the dragon. She wanted to follow Mirabel, but grasped Matt's hand tightly and drew strength to resist her urges from him and for him. For his part, he held Janey's hand because he needed her warmth and compassion. They stood there together, silent, and watched the events unfold inside the barrier.

Holding Maia between her left arm and her chest, Mirabel took the bottle and cap from Magdalena with her right hand and sprinkled the pollen onto the roots of the tree, leaving some in the bottle. She screwed the cap back on with her left hand and stuffed the bottle in her pocket. She stood back as the roots of the tree spread open, creating a portal that spread up the center of the tree. The tree remained solid, but became pliable, bending and molding itself around the opening until it was large enough for Mirabel to walk through.

Magdalena said, "Go now!"

Mirabel took one last long look at Matt and Janey through the web of magic lace, stepped through the portal, and disappeared.

Janey and Matt stood stock still as Magdalena quickly walked over to the tree and bent it back together, closing the opening, almost like folding a zip-lock seam back together. Next, she jumped through the magic web, and as she did, she transformed into a deer and leapt away. The web dissolved. Matt and Janey were left standing in the grove, enveloped in silence.

Slowly, life came back to the grove. A scrub jay screeched down the hill. A rufous-sided towhee started scratching under a shrub nearby, and an oak titmouse bounced around on the branches above them, calling out in its raspy voice *Tsik-a-Der-Der-Der, Tsik-a-Der-Der-Der.*

Janey, still holding Matt's hand, guided him silently down the steep hill. The sky was a rosy pink and burnt orange backdrop and the light was waning fast. Eventually they made their way down the ravine, through the lower groves, around the bend that hid the grove from the driving range, and to the parking lot. Not knowing what to say, they quietly entered the car and Matt drove toward home.

Chapter Seventeen

Mirabel stepped through the tree into a grove devastated by fire. All except the tree she stepped through were dead, now just a pile of charred branches on the ground. The ground was blackened and scorched. While it had been dusk on Gaia when she stepped through the tree, it looked to be early in the day here on Ynys-Avalone. She turned to look at the tree she had walked through; the same tree from her experience in the buckeye grove so many months ago. The tree was no longer glowing white, but was burnt in many areas and otherwise grayed. The tree barely clung to life. She turned in a circle, taking in the devastation as she remembered the former beauty, now enhanced by the memories she had inherited. A well of grief rose up in her, but she pushed it down. There was no time for that now.

Mirabel looked down. Sure enough, at her feet was a pack of supplies, a skin full of water and a snug for Maia. She remembered Magdalena's admonition to never let go of the baby, so she sat down and placed the baby bundle between her thighs, lifted the pack up, looped her arms through the straps, and settled it on her back. Next, Mirabel picked up the snug and wrapped Maia into it and slung it over her shoulder. Still holding Maia, she stood up, then adjusted the strap so the baby sat in front of her right hip.

With all trappings adjusted for her journey, Mirabel closed her eyes and concentrated on her senses, tuning into her belly. At first she had a hard time focusing because the tingle of energy swirling in her palms had notched up considerably. Her memories reminded her that she could consciously dampen the energy, so she focused on her palms and visualized the energy stream spiraling down into a small spark. The tingle abated, but she knew she could awaken it when she needed to.

Now Mirabel brought her awareness back to her belly. At first an unsettled swirl of energy circled round and round, then it oriented itself and she began to feel a tug pulling her off to the right. She turned and the tug responded by gently pulling her straight forward. It wasn't strong enough to physically pull her, but when she stepped toward the pull, the tug continued to prompt her movement forward, so she aligned herself with the subtle force. She decided to take a slight step in another direction, and the sensation of being out of alignment impacted her by pulling the core of her body out of balance, causing some discomfort.

Mirabel decided to test it a little further. She took another step forward, which strengthened her awareness of the sensation. Next, she tried to do the same with her eyes open. The sensations were slightly muted by her vision, but as she tested moving forward, following the tug and stepping out of alignment, her skill at reading her sensation and remaining aligned improved, increasing her confidence. Mirabel hadn't left the grove yet. She thought it relatively safe there, so she practiced for a while until she felt adept.

Before leaving, Mirabel took one last look around at the grove and put her hands on the tree. Her palms responded by pulsing and she realized that before she left, she could use the healing energy in her hands to strengthen, if not heal, the tree.

She thought it would be a good idea to do so. Perhaps Maia Jane would need to return here one day and make her way back to the other world, and she needed to ensure that Magdalena could enter from the other side. If this truly was the last tree and it died, so would the tree on the other side. The two worlds would be cut off from each other forever, and both would perish.

Mirabel focused on her palms again and let the energy loose, allowing the contained spark to grow back into a swirling spiral. She placed her hands on either side of the tree trunk, closed her eyes, and visualized the energy moving into the tree from her palms, making its way into the xylem, the tubes that transport water up the tree, and from there spreading down through the roots and up into the branches. The tree responded by sending out magical, telepathic filaments, like silver threads that entered her and enhanced her vision, showing her what was happening inside the tree. Mirabel saw the glow of energy strengthen the tree's cells, which had been in the process of breaking down. She also saw that many of the cells were already too far gone, particularly on the ends of branches, and more than halfway down several major branches. Those could not be saved.

One whole side of the trunk connected to the dead branches was also dead, too scorched and damaged for life. Mirabel shifted her attention to the roots, sending the majority of the energy there to do its healing work, as strong roots would make a stronger tree. She knew she hadn't done enough to save the tree, but she could make it last a little longer. Then she sensed the connection to the tree on earth and she became aware that the only reason this tree had survived the conflagration in the first place was due to the health of the tree on the other side, which lent life to this tree. At least she had supported the tree enough for it to last a while longer. Finally, Mirabel pulled her hands away and the connection was broken. She consciously sent the spiral energy back down into a spark and opened her eyes. It was time to start her journey.

Mirabel oriented herself to the pull and began to walk. The grove in Ynys-Avalone, unlike on earth, was at the top of a gentle hill. Off in the distance to her right were the most magnificent mountains she had ever seen. Mirabel stopped to admire them. The peaks disappeared into clouds, the mountains pointed and dramatic. They reminded her of the Tetons where her father had taken her once long ago, but they were much more impressive in their stature. Snow lay halfway down the peaks, and she found it hard to judge how distant they were. She remembered her people called them the *Sliobd Corcair*—the Mountains of Mystery. They were named appropriately, because one never knew what might be encountered there. Entering into the mountains could be both enchanting and dangerous—one could encounter a dragon or a winged horse, depending on how clear one's intentions were. The trees there were white, much like earth's aspens, but much larger with gnarled branches and heart-shaped leaves that fluttered and emitted a luminescent light, enchanting all who entered into their presence. Mirabel's people treated these mountains with great respect and typically entered them after weeks of meditation and cleansing, and only to seek healing from the winged horses who could mend broken hearts. The mountains, capped by sparkling white, glowed a deep purple in the distance. At least the devastation on her world had not seemed to dim their beauty from this distance. Mirabel sighed and set out on her way again.

The way down from the grove was much easier than it had been on earth. The walk was gentle—a contrast to the harsh scene of devastation around her. She was grateful for her good shoes and sturdy, comfortable hiking digs. She followed the tug down the hill and into a valley, which she knew had once been a beautiful valley full of singing flowers, and magical trees bearing all kinds of fragrant, flavorful fruits. She could almost taste the lingering sweetness of the fruits on her lips. She knew how the fruit would burst into your mouth, startlingly sweet, and then change, becoming lighter as you chewed. The aftertaste was non-cloying and left a lingering freshness in your mouth, somewhat akin to earth's mint, yet different; more fruity somehow. She longed to bite into one of these and became aware that she was hungry. She needed a break and some nourishment.

Mirabel had to sit down to take off her backpack. Struggling with her trappings, she realized she had put her pack on before she had slung the snug over her left shoulder. When she started up again, she would remember to put the snug on first so she could more easily remove the pack and keep Maia at her side always. She carefully lifted the snug over her shoulders and placed Maia on her legs, then took off the pack. Next, she draped the snug back over her head onto her left shoulder, placed Maia in the center of her lap, and proceeded to dig into the pack. She found packets of dried preserved fruits of her world and packages of unleavened bread. She ate sparingly, yet careful to ensure she received proper nourishment. She needed to be cautious with her food supply, as she did not know how long her journey would take. But she also was sure to eat enough to keep up her strength.

The energy from the food flowed through her body and nourished every cell. The experience of eating was much more enhanced here in Ynys-Avalone.

Next time I won't eat so much. I need less here.

After stowing the food back in her pack, Mirabel took a drink from her skin. The water flowed clear and cool over her tongue and she noticed how the water brought life-giving moisture to her tissues and cells. She marveled at the difference. She thought of Matt, wishing she could share this revelation with him, and suffered a pang of loneliness. Prior to sitting down for a rest, Mirabel had been so intent on developing her new skills, healing the tree, and starting her journey, that she had not paid attention to the loneliness that crept into her bones. Now she was confronted with it. She was all alone in this devastated world and she longed for companionship. She cradled Maia Jane in her arms, warm with love for her daughter. This bolstered her somewhat, but the baby in stasis was not a companion. Mirabel ached for Matt's touch and Janey's compassionate gaze. Bereft and alone, she was responsible for the fate of two worlds. The immensity of the pressure bore down on her, pressing her into the ground, making it hard to breathe.

Sighing heavily, Mirabel slipped the pack back on, made a few adjustments, stood up, and started walking again. If only she could walk away from that pressure. She focused on the tug, ever mindful of its pull, and it lightened the sense of burden a measure as she moved ever forward.

Sustained by her meal, Mirabel walked for hours, up and down over gently sloped hills. The ground beneath her feet was dry and hard, and the devastated landscape around her was devoid of color and changed little as she walked on. She knew she was nowhere close to the Nygel Plain yet. She knew that the land would gradually slope downward to where the flat land of the Nygel Plain began. Even when her world was healthy, the Nygel Plain had always been a trial. To go across the plain to the Shialon Tree had once been a pilgrimage, and every girl in the transition from youth to adulthood had been required to cross the plain as a rite of passage. Of course, the Watchers had always been employed to follow and watch from a distance, ensuring that girls could be rescued if needed. But the need for that had been rare, as most of her people were up to the challenge.

If ever a girl didn't make it, she had to try again the next year, and the next, until she finally succeeded. No girl was allowed the responsibilities of adulthood before successfully crossing the plain and bringing back the flower of the Shialon Tree. The flowers, under the care of a girl, turned to a seed. The girl, now become a woman, planted the seed and cared for the tree that grew from it for life. It was her tree, and her magic would be attuned to the magic of the tree. Like every girl, each tree was different. The flower petals would be dried and ground into powder, which would be used in a rite to honor the Shiashialon and beseech her for a gift. The powder was imbibed during this rite and the girl-turned-woman would incubate by her seedling tree and dream. The young women dreamed the dream of the Shiashialon, who lay sleeping in the void, and during this dream were given a gift symbolizing their magical specialty. Some were given the staff of healing, others the song of the Shiashialon and their voices were infused with great enchantment. They could sing in etheric harmony with the music of her world, their songs hauntingly beautiful and woven with the stories of her people. Others had the gift of working with the plants and trees, or creating beautiful works of art. There was a gift for whatever was needed to make their lives comfortable and fulfilling. Some had the gift of creating beautiful structures. These structures were made with magic as well as craft, and to walk into a village in her world was to walk into homes that blended into the landscape, yet evoked the beauty that gothic cathedral builders aspired to. The builders often crossed over to earth and learned from humans who had a special knack for creating stable structures. These homes were warm and comfortable, as well as beautiful dwellings.

Once a gift was discerned, the young women were apprenticed to an elder with the same gift, who would nourish the talent in their charge until it was fully developed. Once the gift was discovered, her people thrived in their calling. Rarely, if ever, were there feelings of dissatisfaction or a desire to do something different.

Some few children were born male and became great workers of the ethereal magic, and were needed to help balance the forces of change and the dynamics between the two worlds. Many of these were also renowned as great magicians on earth. Only a special few of her people were given the gift of parenthood, which was conferred on those who had a temperament and willingness to pay the ultimate sacrifice for their children—to give their life if needed. This Mirabel's mother had done for her, and she would do it for Maia. Children were not born in this world very often, for her people lived a long, long time. But every child was cherished by all and was seen as a special endowment from the Shiashialon.

And finally, the most revered among her people were those who were given the gift of becoming a Watcher. The gift of the Watcher was the most rigorous and important in her world. The Watchers ultimately held the fate of all people on her world. They were connected to the Weavers, who wove the fabric of the reality for the Shiashialon, for the Weavers were the first children of the Shiashialon. They were the ethereal force behind the manifestation of creation, and their realm was the stars. So intricate, so delicate, and so subtle was the fabric they wove. These magical threads could be tapped into by the Watchers, who would then guide their charges based on their oracular powers.

Mirabel, remembering this, also remembered an article she had read in a magazine on earth and suddenly realized that the string theory in physics was a very rudimentary understanding of this reality. All reality ultimately threaded back to the Shiashialon—she, and she alone, was eternal reality and all beings were part of her. But when humans had chosen fear and disconnection, she had retreated and slept. Now both worlds were in the midst of a nightmare that had started long ago.

There was a legend on her world that one day a child of Ynys-Avalone would be born on Gaia, and being born there outside the patterns laid down, this child would be granted two gifts; the gift of parenthood and the gift of the Watcher. Mirabel knew that some of this fit her story, but she couldn't see how she herself had the gift of a Watcher. She didn't appear to have any skill with oracular powers or the ability to read the delicate fabric of creation, so she figured the legend couldn't be about her or must have been wrong. All she knew was that she had to try to end the nightmare dream of the Shiashialon, so she could dream a new dream to repair the rift. Mirabel would do anything to save her child and those she loved. For that, she was willing to sacrifice her life, as her mother had sacrificed for her.

Mirabel shook herself out of her reverie and stopped plodding. She remained aligned with her course, but she now entered an area of instability. She looked ahead. The path was warped and bent in front of her in unnatural ways. For some time now, a path had been well demarcated and easy to follow, even without the tug. But now she knew that she was about to enter an area where everything would rely on her ability to remain aware of and follow that tug. There was an uncomfortable energy dancing on her skin, making the tiny hairs on her body stand on end. Ragged blue flashes rent the air around her a couple of times as she stood there, making her belly twinge with unease. She thought she heard voices, too—unhappy voices—voices that haunted her.

Feeling alone and anxious, Mirabel realized she was tired and not ready to enter the next stage of her journey. She turned and made her way back along the trail, working against the tug, which made it hard to move very fast. She needed to rest before she continued on, and creating some distance between herself and the instability ahead seemed wise.

Mirabel found a hollow by the trail that made a comfortable resting place and settled down to nourish herself. She ate, feeling the nourishment fill her up, and then drank thirstily from the skin, unthinkingly finishing off the last gulps of the soothing liquid. Suddenly aware that she had just taken the last of her water, she hoped she would find more. Surely Magdalena would have told her if finding water was a concern? Mirabel didn't remember seeing any streams along the way, but she decided to trust that it would be okay and pulled the blanket from her pack. Magdalena had advised her to cover herself and Maia with it when they slept, so she settled under the blanket with Maia lying inside the curve of her body, still wrapped in the snug, which remained slung over her shoulder. Mirabel soon fell into a fitful sleep.

Chapter Eighteen

att grieved Mirabel's absence. His evenings at home were long and lonely. The house felt empty. The warmth and magic that Mirabel had brought when she moved in was gone. Many evenings he sat for hours in the rocker in Maia Jane's room, dismayed by all that had happened. And with no one around to see him, he cried. He didn't know what to do with himself without Mirabel there. So, when Janey told him her apartment complex was being renovated, he quickly offered his place as a temporary home during the construction. He didn't want to be alone with his grief. Janey knew Mirabel better than anyone, and he knew that her presence would lighten the burden, if even just a little.

Matt removed everything from his home office, finding space for it in his office at the bike shop instead so Janey could have a room for herself. Janey and Tarsi moved in and made it their new home for the time being. Janey's easy chair took up a corner that overlooked the garden Mirabel had put in, and Tarsi took to the space almost immediately. She loved being able to go outside and soon became queen of the garden, keeping it safe from rodents and intruder cats.

Matt's home was spacious, and it felt so empty and forlorn without Mirabel. Women had a way of making a house a home, so he was glad to have Janey there to lend her feminine energy to fill the lonely space. They had no one else to share their secrets with, and they found it comforting to be around someone who truly understood the depth of their feelings toward Mirabel.

Of course, Matt had to create a story about the whereabouts of Mirabel. He told everyone that the death of Maia Jane had shattered their marriage; that Mirabel had gone back to Montana to get away and be with her family. Their friends never knew that she didn't have family left there and it didn't matter. He told them that he was waiting for her to return. If anyone asked about Janey moving in, he let them know it was temporary until her apartment was renovated. No one ever really questioned him any further. They knew how devastated he was. They preferred to avoid the intensity of his grief, and avoided the subject. He felt grateful for Janey, and she understood because she felt it, too.

Janey had a harder time with explanations. Her friends were more intuitive and sensed there was more to the story than she was willing to tell, so they worked hard to draw it out of her. Their intentions were good, but they were relentless, and Janey finally had to draw a line in the sand and let them know that she appreciated their concern, but out of respect to Matt and Mirabel, it was none of their business. This chilled some of her relationships and made Janey grateful for the new emotional bond she and Matt shared.

They left the nursery as it was. For Matt, the space reminded him of the essence of Mirabel and Maia Jane. He wanted to keep it for Maia, imagining that one day she would come back and he would have a room for her. Janey liked to sit in the room when Matt was at work and she was home alone. Tarsi also made the room her haunt when she wasn't out in the garden, and Janey often found her sleeping in the crib during daytime hours. Matt never said anything about Tarsi co-opting the crib, so Janey just let her sleep there. If Tarsi was in the room when Janey came in, she would leave the crib to greet her, then curl up on her lap. Janey felt like the room held some of the magic she longed for, and she imagined that was why Tarsi spent so much time there.

Janey dove into her work at the store. Her tarot readings grew into aura and tarot readings. During her sessions, she slipped into her dragon skin. She noticed the change one day when a new client had come to see her. That day, Janey sat in the plush chair provided for readings with her eyes closed, preparing for her upcoming session. Opening her awareness, she found the inner doorway and slipped through and into her dragon, feeling the surge of energy as she merged. She opened her eyes and her next client was standing before her, waiting. Janey immediately noticed a pink halo dulled by gray edges surrounding the woman. The woman's shoulders sagged and Janey could feel the sadness seeping off her. She led her back to the reading room, gestured for the woman to sit, and prepared the cards for the reading. She asked for the woman's name.

The woman looked across the table at her and said, "Melissa." She paused, still looking at Janey. "Who are you? I never felt...well...I know you can help me. You have power, don't you?"

Janey nodded, looking out through dragon eyes now. The gray and pink in Melissa's aura battled each other. The pink had briefly flared when Melissa recognized her power, then retreated when Melissa looked down, embarrassed by her exclamation. Janey knew if the gray ultimately won, Melissa was at risk for cancer or some kind of illness. The cards she pulled said the same thing. Janey gazed across the table and said, "You feel betrayed, is that so?"

"Yes, how did you..." Melissa began to cry. "My best friend and my boyfriend, I found them together. Why does this always happen to me? So many times I have been betrayed. My work, my lovers, my friends..." Her voice trailed off and she looked away.

"What is the root of the betrayal?" Janey drew a card. "Someone close to you, when you were young."

Janey reached across the table and took Melissa's hands for a moment, gazing warmly into her eyes until Melissa sighed. Janey took her through a visualization. She surrendered herself to the dragon and allowed the dragon to send a shower of golden fire over Melissa. After the visualization, Janey opened her eyes and looked across the table at Melissa. A predominantly pink halo surrounded her, with vestiges of gray here and there. Janey gave Melissa instructions on how to enhance the pink aura and her power for self-healing, gave her a hug, and sent her on her way.

After that, Janey's readings were like this more often than not. She was a favorite among the clientele of Mystic Dolphin and in high demand. At home, Janey guided Matt and tended to his aura. She taught him to meditate and did hands-on healing on him, which calmed and fortified him.

Matt and Janey's lives wove into somewhat of a rhythm. They cared for and supported each other. They both missed Mirabel, and Matt in particular grieved heavily. He had lost almost everything when Mirabel left with Maia Jane. He wasn't one for moping around though, so he dug himself into biking when he wasn't at his bike shop.

One day Matt decided to ride on the trail by the driving range. When he got to the parking area, he noticed a lot of large equipment parked in the lot, and saw that the gate had been removed. Knitting his brow, he rode around, scoping out all the big grading equipment, and wondered why it was parked there. He looked up at the trail and noticed it had been widened, and had obvious tracks from large trucks driving up and down it. His heart skipped a beat and he felt disturbed. Wasn't this planned open space already purchased by and managed by the Mt. Diablo land trust?

Worried, he decided to ride up the trail. He followed the big tracks around the curve by the driving range, and then around the hill that hid the buckeye groves. When he got around the hill he stopped suddenly, stunned by what he saw. The lower grove had been razed. The trees, now a quagmire of logs and branches, were all piled up in one corner. Matt got off his bike and ran into the devastation. He turned in circles, taking in the damage. Clenching his fists and working his jaw, rage rose from deep in his belly as he stood there staring out over the ruins. *How could this happen?* He looked up the ravine. At least it remained intact and there were no signs of heavy equipment on the trail past the first grove.

Finally realizing he couldn't contain this on his own, Matt picked up his cell and called Janey.

"Matt?" Janey answered.

"Janey, they're destroying the grove."

"What? Where are you? What do you mean *destroying the grove?*"

"I decided to ride on the trails around the buckeye groves today—you know, Mirabel's groves. They've demolished the first grove. I can't believe it!"

Janey, shocked, was completely silent. It had never occurred to either of them that the groves could be destroyed.

"Janey, we have to do something. We can't let this happen!"

"Can you wait there for me? I'll get my things together and drive over right away."

"Yes. I'll meet you in the parking lot. I want to check on the Mother Grove. Hurry, please. I feel sick about it."

• • •

Janey changed into hiking clothes and took off for the open space immediately. The first thing she saw as she drove up to the parking lot was all the construction equipment. Her heart dropped into her belly. Fear and rage clawed at her chest, and her breaths came in sharp intakes. She couldn't quite grasp

163

the concept over the phone, but the large equipment made it real. She parked the car and ran over to where Matt waited by the trail. They decided to check out the upper grove first, and then wait to see if any workers showed up so they could find out what was going on. They were relieved to find the second grove and the Mother Grove still intact. Only the lowest grove had been destroyed. By the time they got back down to the parking lot, trucks filled the lot and a crew of workers milled about, waiting for something. Matt approached one man to see what he could find out.

"What's going on here? Why is all this equipment here?"

"Got a project to build a new clubhouse for the golf course," the guy said, nodding toward the old clubhouse across from the parking lot.

"But this is supposed to be open space. It's protected."

"We're just doin' our job here, it's not my business why. Seems the city approved it. The club owner's putting in a new home, too, so he's close to the club. It's good. It's work for us."

"You can't! This is protected space!"

"It ain't protected no more. I got work, that's all I care about. Now you git outta my way. We got work to do."

"We'll see about that," Janey announced as she walked up to the conversation, chin jutting out and hands on her hips. She tugged on Matt's arm. "Come on Matt, these people aren't behind this. We need to go to the city."

They put Matt's bike in Janey's trunk. She tore out of the parking lot and made her way through the residential streets to downtown Walnut Creek, heading straight for city hall.

Janey got out of the car and marched into the building. Matt followed quickly behind her.

Janey walked up to the receptionist. "I want to talk to the city planner."

Looking up at her, the receptionist said, "Do you have an appointment?"

"No, but this is urgent," Janey replied.

Matt stood by her side. Four eyes now bore down on the receptionist, imploring her to call the planner.

"Can I ask what you need to see the city planner for?"

"Yes," Janey replied, jutting her chin out again. "We went to the open space by the golf course today and there is construction going on. It's supposed to be protected open space. We aren't leaving until we talk to someone."

"What is your name, miss?"

"Janey. Janey McGann."

"Well, Miss McGann," the receptionist said resolutely, gesturing to the lobby chairs, "why don't you take a seat and I'll go find out if he can see you."

Matt spoke up. "Tell him I am a local business owner in Walnut Creek, Matt Gallagher. I own the Shell Ridge Bike Shop and Sports Bar. I pay my taxes and I demand an audience."

The receptionist nodded at him and walked off.

Janey and Matt sat down and waited impatiently. Finally, the receptionist came back and said, "The city planner has left for the day. You will have to come back some other time."

Janey could tell she was lying, but she was just mad enough that she didn't care about anything but stopping the destruction of the grove, so she got up and walked down the hall and started looking for the city planner's office herself. Matt followed close behind.

The befuddled receptionist started after them, yelling, "Stop! You can't just barge in." Realizing she wasn't going to be able to stop them herself, she went back to her desk to call security.

Janey found the office marked by a placard that read, City Planner, Jay Reed. She opened the door and marched in. The city planner sat at his desk, and suddenly stood up when Matt and Janey burst through the door.

"Excuse me!"

Janey looked him straight in the eye as she moved to stand directly opposite the desk from him and said, "Mr. Reed, can you tell us why a new clubhouse for the golf course is being built on protected open space?"

"I'm sorry, Miss McGann and Mr. Gallagher, but you can't just barge into my office when I am in the middle of an important project. Common courtesy demands you make an appointment."

"Well, we tried that and fully intended to wait for an appointment until your receptionist lied and told us you weren't here. Besides, this is urgent. It looks like construction on the clubhouse has already begun and I intend to stop it. That is protected open space and I know there are some heritage trees in the area, so I am sure it is out of ordinance. Was a site assessment done?"

"The club owner jumped through all the hoops and the project was approved by the city council in an open session. The public had every opportunity to object and no one did, so we moved ahead," Reed replied.

"We'll see about that!" Janey said and repeated her question. "Was an assessment done to determine if heritage trees were in the vicinity?" Janey knew it was a long shot to go down this route, but her anger led the charge and she followed her gut instincts.

Matt was angry too, but also pleasantly surprised by Janey's moxie, which he hadn't quite seen at this level before. He could see it was working. The city planner showed signs of getting a little nervous and he started obfuscating.

"Well, Miss McGann, I can't keep track of every little detail in my head and will have to go back to look and see if an assessment on heritage trees was done."

"And what about the horned lizards?" Janey added. "They are endangered and I have personally seen them in this habitat. If I find that the proper assessments weren't done there will be hell to pay."

"Now miss, the club isn't taking up the entire open space, just a corner, and the golf course will be incorporating the shooting range, opening it up for recreational as well as police use. In the long run, it will save the city money and add value for the citizens. The horned lizards will have plenty of space to roam."

Matt said, "I'm the owner of Shell Ridge Bike Shop and Sports Bar. When the bikers find out about this, they aren't going to be happy. They use those trails extensively."

The city planner turned red in the face, clearly getting flustered. "You will have to take this to the city council. They are the ones that voted on it. I just implement the plans."

Janey knew that was partly true and partly an excuse. If the city planner had been doing his job, the i's would have been dotted and the t's crossed. Something was clearly amiss here, and that at least gave her some hope. She didn't really have a plan when she came in; all she knew was that she had to save the groves—and more importantly, the Mother Tree in the middle of the upper grove.

Realizing that they couldn't do anything else there, Janey and Matt walked out of the office, but only after Janey turned and threatened, "We aren't finished with this."

• • •

As soon as Janey and Matt left the office, Jay picked up the phone and called the mayor. "Ed, I think we have some trouble. I told you we should have done all the assessments on that clubhouse project, and now some environmental group or something has just caught wind of it. They were in my office today asking some uncomfortable questions."

Ed responded, "Now Jay, don't you worry about it. The construction has started, it's already too late, and those folks will just have to live with it." On that note, he hung up on Jay.

Jay shifted in his seat. He always hated confronting the mayor. The mayor was an arrogant, incautious man, and Jay knew all too well how close Ed had gotten himself to the wealthy owner of the golf course. The mayor was often at the course and Jay suspected that his membership to the club was a gift for political favors. The owner of the club, John McNulty, had a way of getting whatever he wanted since Ed had been appointed mayor. Jay worried. He reported to the council and the mayor controlled the council. He could lose his job if he pissed the mayor off, and he was likely to lose his job anyway if it came to light that there were certain irregularities in the project. Now he was between a rock and a hard place.

• • •

Janey and Matt made their way back to the house and sat down at the kitchen table to discuss a plan of action to stop the construction.

"We can put an announcement on the Bike Shop Blog and let the bike community and customers know about it," Matt offered.

"Yes," Janey said, "that's a good idea, but I think we need to have a bigger action. We should plan a protest and get the word out. I think we need to dig a little deeper to find out what was done—or rather *not* done—before the construction began. We might be able to pull in the Environmental Protection Agency or the Sierra Club or something, take it beyond just Walnut Creek to the larger community. I will also make an announcement to the Mystic Dolphin email list. Most of the regular customers who go there will support our efforts as well."

Janey and Matt worked through the evening, calling for help and creating and sending out the message. Janey decided to spend the next day digging into the city planning records. Matt had gotten enough bikers together for an immediate action at the construction site. They were going to do a "bike-in" at the site to stop the construction.

Chapter Nineteen

After a restless sleep, Mirabel awoke suddenly to a loud crack. She peeked out from under her blanket and saw a lightning storm in the distance, near where she had encountered the instability before backtracking to rest. It made her nervous. She thought the instability may be increasing, and decided she should not linger more than necessary. She sat up and spread the blanket in front of her, carefully settled Maia between her knees, pulled the pack up next to her, and took out breakfast. As she ate the unleavened bread and bits of dried fruit, she remembered that she had taken the last of her water the night before. She craved the magical water and reached for the skin, hoping to squeeze out a few remaining drops. The skin was heavy, as if full of water. Grabbing it with one hand, she uncorked it and water flowed out of the opening, over her hand and into her lap. It was full. No wonder Magdalena never mentioned water in her instructions. The skin was magical and had replenished itself. Her heart expanded as gratitude filled her. Mirabel looked down at Maia Jane between her knees. Feeling hopeful, she decided to sing her a lullaby. The memory of a song from her world rose to the surface and she began to sing:

Sleep my little one, sleep, and I will sing a song
A haunting loving tale of the first Liouradion
Liouradion, Liouradion, my sweet Liouradion
Called to the Silent One, mathair Shiashialon
You traversed the perilous plain, courageously alone
Liouradion, Liouradion, my brave Liouradion
To worship at the Shialon Tree, child of the Shiashialon
Whose branches wove the sky, eternity roots adorn
Liouradion, Liouradion, my sacred Liouradion
You dove betwixt two worlds, trusting to a fate unknown
For the tree was nigh on dying, my sad Liouradion
Liouradion, Liouradion, my sad Liouradion
Falling far, falling deep, swept beyond anon
Vastness unmarred by time, your existence quite undone
Liouradion, Liouradion, my dying Liouradion
She found you lying there, the fair Shiashialon
And between your heart and hands, fair seed of the One
Liouradion, Liouradion, my fair Liouradion
She sowed the seed, and the Shialon Tree grew anew,
And in honor, inside it she placed you
Liouradion, Liouradion, my shining Liouradion
Honored is your hallowed soul, our memories forever one
Liouradion, Liouradion, my shining Liouradion

Mirabel sighed, now pulling up her memories of the first Mirabel, her namesake, and the first Liouradion. This story and song had only just surfaced, and now she understood that she had been named in honor of the first Liouradion, who had sacrificed her life to bring the seed of the Shialon Tree to the Shiashialon so that it could be renewed. The original Mirabel was the reason her people had their ancestral memories, which had been granted to them by the Shiashialon after Mirabel had sacrificed her life to bring the seed of the Shialon Tree to her.

She bowed her head in devotion to her as she held Maia Jane close, reluctant to leave behind this moment, but it was time to go. Adjusting her burdens, she began down the trail. It didn't take long before she arrived at the edge of the instability.

Mirabel paused and looked around. Knitting her brow, she contemplated the Sliobd Corcair. The mountains seemed to be much closer than she remembered. Yesterday she would have sworn that she had traveled parallel to them, and didn't remember drawing any nearer to them. She must have been preoccupied. Right now she had other concerns. The blue flashes had ceased, but uneasiness crept into her toes from the ground and made its way up her legs and into her spine. The energy agitated her. She pulled Maia around to her chest and wrapped her arms protectively around her. As she stood there deciding what to do, she could feel the land buzzing.

A sudden blue flash rent the air right next to Mirabel and blew her backwards, landing her solidly on her rear. Fortunately, she was still holding Maia, but she sat there stunned for a moment, and took a deep breath to still her pumping heart. Then she noticed that the ground wasn't buzzing anymore. She speculated that the buzzing indicated a preliminary build-up of energy prior to the flash. Next time she would be aware and move away—fast.

Still cradling Maia in one arm, Mirabel pushed herself up off the ground and prepared to start back down the trail. That was when she noticed she couldn't feel the tug in her belly. She panicked. She turned this way and that, but the blast had blown her off the trail and she wasn't sure to which side it had thrown her. Should she move left or right? She didn't know, so she just stood there, paralyzed. She wanted to scream, but she knew it was pointless. She felt utterly alone and wished that Matt and Janey were with her. A picture of Janey's brown eyes gazing compassionately at her came into her consciousness, and with it came a measure of calm.

What would Janey do?

Mirabel closed her eyes, which strengthened the image of Janey in her vision. She heard Janey's voice telling her to breathe deeply and to trust herself. She remembered the cloak of protection that Janey had woven for her out of love and energy, and she imagined pulling it around herself and Maia. Next, she heard Janey telling her to let her grounding cord sink into the earth and make its way down to the core. Mirabel heard Janey's voice so clearly in her mind, she almost felt as though Janey stood next to her, calming her further. She concentrated on following her internal cord, and that's when she noticed that the cord didn't feel like it went straight down, but instead was making its way to the left. She followed the direction for a few steps and stopped. She still couldn't feel the tug, but in her mind's eye, the cord led her further to the left. Mirabel took one step at a time, pausing between each to make sure she still followed the direction the cord was leading her. After about seven steps, she began to feel a slight pull on her belly, and moved more quickly toward that feeling. Sighing in relief, Mirabel soon found herself back on the path where the tug pulled her forward with the familiar force she remembered.

"Janey," she whispered, "thank you again, even though you aren't here."

Mirabel couldn't pause for long because she noticed the buzzing at her feet again, so she quickly followed the tug forward. As she did, the buzzing sensation lessened. After a few moments, she heard the crack of a blue flash behind her. Mirabel spent the rest of the day practically running to avoid the flashes, going by the intensity of the buzzing, which gave her an indication of how close she was to the nexus of the upcoming flash of energy. More than once she had to backtrack in order to allow a flash to occur ahead of her and still remain on the trail, but she didn't want to risk getting off it again. Her senses were alive and she now had an acute awareness. Mirabel became adept at reading the air around her and the ground at her feet, while remaining fully conscious of the tug, which got stronger as she moved forward.

Finally, she reached an area that was more stable, but now the terrain was getting rougher. The barren land still sloped downward, but there were large cracks in the ground in and around the trail. Each time she came to a crack, she had to climb down, then up again, and it was exhausting work.

Tired and hungry, Mirabel decided to break for a rest. The dark of evening had begun to creep in. Directly ahead was another larger break in the ground, and she climbed down into it, took off her pack, and sat with her back against the ridge, Maia in her lap. She ate her dinner, pulled the blanket around her, curled around Maia, and quickly fell asleep.

Mirabel's sleep was full of dreams. Faces swam by, young women pulled at their hair and wept, and a dense fog smothered everything. She woke up when it was still dark out, and shivered from the cold. She wrapped the blanket closer around her while poking her head out to survey her surroundings. A thick fog had rolled in and lent a chill to the air. She pulled the blanket over her again and tried to go back to sleep. Then she heard a voice. Someone called out mournfully in the distance. Perfectly still, she listened with all her attention. She thought she heard her name in the mournful cry. Remembering what Magdalena had told her about her lost people, Mirabel buried her head deeper under the blanket, pulled Maia Jane close, and fell back to sleep.

Chapter Twenty

$\mathcal{M}$att met a cadre of bikers at the open space parking lot amidst all the construction equipment. It was still early, and the morning air was crisp. The sun was just breaking over the hills, sending shards of light across the parking lot and beyond. They had come early to arrive before the construction workers they knew would show up soon. Matt called all the bikers over to him near where a gate had once separated the open space from the golf club and the residential area that bordered it. The gate had been removed in order to let the equipment and trucks have full access. Deep, textured tracks of large equipment snaked up and down the hill, ruining the trail for the bikers and hikers alike.

"John, you and Sammy take a group of about five with you. Ride up the hill, if you can, and make a left when the trail forks, then ride around by the driving range. Once you come around the hill on the left of the trail, you will see where they have cut down all the trees and piled them up. Spread yourselves out across the way and don't let any equipment pass. Eric, you can help me pull this chain across the parking lot opening. That will hold them up for a bit. Jill, I'll let you lead the rest with the protest signs. You can find the signs in the back of my truck. Some of you might think about hiking up the trail and spreading out with your protest signs, but we should keep a good group down here. It will be more effective. Any questions?"

No one had any questions, but there was an excited buzz as everyone spread out to take up their respective duties. Matt and Eric pulled the heavy chains out of the truck and wrapped them around the posts on either side of the parking lot opening, hoisting them up and tightening them, then locking them in place with heavy-duty locks. Next, they positioned themselves, arms crossed, in front of the chains. Meanwhile, John, Sammy, and the other bikers made their way up to the destroyed grove. Jill led a group of protesters in a chant as another biker passed out signs: "Open space is sacred space. No new club! No new club!"

Soon work vehicles started rolling in and were stopped at the chain.

The supervisor hung out the window of his large truck and said, "Hey, whadda you think you're doing? We got work to do!"

"Too bad," Matt said. "No work for you today. Go back where you came from!"

"What's this all about, anyway?" the supervisor bellowed.

"We're protesting the improper use of open space and we're gonna stop this tragedy today," Matt retorted.

The crew started parking their trucks along the street, gathering where Matt and Eric stood. The protesters, carrying their signs, made their way over to surround Matt and Eric in a protective circle.

"We'll see about this," the supervisor said as he pulled out his cell phone, and made a call, looking at Matt and the protesters as he spoke.

In the meantime, Matt started to spur the bikers and regaled the construction workers with tales about the beauty of the open space, and how he and the bikers used the space to be out in nature. He talked about the rare horned lizards that delighted, the stature of the oaks, and noted the possibility that a heritage tree resided on the space under construction. He talked about how the open space was land for all citizens to enjoy. He pointed to a young construction worker and asked, "Do you have kids?"

The construction worker nodded.

"Do you want your kids to be able to enjoy horned lizards, hike this land, and enjoy all the wildlife here? What are you going to tell your kids when the oaks are gone and the coyotes, foxes, and mountain lions must go elsewhere? Do you want to be the reason your kids lose this rich heritage?"

The construction worker, agape, shook his head. The supervisor glared at him. Another worker, seeing the look, hit his arm with the back of his hand.

Matt finished his speech and the construction workers milled around in front of the protesters while the protesters chanted. Matt and Eric stood, chests high, arms crossed. They were at an impasse, but Matt knew it wouldn't last long. The supervisor had called in reinforcements, and Matt wondered when the police would show up. He was ready to risk being thrown in jail over this. In fact, he thought, *I will fight to the death for this*. Mirabel's sweet face appeared in his mind's eye. He would do anything for her. Even if he had to chain himself to the tree to keep it safe, he would. He only hoped that the other bikers would be as dedicated.

Matt knew they all felt strongly about protecting their space. He didn't always agree with the way some of the bikers treated the trails; sometimes they rode on trails they weren't supposed to, unable to resist the thrill of the difficult terrain, and he knew that caused environmental damage. But that was nothing like the damage a new clubhouse would cause. The only thing that really mattered to him now was the safety of the tree. If there was any hope that Mirabel or Maia would return to him someday, that tree had to be safe.

Janey had gathered some forces of her own. She had gone to visit the Sierra Club in Oakland and managed to meet with the director to try to convince him that the Sierra Club needed to intercede and help hold up the construction. She ran into some roadblocks, as the Sierra Club was deep in a battle to drain the Hetch Hetchy Reservoir and return the valley to its original state. They weren't having much luck, but it was their primary focus, so she was having a hard time getting the director onboard with what was happening in Walnut Creek. But Janey persisted and refused to leave until she had a commitment. Finally, the director relented and said he would send someone out to investigate. Janey thanked him, but told him she wouldn't leave until she met the investigator and could take him out to the site.

The director looked at her and shook his head. "Miss, I could use someone like you on my team. Have you ever considered working for an environmental organization?"

Janey smiled and looked him straight in the eye. "Well sir, if you help me fight this battle in Walnut Creek, I'd be happy to help you with Hetch Hetchy and any other battle you take up. I know this may seem like a minor issue compared to Hetch Hetchy, but there is a lot hanging on this; maybe even the world itself."

The director raised an eyebrow at this. Janey was a little relieved that he didn't take the bait. They sat in the office, staring across the desk at each other. Finally, a young woman knocked at the door and entered the office.

"Ah, Julie, thank you for answering my call. Julie, this here is Ms. Janey McGann. Janey, meet Julie Ehrensaft."

"Nice to meet you, Ms. McGann." Julie shook Janey's hand.

"Oh, please call me Janey. Nice to meet you, too. May I call you Julie?"

"Yes, that would be nice." Julie turned to the director. "Dan, I am assuming the reason you called me has something to do with Janey here. I was just preparing that report you asked for about my trip to Hetch Hetchy last week. I was hoping to get it to you today."

"Of course I want you to finish that report, but one more day isn't going to matter. Ms. McGann here is pretty persistent and she has a concern that is closer to home. Would you mind going out to Walnut Creek with her to check on it?"

"I can do that, but I don't understand why this takes precedence over Hetch Hetchy? We've allocated almost all our resources to that battle and it seems a little strange to get distracted from it now."

"Janey, would you explain to Julie here what's going on in Walnut Creek?"

Janey went into another impassioned dialogue about the construction taking place in the open space, and how she thought that a heritage tree could be involved. Janey had a way of mesmerizing people when she really hit her stride, and by the end of her dialogue she had won Julie over. Hetch Hetchy was put on the back burner in Julie's mind for the moment.

"I'd be happy to go out there and do a preliminary assessment with you, Janey. Let me go gather my camera and notebook and make a call to Zipcar. I will follow you out there."

"Oh, I can ride with you," Janey said. "I took BART into Oakland. I'll give directions. We've got a protest organized out there already. I imagine things are getting heated up."

Julie left to gather her things and Janey turned to the director. "Dan, thank you, and you won't regret this. I do appreciate what you are doing for us." She shook his hand and went out to wait for Julie in the lobby.

Julie returned with her equipment and they made their way to the nearby Zipcar location to get a car. Julie looked at Janey and said, "Zipcar is great! This way I can take public transportation, but when I need a car to get to a location, it's handy to have a Zipcar. The Sierra Club covers the cost for me. They encourage us to do the right thing environmentally, as you can imagine."

"That's great," Janey smiled.

The two of them chatted all the way out to Walnut Creek, and by the time they reached Lafayette, they had bonded. Janey explained the magical buckeye groves, and her love of trees, but she didn't mention Mirabel or the real reason for her quest to save the grove. She didn't need to. Julie had already become a fast ally.

They arrived to pandemonium. By now the Walnut Creek police had arrived, and the protesters had chained themselves together and were standing in front of the path. Matt and Eric were down on the ground in handcuffs, and the police were preparing to drag them to a waiting car.

Julie parked the car and she and Janey quickly got out. Janey walked straight up to the police officer, put her hands on her hips, her feet hip-length apart, and confronted him. "Officer, this man has a right to freedom of speech by the first amendment. You have no right to arrest him."

"Oh, yes I do, miss. He was disturbing the peace and the good neighbors of this community. Now you get out of my way. I've got to get these two down to the station to book them."

"Sir, my name is Julie Ehrensaft," Julie stated as she walked to stand next to Janey. "I work for the Sierra Club and we believe this construction is happening here illegally. I am here to investigate."

The supervisor was standing nearby and overheard Julie. "Oh, jeez," he said, and picked up the phone to make another call to his boss, Spencer Wright, owner of the Mount Diablo Construction Company and friend of the mayor. "Spencer, we got more trouble. The Sierra Club just showed up. I thought we had it under control when the police got here, but now I don't know."

"All right, Gus," Spencer sighed. "Let's try to keep this quiet. Tell your crew to go home for the day. Tell them you will call them tonight to let them know about work tomorrow. I will take it to the mayor and get a restraining order if I can.

The mayor has a stake in this and he will come through. I don't want this to get any more publicity if we can help it."

The supervisor walked over to the police and asked if one of them could step aside with him. Since he represented Spencer Wright, who had made the complaint with the police, the officer went with him.

"Sir, we appreciate you coming in to help us. I just spoke with Spencer and we'd like to try to keep this quiet. We're going to drop the charges for now and Spencer will take it up with the mayor."

"You sure?" the police officer said. "We can haul these guys down to the county jail and keep 'em overnight."

The supervisor shook his head. "Thanks officer, but that is the boss's decision."

The officer went back over to Matt and Eric, unlocked the handcuffs, and hauled them roughly to their feet. "You guys lucked out this time. See that you keep the peace. No more disturbing this good neighborhood with your antics."

Matt looked him in the eye and said, "Officer, I will do what I need to save this open space. This construction was started illegally. You should be arresting the club owner, not me."

The officer shook his head and walked away.

Janey ran up and hugged Matt. "You're so brave! I am so proud of you. Matt, I'd like you to meet Julie." She turned to Julie. "Julie, this is Matt. He organized this protest while I went to your office. Matt feels just as strongly, if not more strongly, about this cause than I do. Matt, Julie is from the Sierra Club. I promised you I'd get someone out here. She's come to assess the site for environmental cause to stop the construction." Janey was practically bouncing, she was so excited—and hopeful.

"Pleased to meet you, Julie. Thanks for taking up our cause. What can we do to help you?"

"Well," Julie said. "I am impressed with your organizing and it seems you are at a temporary impasse. Can you show me around, fill me in on the details so I can get a report together for Dan, the director?"

"Sure I can," Matt said. "Janey can come with us. Let me go thank all the bikers who came out today to help, and send them home. I don't want to use them all up on the first day. I am sure there will be more to come."

Matt called the cadre of bikers around him and thanked them. By now, the crew that had gone up to the grove had made their way back down, as they had been keeping in touch via cell phones. They were a little disappointed to have been left out of the action at the parking lot, but Matt assured them that the battle wasn't over, and that they would see action soon enough. He told them all they had earned a free pitcher of beer and lunch at his sports bar, and sent them on their way. Next, he made a call to the sports bar to make sure that the manager was prepared for the onslaught of hungry, thirsty protesters.

Finally, he walked back over to Janey and Julie and they started up the hill toward the grove. When they arrived, Julie sucked in a gasp at the site of the destruction.

"It was so magical, Julie," Janey said. "I wish you could have seen it before they tore it down. But follow me. There is another grove up the ravine. You can see that one in its full glory. We can make our way up the hill to what we call the Mother Grove. I think there may be a heritage tree up there. There is an ancient buckeye up there and I noticed a grand old oak off to the side. After that we can hit the trail around on the other side of the driving range and Matt can show you the horned lizard habitat."

They gave Julie a full tour of the area, and she took numerous pictures and made lots of notes. They ended the tour on the trail where Matt had seen horned lizards in the past, and Julie said, "It would be great if we could get a picture of a lizard."

"That will take time, as they don't tend to come out and pose for pictures," Matt laughed.

"Do you think you can get a picture?" Julie looked up at him.

"Well, I have one already. I was so fascinated by them, and I saw one on this trail one day several years ago. Luckily, I had my camera. I actually have the snapshot on the wall in my office."

"Great. Do you have a digital copy you can send me?"

"Yes, I can do that."

"Can you send it this afternoon? I'd like to get back to the office and start my report. Since the construction is imminent, the sooner I get the report on Dan's desk, the sooner he can take action."

They walked back down to the parking lot, and Matt and Janey saw Julie off. As they watched her drive away, Matt put his arm around Janey's shoulders and looked down at her. "Janey, I don't know what I'd do without you."

They stood there for a while, arm in arm, and Matt finally sighed, "I wonder where Mirabel is and how she is doing? I'm scared for her, Janey. I just wish I knew if she and Maia are safe."

Chapter Twenty-One

Mirabel peeked out from under her blanket. Dense fog still permeated the atmosphere. She sat up, cradled Maia between her knees, and thoughtfully ate breakfast. She gathered Maia into her arms, crooning over her for a few moments. She felt it important to talk to Maia, to sing to her and let her know how much she loved her even though Maia was in stasis. Mirabel trusted that Maia would receive her love.

Mirabel stood up and prepared to start down the trail again. The terrain continued to get rougher, and the fog made it impossible to see very far. There were more rocks strewn along the path, and the trail meandered up and down over small ridges and in and out of ravines. The vegetation was sparse and most of it was dead. The trail was becoming less visible as Mirabel traveled, and she relied more heavily on the tug in her belly than she had when the trail was more clearly visible.

As she wandered over the ridges and ravines, Mirabel's mind drifted to Janey and Matt. She wondered how they were doing and hoped they were bonding. She missed Matt's arms around her and thought of all the lovemaking that had happened in their home. She knew now that "happily ever after" with him was never meant to be, but she still longed for his touch and was grateful for the love they had shared in their time together. Mirabel thought about Janey, too. She had come to realize that Janey loved her every bit as much as Matt did. Janey had been the truest friend to her; her muse of sorts. She had come to ask herself daily, *What would Janey do?* Mirabel laughed a little at this. She had seen bumper stickers that read, *What would Jesus do?* Somehow, Janey had become her Jesus of sorts. *What would Janey do?* became a mantra that kept her steady during her journey. She patted Maia at her side and said aloud, "Oh Maia, I wish you could have known Janey, she would have made a great auntie and you would have adored her."

Lost in her thoughts, Mirabel had mindlessly been following the tug, but she was surrounded by the heavy fog that had rolled in while she had been sleeping, and now had lasted well into the day. Her disquiet accentuated her loneliness. As she moved forward through the fog, it penetrated her and slowed her down. She started to droop and drag her feet. A sadness began to creep in, much like the sadness she had felt in her earlier years before meeting Matt.

Suddenly, Mirabel wanted to sit down and weep, feeling hopeless in her travels alone to the tree. What was she going to do when she got there? Now she feared this quest was quite fruitless, but she continued to drag herself forward anyway. *What else am I going to do?* The weight on her shoulders increased, until finally she dropped down onto her knees and cried, Maia cradled in her arms. She knew she was walking toward her death, and she wanted to turn around and run back to the buckeye tree and to Gaia. She sat there for some time, her head hung low. And then she heard someone calling. The voice was sweet and feminine, but desperately calling out names, as if searching for someone...anyone.

"Meara, Meara where are you? Oh, Meara, I'm lost. Meara? Melusine? Melusine, can you hear me?"

The calling was punctuated by crying. The voice would stop and Mirabel could hear sobs, then it would start up again. Eventually, she heard the woman call her name.

"Mirabel. Mirabel, can you hear me? Mirabel, I can feel you. Come, come to me."

Mirabel's hopelessness transformed into longing. She was drawn to the voice. She desperately wanted to find the caller and soothe her. She wanted to let her know she was coming. She called out. "Who are you?"

The calling stopped. After a few minutes Mirabel heard, "Meara, is that you? Come, come to me. The fog. I can't see you. Oh, Meara, I can feel you near."

Mirabel stood up and adjusted her pack. She stepped off the path to make her way toward the voices, now pulled almost magnetically by the longing in her chest. *Yes,* she thought, *yes. I will meet my people. This woman needs me. I will go to her and it will be all right. I won't be so lonely and she can go on my quest with me.*

Mirabel, in a trance, left the trail. She didn't notice that she had stepped into even heavier fog. Every part of her longed to see and touch this woman.

"Meara, oh Meara, there is someone else there. I can feel a child. Meara, are you with a child?"

Mirabel stopped in her tracks, suddenly remembering herself. She heard Magdalena saying to her, "They will reach across the gap toward Maia..." She looked down and realized she had, at some point, unconsciously taken Maia out of her protective snug. Panicked, Mirabel turned to go back to the trail, but was mired in fog. She didn't know from which direction she had come, and now, despairing, she knew she had made the mistake that Magdalena had warned her against.

"Meara, are you coming? Why is it taking you so long? Let me hold the child. Oh, a child. How I have longed for a child. Come, let me see."

Mirabel placed Maia back in the snug as quickly as she could. The voice still tugged at her, threatening to put her back into a trance again. *Now what?* She couldn't feel the tug on her belly. She was lost. She sat back down and wept, feeling hopeless again. She cried until she was exhausted.

"Meara, why don't you come to me?"

Mirabel sensed arms reaching toward her. She wanted to run into them; to do anything to assuage this fear and loneliness, but the weight of Maia, now resting in the snug in her lap, reminded her to resist. *Oh, what am I to do?* A wave of anger came on. Mirabel clenched her fists and her stomach twisted. *Well, I've royally messed this up. It's all my fault. I've failed. I've failed! How could I fail?* She trembled, desperate, hopeless, and angry. All she could do was sit there and wrestle with her emotions until she was so exhausted she fell into a fitful sleep.

Mirabel woke up sometime later and covered herself with her blanket, then fell back to sleep again. In her dreams she saw her people wandering around, crying out, hopelessness and desperation written all over their bodies. She would wake for moments, then drop back into sleep again. And then the dreams shifted. Suddenly, she found herself sitting on Janey's old Navajo blanket by the oak tree, with Janey sitting across from her and chanting. Mirabel saw the electric blue light emerge from Janey's chant and wrap itself around her in a protective cloak reminiscent of the cloak Janey had created for her on Gaia. After this dream, she fell into a more peaceful sleep, still surrounded by fog, but wrapped in her blanket, Maia cradled by her side.

Chapter Twenty-Two

Startled, Janey woke from her dream. She had been sitting with Mirabel on her Navajo blanket near the oak tree where they had done their rituals together. In the dream, she was chanting and could see blue plumes, like cool flames, emerging from her words. The words she chanted made no sense to her, and as the flames emerged, they wrapped around Mirabel and created a shield.

How odd.

The dream was so vivid, she couldn't shake the feeling that she had actually been there with Mirabel by the oak tree. Janey closed her eyes and imagined herself back in the dream. She could feel another presence there, too. In her imagination, she turned and looked behind her. That's when she saw the silhouette of a white deer. She opened her eyes again.

I wonder how Mirabel is?

Checking in with her body, Janey noticed tension in her belly when she thought of Mirabel in her world, but not when she thought of her by the oak tree where they did the rituals. She couldn't shake the fear that arose out of that tension. She sat up to look at the clock. It was 3:00 a.m.

She lay back down and thought of the big day ahead. Today she was going to the grove and construction site with Matt and another party of bikers. She had managed to rally up a group of friends and acquaintances from Mystic Dolphin to join them. She knew it could potentially turn into a skirmish with the construction crew and the police. Janey also worried about Matt. She had never seen him so angry. A hardness had come over his features, and even though he was a gentle soul, something new had entered that scared her. He was desperate and not thinking clearly.

Janey had already done some spells and chanting before going to bed, setting up an altar in the center of the nursery. She had placed four candles around the periphery in blue and green; blue for tranquility, green for strength and life. She had placed a white candle in the center for hope and peace. Next, she had sprinkled the flower essence of Oregon Oak around the circle for support and to strengthen resolve. She also had made a tincture of vodka, Oregon Oak, and Miracle Essence, and had imbibed it, praying for hope and miracles. Matt had put off her invitation to join her in the ritual, saying he didn't believe it would do anything, that it was time for action, not "airy fairy" stuff. That had hurt her feelings. Before this, Matt had never brushed off her spiritual practices. She thought about sneaking some of the tincture into Matt's drink at dinner, but Janey felt it wasn't ethical to secretly give him a tincture without his permission.

Janey tried to go back to sleep, but she couldn't shake her fear. Her mind churned out a stream of endless stories that all ended tragically. Finally, she got up and went into the kitchen to make a cup of chamomile tea. She filled the teakettle with water and started heating it up, added the tea to her favorite teapot, and sat down with her cup to wait. When the kettle whistled, she poured the water over the tea and took the teapot to the table with her, letting it steep for a few minutes before pouring a cup for herself. She sipped it, still distracted by her thoughts. Eventually, it brought a measure of calm and she sat there, staring into the cup.

Unexpectedly, she saw an image of Mirabel in her tea. She was sleeping, curled around Maia. They were surrounded in a shroud of fog. The fog looked heavy and dense, and had a mournful feel about it. She wasn't sure how she knew that, she just did. Janey closed her eyes and recalled her dream. She allowed her consciousness to drop into it and the images strengthened. She saw herself chanting and observed blue flames emanating from her fingers. Warmth and protection spread from her center along with the blue flames. Consciously, she sent this toward Mirabel, where it enveloped her. She added love and wove in the flower essences she had imbibed earlier. She moved deeper and deeper into a trance as she held these visions and feelings. And as she did so, a calm and stillness seeped in.

• • •

Matt stumbled into the kitchen to find Janey staring into a cup of tea. She didn't notice him. He had tossed and turned for hours and couldn't sleep, so eventually he gave up. Desperation and anger prevented sleep and he couldn't shake the feeling that Mirabel was in danger. It made him itchy and anxious. Furthermore, he was angry with himself for the way he had callously brushed off Janey when she had asked him to join her in a ritual earlier. Her crestfallen face had said it all; he had hurt her feelings deeply. He had been excoriating himself throughout the night and his mix of emotions was near unbearable.

Matt looked at Janey, seemingly in a trance over her tea, and his heart ached, wanting to stretch and tear itself from his body. *I wish Mirabel were sitting here having tea like we used to.* The intensity of the feeling overwhelmed him. He stepped back and knocked over an umbrella that leaned against the shelf. He looked down at it, confused. Why was an umbrella in the kitchen?

The noise startled Janey and she looked up at him. "Matt? What are you doing up?"

Matt looked at her, trying to keep the tremble out of his voice. "I could ask the same of you. It's four o'clock in the morning. What are you doing up?"

Janey looked up. "I had a dream about Mirabel and then I couldn't sleep. I had a feeling that she was in danger, but now it has passed. I've been sitting here with a cup of tea doing my best to send protection her way."

"Do you feel the danger has passed?" he asked earnestly.

Janey nodded.

"I couldn't sleep, either. I also felt Mirabel was in danger. Janey, I am so worried about her I can hardly stand it."

"I know how you feel, but strangely, I have this feeling circumstances have changed and she is safer now," Janey said, trying to comfort Matt. "Maybe it would be good for you to have a cup of tea, too. I am drinking chamomile with mint. It is soothing and calming."

Matt sat down. "If you think it will help settle my nerves. Janey, I want to apologize for brushing you off earlier. You didn't deserve that. It's just I've been so worried about Mirabel, and the trees, they can't..." he trailed off. "I lost hope."

She reached across the table and grabbed his hand. "Matt, I know. This is not easy."

"Thanks for being such a good friend to Mirabel and, to me. Without you, who knows..." he trailed off again.

Janey sighed audibly.

Hearing her sigh, Matt looked back over at Janey, who now looked down into her tea.

"Janey, you know I love having you here. You take such good care of the house and me. But I would understand if you decided to leave. You have a life you should live."

"This is my life now. This is the most important thing I will ever do. I am in this as deep as Mirabel."

Matt appeared to be at a loss for words.

"It's almost daylight. Perhaps we should get ready for the day ahead. I can fix breakfast," Janey offered, trying to wrest the conversation away from its present course and Matt's hopelessness. They both had to think of Mirabel. *No feeling sorry for yourself.*

"Okay, Janey, you're right. I'll go start loading up the signs in the truck, but you don't have to fix breakfast. I am capable of fixing my own breakfast, you know."

Matt went out to the living room to collect the signs and started loading them into the truck while Janey pulled together a breakfast of oatmeal sprinkled with granola and cinnamon. She split a banana in two and added a generous offering of strawberries. *At least we can eat well,* she thought.

They both ate quietly, their silence occasionally punctuated by a comment about the logistics of the day. When they finished, they got up from the table and started cleaning up together.

"Did you ask your group to get there before 8:00 a.m.?" Matt asked.

"Yes, it's a bit early for that group, but I think they will be there. The shop doesn't open until 10:00, so a few of the shop employees will have to leave by 9:30. There should be a good group of clientele there, too."

"Good. I've got a few more bikers to join us this time. Jill's a social media expert. I asked her to spread the word. Maybe we'll have some new folks we don't even know."

"That would be great. Maybe we'll hear from the Sierra Club today, too."

They grabbed some water and snacks and made for the door. On the way to the site, Janey focused on her breath, trying to calm the squirrels in her belly. She was worried about what the day would bring. Her mind wandered back to her fears about Matt's state of mind and the possibility of him getting embroiled in a more serious altercation with the construction crew or the police. She hoped it wouldn't come to that.

Chapter Twenty-Three

Mirabel woke up and saw that the fog had passed. Relieved, she ate a quick breakfast and packed up her things, keeping Maia wrapped tightly in her snug and close to her body. She started down the trail, more hopeful this morning, and glad for the rest she had taken. As she walked, she marveled at how different she felt now compared to the despair she felt before her rest. Then she remembered her dream about sitting under the oak with Janey.

Janey, somehow you were with me. I don't know how or why, but you were there.

Thinking of Janey reminded Mirabel of how she had used her grounding cord to find the trail the last time she had been thrown off. Sure enough, it guided her back to the trail.

"That was a close call," she said aloud, patting Maia. "I won't do that again."

The trail straightened out. Mirabel looked off at the mountains to her right again. *That's strange...they seem farther away today. I guess that's why they call them the Mountains of Mystery.*

Eventually she came into a valley of lakes and ponds. The trail wandered around and between the bodies of water. The water was murky and unpleasant; totally different from Mirabel's memories. Once upon a time, this land had been beautiful. Fairy lights hovered and danced over the water, and delicate orange-pink water flowers had perched atop a triad of blue-veined, iridescent leaves. The shores were covered with green moss, pleasantly soft and velvety on the feet, and charmingly sprinkled with tiny, tinkling flowers. Trees, like willows with graceful, hanging, flowered branches, swayed in the soft breeze while small, colorful, butterfly fairies flittered among the hanging fronds. Large, flat-topped rocks covered with different shades of soft mosses were strewn along the shoreline.

The beautiful naiads that inhabited this water liked to loll about the rocks and preen, diving gracefully into the water, and laughing deliciously as the girls on their journeys strolled into the valley. The water flowers sang an enchantment song, which the young girls journeying through this part of the plain had been told to overcome as they made their way through this area. This part of Mirabel's world was called Shaitair Duma, land of enchanted lakes.

The girls' trial, they were told, was to keep going, to pass through and resist the lure to swim out to the flowers and dance with them. One touch of the flower would take the girl into an ecstatic water ballet, the hovering lights dancing in choreography with the enraptured girl. The movements would stimulate the leaves. These sent out tendrils, catching the girl as she eventually fell into a trance. The tendrils would hold her there in a delicate woven mat of purple at the water's surface while she dreamed the dream of the flower's making—a dream of a lover. During the dream, the tendrils did their own dance on the girl's body. The flower could pick up the fondest fantasy of the dreamer and reproduce it in a dream that somehow mimicked just the right touch and pressure to create an ecstatic explosion of pleasure, which the plant would then absorb, transforming the flower into a seed. The seed would be enfolded in the triad of leaves to be nurtured before it dropped into the water to form a new plant. As the ecstasy faded, the plant would release the girl, who would abruptly awaken from her dream as she dropped under the water into the arms of a waiting naiad. The water naiads always mirthfully carried the girls safely back to shore, where they promptly fell into a sleep until all the effects wore off.

No girls had ever been harmed by this symbiotic dance of pleasure. The trial was nearly impossible for the girls to pass. If they didn't make it past, they had to wait for days to commence on the last leg of the journey. Upon their return from the pilgrimage, they endured the giggles from all the other girls waiting for their own journey, and the knowing smiles and gentle banter of the women responsible for greeting them. In fact, most girls didn't make it past the trial, and they likely didn't try too hard. The ecstasy they experienced was legendary, and most girls didn't *want* to pass the dance. Those who did could never have children, but they had a special talent for healing, and this was one way that healers were sorted out. The flowers assured that the girl's first experience of orgasm was ecstatic. Mirabel speculated that perhaps the flowers had something to do with her people's reproductive cycles as well; perhaps it awakened their wombs and allowed for the parthenogenetic birthing of her people. Her world was full of myriad, interwoven, magical effects that were sometimes bewildering and complex.

Mirabel remembered the ecstasy she had shared with Matt. Had he awakened her womb? Janey had given her some herbs, some of which had enhanced her pleasure. *Were those herbs somehow related to the flowers?* She knew that Janey also worked with flower essences and had given her a bottle of what she said was her "special" mix with a twinkle in her eye. Then she remembered the dream she had when Janey had done the cloak and fertility ritual, and smiled.

Bringing her thoughts back to the flowers, Mirabel realized they reaped benefits, too. They could not produce a seed without the orgasm of the host. The girls themselves learned a few things about pleasure and hence made better lovers, even if they had to face the good-natured jesting from their elders as a result. In her world, pleasure was a value. Mirabel smiled as she thought of this and looked back over the now flowerless, murky waters. Her shoulders sank heavily. So much on her beautiful world was lost. How could she ever reconcile her memories with the present reality? She grieved for herself, but she grieved more for Maia. She wished Maia would one day have the opportunity to make the journey herself, in a renewed world.

Eventually Mirabel passed the land of the lakes. Up ahead she saw more fog. This fog was darker and ominous. She walked toward it as tendrils of mist drifted toward her and wrapped around her. She paused and adjusted Maia, making sure she was completely surrounded and protected by the snug. She peered into the fog, but found it useless to try to see into the impenetrable mass. Just in case, she checked in with her belly, and sure enough, the tug was pulling her directly into the fog. Her stomach churned and she suddenly felt tired and scared. "What would Janey do?" she whispered down to Maia. "What would Janey do?"

She took a step forward and the fog continued to curl around her. She took a few more steps and was completely enveloped. Tendrils, like spider webs, curled around her face and the uncovered skin on her arms. The silence in this fog pierced her, stabbing at her soul with shards of nothingness. Mirabel took a few tentative steps forward. Emptiness and desolation were the magic of this fog, but she bowed her head and continued to move. Every step dragged her further down into emptiness. She wrapped her hands around Maia protectively, and to help her feel something other than desolation. The shards of nothingness cut away at her as, step by step, she moved forward. It left her both numb and at the same time filled with dread. Horror darkened her soul, like black fingers squeezing the hope from it. Forcing herself out of desperation, Mirabel started to chant "What would Janey do? What would Janey do? What would Janey do?"

Mirabel had to do something to hang on to a semblance of life. She closed her eyes and imagined Janey sitting across from her under the tree. She relied on her feet and belly to navigate, the tug now her only hope. Though it took her into this dreadful emptiness, it was her friend who led her forward, step after step. The fog was like a nightmare that Mirabel wanted to escape, but couldn't force herself to awaken from. Moving through it made her feel as though she was a long, long way from consciousness, trapped in a dense thickness, and yet she found strength with her hands on Maia and in her chant. Step by agonizing step she moved forward. It got darker and tendrils of dark fog caressed her, chilling to the touch. The silence turned to a high-pitched trill, constant and dissonant. Nothingness tore at her soul and the discordant trill tore at her body. She covered her ears to block the sound, but to no avail. The sound surrounded her inside and out, and the action of taking her hands from Maia weakened her. She stopped and placed her hands around the snug again, gritted her teeth, and moved forward. "What would Janey do? What would Janey do? What would Janey do?" she chanted through her clenched jaw.

Tears streamed down her face, unnoticed. She bent over and stumbled forward. The chill of the dark fog entered her bones and she began to tremble. She slowed, then halted. She wanted to collapse and disappear. Nothingness called to her, a siren song now appealing against the weight of the trill and the malignant chill of the dark fog. She felt her life force draining away and wanted the nothingness to take her.

A shriek rent the air—close, very close. Mirabel suddenly knew she was in great danger. It was a specter—a vampire of the soul. She cowered on the ground, scrambled to get the magical blanket out of her pack, and covered herself and Maia with it. She didn't know what else to do.

"Skree euwwwww..."

She could feel it pass over her, so near.

"Skree euwww eeeee..."

The blanket lifted as the specter passed, threatening to expose her, but Mirabel clung to it, grasping Maia under her and shivering in terror. The screech tore into her, and like the malignant fog and the unbearable trill, it threatened to rip her soul apart. What would facing a specter do to her? She didn't want to know. Hearing it was bad enough; she didn't want to see it, too. She imagined it would split her soul from her body and fling it into the nothingness, and she would disintegrate...and what would become of Maia? *Oh no, Maia, oh Maia...noooo.*

"Skree errrreuwwwww..."

Mirabel wanted to scream, but her throat became a prison, her voice locked inside it. She desired only to run. Filled with madness and now ready to throw the blanket off and flee as far as she could from the terrors, she pulled Maia closer, readying herself.

As Mirabel rose to run, she saw Magdalena's face and crouched back down as the specter narrowly missed her. Magdalena was radiant and smiling. Mirabel thought she heard Magdalena say, "Mirabella Shialon, my child, find the stillness inside you. Drop deep inside and find the Shiashialon. She will carry you through. Even sleeping, she will carry you through. There cannot be nothingness. There is hope."

Mirabel dropped deep inside herself. Down she went, into the darkness inside her, falling, and as she fell, she began to drift, as if upon wings carrying her gently down into the soft, velvety blackness. In the center of that blackness she began to sense a light. As she dropped down, the light grew in strength. It emanated warmth, a dazzling light radiating an ocean of love. Mirabel heard a silent voice, the voice of the Shialon calling to her, softly without words, but with meaning. "Come, my child, I wait for you..."

A longing swelled in Mirabel's heart, and along with it came hope and strength.

The specter passed over one more time and then was gone. Mirabel stood up, cradling Maia in her arms. Keeping the blanket wrapped around them both, she began to move forward again, step by step. She walked for hours, the longing in her heart pulling her forward, gaining strength with every step.

Finally, the fog broke and the dark tendrils released her. Mirabel moved into a huge clearing bound by fog for miles around. But she could see the sky now, filled with stars—clear, bright stars like diamonds piercing the darkness with crystalline brilliance. She fell to her knees and sobbed with relief as she gazed up at the sky in awe of the beauty.

Mirabel looked toward the center of the opening. The ground rose gently in front of her and she followed its curve upwards with her eyes. Then she saw it—the One Tree. It stood tall and broad. The tree was quite far away, but she could sense its immensity. Its broad, white trunk rose proudly upward from the ground and gracefully curved into branches that swept outward and up toward the sky full of stars, while the lower braches swept down, benevolently caressing the ground underneath. She saw the humps of roots snaking outward into the land around and intuitively sensed the depth of its taproot, rooted in eternity. This was the Shialon Tree, the mythological tree at the core of all stories of creation. It was so unbearably beautiful, Mirabel could not tear her eyes away from it. This tree was the gateway to the Shiashialon and life itself. Mirabel wanted to run toward it, but she was spent. The journey through the fog had taken all her strength and she desperately needed to nourish herself and rest. She ate and fell into a deep, deep sleep that lasted for days.

Chapter Twenty-Four

Janey and Matt drove into the parking lot by the open space. Other protesters were beginning to straggle in both by car and mountain bike. Matt stepped out of the truck and they gathered around him. Janey watched from the car as Matt greeted each person. Even in his distressed state, he was magnetic and inspired a sense of loyalty and purpose in those around him. He radiated authenticity, and even the newcomers and customers from the Mystic Dolphin who hadn't met him before were drawn to him, gazing at him and exhibiting rapt attention to his every word. Janey smiled to herself. *If only he knew.* She was aware of how he always questioned himself and was oblivious to the adoration. She was grateful for the worship he inspired, as it was exactly what was needed right now. The more people drawn into and committed to the action, the higher chance of success they would have.

Janey was tired. She hadn't had much sleep the night before and she had a niggling feeling of trepidation just under the surface of her skin. She didn't like it. Over the years she had learned to trust her intuition, and something didn't bode well. On the other hand, the crowd was growing at an astonishing rate, and looking at the crowd gave her hope. The two feelings, hope and unease, battled within her as she finally stepped out of the truck and moved toward the growing crowd.

Friends and customers from Mystic Dolphin greeted her and parted as she made her way toward Matt and the cadre of bikers at the center of the crowd. The construction crew began to pull in. They all had looks of dismay on their faces as they were forced to turn around and backtrack to look for a place to park. Down the street, residents were beginning to filter out of their houses, looking somewhat confused and distressed about the invasion of their neighborhood.

Matt started directing his crew of bikers, assigning duties and delegating leadership among them. All were armed with cell phones and walkie-talkies for back-up. The bikers led groups of protesters, carrying signs they had made, up the trail. More people were trickling in from adjacent streets and bikers continued to ride in.

Janey, amazed by the size of the growing crowd, remembered Matt had mentioned Jill was a social media master. This crowd had to come from a media campaign gone viral. *She's truly a social media doyen.* Janey startled when her phone rang. She dug it out of her pocket and answered, "This is Janey."

"Janey, its Julie. Are you at the site?"

"Julie, hi, yes. It's amazing, you should see the crowd!"

"I know. I'm trying the get there myself and running into a traffic jam. I had no idea the people of Walnut Creek would end up being so passionate about their open space. Janey, it's amazing. How did you pull this off?"

"Oh, it wasn't me." Janey thought back to the amplifying spell she had done for today's action before going to bed—before her dream and all that had happened that morning. *Could it be?* She was suddenly aware of her power. "Well, we have a social media maven on our side. Looks like her campaign was successful."

"Make sure you introduce her to me," Julie said. "We could use one of those at the Sierra Club."

"Sure," said Janey. "Julie, did you have any luck getting the EPA to put a hold on the project?"

"Actually, that's why I am calling. Yes, we were successful and Dan is delivering it to the city planner as we speak."

"Oh Julie, that's wonderful! I'll be waiting in the parking lot area for you if you can make your way through the crowd."

• • •

The construction crew formed a small group milling around in the clubhouse parking lot across from the open space area. The supervisor was there, as well. He herded them in and prevented them from taking off. They looked cowed by the crowds and even more so by the ongoing ranting of the apoplectic supervisor. He did not like having his day upended; he preferred things regular, orderly, and going by plan. This burgeoning protest was decidedly unexpected and outside the plan. Being a man barely tolerant of even the smallest delays, he was now beside himself. He had already threatened to fire any crewmember who stepped off the clubhouse grounds and was currently yelling into the phone at his boss, Spencer.

Spencer was none too happy himself, and would have liked to have punched the supervisor in the face about then. The supervisor was dependable and got the job done, but he got on Spencer's nerves with his abrasive style. Spencer liked things genteel. He imagined himself a sophisticated man and it annoyed him that the supervisor brought out the dark side of him that he worked so hard to keep under wraps. Things appeared to be falling apart quickly, and the mayor wasn't answering his calls.

The mayor was down at the office having a meeting with the city planner, Jay Reed, who was realizing that he was going to be the fall guy. He sat across from the mayor, humiliated. The mayor had just served him his pink slip, and he was not even allowed to go back into his office to retrieve his things.

The mayor said that the secretary would collect any personal items and mail them to his address. Jay had to sit and wait under the smug gaze of the mayor while he called the security guard to come escort him out of the building. Jay was in a state of shock. He should have seen this coming, but instead he had buried himself in his work, hoping the whole thing would pass without incident. He had tried to accommodate the mayor and the club owner, thinking that if things got out of hand, they would protect him. *I should have known better.* Now he was being sent from the office with his tail between his legs.

To make things worse, he had just found out his wife was having an affair with his neighbor. The day before he had left the office early. The stress had gotten to him and he decided to leave at 2:00 p.m. The scene he walked into at home was now seared into his brain. *I should have seen the signs there as well.* Sheila had never been very affectionate, but her stunning looks had made up for that. Lately she had become more distant. He thought perhaps he had been working too hard, so he stopped by the store to pick up some flowers and a bottle of wine. He hoped they could spend a nice evening together and that it would lead to some physical stress relief. Little did he know that Sheila had been relieving her stress with their neighbor Jim, whom he had thought was his friend. They had shared many barbeques with Jim and Nancy. *I wonder if Nancy knows what's going on between my wife and her husband?*

It was so embarrassing. He had come in through the back door, flowers in hand, to find his wife and neighbor up against the dining room wall. Sheila had on an apron and nothing else. Jim had her pinned to the wall, going at it quite hard, and Sheila was making noises that never occurred in their bedroom. Jay interrupted their little party. Dismayed and disgusted, he immediately walked right back out, turning his back on their surprised faces. He couldn't bear the thought of going back home, so he went to the Marriott on Main Street in Walnut Creek and stayed the night, coming to work in the same clothes he had worn the day before, only to face the indignity of being fired. The whole world was against him. *Betrayal. That is the name of the game I'm in.*

After Jay left, the mayor called the paper to make an announcement about the impropriety he had discovered between the city planner and the owner of the club. *I'll be damned if I'm going to take the fall for this,* he fumed to himself. The club owner had been pushing him for months to get his new clubhouse, and the mayor had finally relented when the club owner had promised a significant donation toward his campaign for state senate. Scheming, he tapped his fingers on the desk. *In fact, I might be able to work this into some good publicity for the campaign. If I play this right, I might just be seen as the whistle blower and win the public's favor.* It was time to shut down the construction site. His next call was to Spencer. After he talked to Spencer, he planned to go to the site and make a public announcement.

• • •

In the meantime, Matt went up to the Mother Grove and stood by the tree alone, away from the crowds. He knelt before the tree and placed his wedding ring at the base. He made a vow out loud to Mirabel. "I will protect this tree with my life if I have to."

Matt didn't realize he was being filmed by a local reporter, Sue Ellen Joseph, who had followed him up there after realizing that he was the leader of this action. The protest had taken everyone in the newsroom by surprise. Since she lived nearby, it was easy for her to get to the scene first. She had her IPhone to capture impromptu videos while she waited for the camera crew to arrive. This story could be her big scoop. She rarely had an opportunity to get a scoop over the other reporters.

• • •

Janey met Julie in the parking lot. Julie ran up and hugged her.

"Janey, this is amazing! Where's Matt?"

"I don't know. Earlier he was giving out directions and delegating tasks. He told me he was going to ride up the trail with some of the other bikers and lead an action at the groves. Let me call him and let him know you are here."

Janey dialed and listened as the phone rang, but got no answer, so she texted him. She looked at Julie. "Maybe he's out of range up there."

"Well, I was hoping he would be down here when Dan called so I could personally deliver the good news that the project will be stopped to save the horned lizards."

Julie didn't know that Dan had already reached the city offices only to find that the mayor had already left. He also learned the city planner was "no longer with the city." The secretary told him that the mayor had gone to the site, so Dan decided he would go there himself. He was curious, after all. The size of the protest and the ensuing traffic jams were all over the news that morning, and he couldn't resist the opportunity for a little publicity. *I'd love for the Sierra Club to have their stamp on this action.* Perhaps the publicity would help the Hetch Hetchy campaign. Dan took the legal stay, got back into his car, and headed over to the site.

He pulled into the site just as the construction crew was leaving. He at least didn't have to walk far, unlike Julie, who had to park on neighboring streets several block away. Dan walked up to the club parking lot just as a buzz was developing about the mayor's arrival. The police presence had ramped up, and many local news channels had also appeared on the chaotic scene.

Julie waved him down and she and Janey made their way over to him.

"Dan, isn't this amazing!" Julie said when they got to Dan's side.

"Sure is. I wish we could instigate this much passion, but I am not sure it's great for the wildlife in the area. Hi, Janey. How did you and your team manage to pull this off?"

"Oh, we have our ways," Janey smiled. "A little of this and a little of that."

"Well, my earlier job offer stills stands."

"Thank you, Dan."

"Well?" Julie stood with her hands on her hips. "Did you deliver the stay to the mayor?"

"No, when I got to the mayor's office he had already left for the site. There he is, over there." He pointed. "Looks like he is directing people to set up a makeshift stage. I would guess an announcement is in order. Let me see if I can make my way over and get his attention."

"We'll follow," said Julie. She turned to Janey. "Come on, let's go provide back-up."

"Okay, I'm with you!" Janey replied, falling in step behind Dan and Julie.

Dan approached the mayor. "Excuse me, Mayor Hauser."

"It'll have to wait," the mayor said. "I'm about ready to make an important announcement."

"Well," Dan said, "you might want to add this to your announcement. I am the director of the Sierra Club and we've done an environmental assessment of this project."

"Hmmph," the mayor said. He didn't want the Sierra Club to pre-empt his party. "We're closing the project down due to our own assessment. I just fired the city planner today for improper conduct and lack of protocol. The Sierra Club ought to be happy that the City of Walnut Creek stands behind its commitment to the environment. If only I had known more about the project earlier, I would have never let it start."

Dan stood there, open-mouthed at the obvious lie the mayor was telling. But then he shut his mouth and decided to hold back on saying anything about it. The end result was the same, whether it came on behest of the Sierra Club, or from a cover-up by the mayor. It was clear he wasn't going to make any headway.

Janey stood with her hands on her hips, perplexed and angry. She was glad they were stopping the project, but she hated how the mayor was playing this out to his advantage. *Where is the justice?* It rubbed her the wrong way. She actually felt compassion for the poor city planner. It was clear he had become the fall guy. She wasn't sure what she wanted to do, but she felt mighty uncomfortable at that moment. Her intuition nearly screamed at her that something was amiss, but she just couldn't put her finger on it.

• • •

Matt finished his ritual at the Mother Tree and made his way back down to the protest. He wanted to find Janey. Right now, he wanted to be near her. *Her magic brings me hope.* He needed her. The intensity of all the emotions that swirled around inside him overwhelmed him. Matt was so wrapped up in his thoughts he never noticed that he had been followed.

• • •

Sue Ellen Joseph, adept at reading people, had seen when Matt was getting ready to wrap up his ritual. She quickly and quietly made her way back down to the crowds. She was in possession of a nice little human interest scoop that no other reporter had, and she was anxious to get back to her crew and do a quick taping to present it to the evening news director. Sue Ellen arrived at the scene outside the club just as the mayor was stepping up to the hastily erected stage.

Matt arrived a few minutes later and searched out Janey. He found her with Julie and Dan. He hadn't yet met Dan, and Janey quickly introduced them. They fell silent as the mayor started to speak.

"Fellow citizens of Walnut Creek, as mayor of this great city I am inspired by the passion of this citizenry for our heritage and this beautiful landscape at the foothills of our special landmark mountain, Mt. Diablo. This open space is used extensively and is revered by our citizens. As mayor and head of the city council, I hold that sacred. It has come to my attention that improper means were utilized to acquire the permits the construction at this site required. Had I known about this earlier, I would have never let this project go forward. I have fired the responsible party, our city planner Jay Reed, and have sent notice to the club owner, John McNulty, that I am shutting the project down. Furthermore, the city has decided to use its discretionary funds to protect the heritage trees on this site and make improvements to the oversight of this public property."

A cheer went up from the crowd.

• • •

John McNulty watched from a window inside the club, red in the face. *That bastard. I've been used!* But he knew the game was up. He was going to have to come up with some public scheme himself to apologize to the people to regain his standing in the city. *Perhaps I will donate funds to create a commemorative plaque for some of the heritage trees on the golf course. I can do some improvements to the trailhead parking lot area, like a bathroom.* He was tired of the hikers and bikers using the club as a public bathroom anyway. He could kill two birds with one stone. He found this hard to swallow and wasn't happy about it, but he would find some way to eventually get back at the mayor, especially after all the money he had donated to his campaign for higher public office. It galled him.

• • •

The mayor was winding down now, encouraging folks to go on home and assuring them that this open space was now safe. Janey, Matt, Julie, and Dan were standing together. Dan turned to Julie.

"Well, looks like our work is done here for now. We should get back to the office and dig back into the Hetch Hetchy project." He turned to Janey. "I'm serious about that job offer, Ms. McGann. Do you promise to call me in the next few weeks so we can discuss designing a position for you?"

Janey smiled and said, "I'll be in touch." She didn't want to disappoint him right after their help. She was all for saving the environment, but now that she knew the truth, she wanted to dedicate her time toward magic and saving both worlds.

After Dan and Julie left, Janey turned to Matt and hugged him. "We did it, Matt, even if it didn't occur the way we thought it would. The public action worked and I guess the mayor had no choice. I heard he was running for state senate and I guess he didn't want to rile the public before the election even got started." Janey didn't mention to Matt her unease and that something felt amiss. *What can I tell him?* Besides, he had been so tense. He had earned the right to celebrate their victory.

"We did this together, you and me, with some help from our friends," Matt said.

Those friends were beginning to gather around. Matt put his arm around Janey and announced a party at his pub, with free beer for anyone who brought in a sign or other proof that they had attended the protest that day. Cheers went up all around.

Chapter Twenty-Five

Mirabel had stopped taking breaks during her travels, and had eaten little since her goal had come into sight. She just wanted to get to the tree. The tug on her belly was stronger now, and as she made her way closer to the tree, it grew in stature and in presence. She could feel the life emanating from it as it pulled her into its aura. There was a deep magic in the tree and she longed to be near it—to touch it and linger under its mighty branches. Finally, she could walk no more and she sat down and ate. After a quick meal, she cuddled Maia in her arms and spoke to her.

"My little Maia Jane. We're nearing the end of our quest, and soon you will be in my arms awake and I will get to see your beautiful little face with life in it. I may not get to stay with you long, and I don't have any idea where our journey will take you once we reach the tree. Our Liouradion, Magdalena, told me the answers would become clear when we reached the tree. How I wish I could watch you grow." Mirabel rocked Maia. "There are people I hope you will know someday. There is Matt; he could've been your father if our people had fathers. He loved you, even after he found out you were not his child, but I know you will always be the child of his heart. You should've seen his thighs, Maia, made to make a young girl blush. Someday when you are older, I could tell you a thing or two about strong thighs in the bedroom, and I wish I could experience that again. But that is not for now. Most of all, he made me laugh. Back then, when we first met, I could be so sad all the time. His gift of laughter was magic to me. I think he made you possible. I hope you will seek him out. He would wrap you up in his love just like he did with me."

Mirabel gazed off into the distance, then closed her eyes. She wanted to see if she could feel Janey. After a few moments she looked back down at Maia. "Then there's Janey, my little one. She is special. I've never met anyone like her. She could be so outspoken and kind of sassy, but there was no one alive who could match her compassion. Just to have those two loving brown eyes focused on you was to know that you were loved and held. She was the best friend I ever had. I miss her, Maia. She and Matt made me whole, kept me together until I found out who I was. You see Maia, all my life I didn't know who I was. I knew I was different. It made me horribly sad. I never knew why I was so sad until the day I read the letter from my real mother, your grandmother, Melusine. I never met my mother. I only know her through my memories. I am so grateful for the memories now. A girl should never be without a mother's love. Now I can see her in my memories and I see her holding me, her only child, by one of the magical trees in Scotland before they tore it down. She suffered greatly there to save me. That means she saved you, too, little one." Mirabel rocked and patted the bundle. "She sacrificed her life for us. She left us in the protection of Magdalena, whom I am sure you will come to know. She is your Liouradion, too. Now it is coming close to being my turn to sacrifice myself for you in turn. My sweet little Maia, I hope I am the last to make this sacrifice. I want you to live the life our people once had here in this place where magic and beauty were woven together so artfully. I hope our home can be renewed, and that it will also renew earth in turn. I love both worlds. They are both a part of my broken heart."

With that, Mirabel lay down and threw the blanket over herself and Maia. After her rest, she would embark on the final leg of her trip. Her dreams were filled with the whispering calls of her people, but no matter how hard she listened, she couldn't quite understand what they were telling her. The tree communicated with her as well, through sensation, but similarly she couldn't quite grasp its meaning. She knew there was love in that communication, and answers, but she wasn't quite close enough to understand. Despite the dreams, her sleep was deep and restful.

Mirabel woke in the morning, threw off her blanket, and cradled Maia in her lap. She expected to make it to the tree today. But, when she sat up and looked toward the tree, she was astonished to find herself at the foot of the mountains. Somehow, the Sliobd Corcair had placed themselves between her and the tree. After staring at the scene in front of her in confusion and dismay, Mirabel searched her memories to see if she could find any that indicated that the mountains moved from place to place, but she found no tales or memories of this being so. She stood up, holding Maia in her arms, and looked up the steep slope, trying to determine whether she could climb over the mountains, but she knew she wasn't prepared for the snow and ice she would have to traverse if she made that choice.

The slope was covered with trees that looked like they were barely clinging to life. Mirabel remembered their former beauty, but now most were almost barren; what had once been beautiful, gnarled branches with fluttering heart-shaped leaves now were bare. The once beautiful white bark was now grayed and peeling. They reminded her of the aspens she knew as a child on Gaia. With her heart in her throat, she mourned the destruction of these legendary trees. But that was the least of her worries. She was so close, and now impossibly far. Frustrated, she abruptly sat back down again, placed Maia between her knees, and put her hands on her head, at a total loss about what to do. She sat there for hours, unable to make a move. Even her mantra, "What would Janey do?" didn't help this time.

Deciding to nourish herself, Mirabel pulled her pack closer. As she did, she heard something large lumbering through the trees, coming her way. She didn't know whether to be alarmed or happy. She had done no cleansing ritual, so who knew what she might come upon? She decided it would be prudent to hide. She stood, Maia in her arms, and grabbed the pack, then scanned the area. Off to her left she saw a small overhang with what looked like a small cave under it. She quickly made her way there and backed into the small cave. It didn't go deep, but it was enough to hide her.

Mirabel peeked out to see what was approaching. She heard it crashing through the trees and muttering to itself in a trumpeting voice in a language she couldn't understand. Finally, it came into view and she saw that it was a manticore. Its tail had lost its stinger and its mane was shaggy and sparse. Its wings were tattered and it looked as though it could no longer fly. It had a face that appeared to be a cross between a human and a lion. Turning toward her, it sniffed the air and grimaced. Mirabel could see a row of sharp teeth and knew she was in danger. She knew manticores were uncommon and untrustworthy. Her people rarely encountered them unless they came to these mountains. They were dangerous carnivores, but usually feasted on other mountain creatures and left her people alone. Once upon a time one had crossed over to earth and kidnapped unsuspecting humans, which they dragged back to the forest to feast upon. This had been the source of all the legends she had learned about in her studies on Gaia. Now her memories showed her that her people had to destroy the portal tree the manticore had used to cross over. This had aggrieved them seriously, as they loved all trees, especially the portals. But it was too dangerous to allow such a creature to cross over. Humans on earth would not know how to fight them.

This manticore was painfully thin. Its ribs stuck out below its ragged mane hairs. Mirabel pitied it, and she imagined it must be ravenous, but that would also make it even more dangerous. Right now it sniffed the ground where she had been sitting, and looked around, muttering to itself. Mirabel wondered if her magical cloak would protect her, but she was afraid it would make too much noise to get it out.

The manticore sniffed the ground and followed her trail, headed straight toward her hiding place. Mirabel backed as far as she could into the little cave, holding Maia close to her body. Magdalena hadn't said anything about what to do if she ran into such creatures. She may not have known how severe the instability of her world had become—enough to move mountains and put Mirabel in danger from creatures her people had rarely encountered.

Mirabel searched the floor of the cave, wishing she had at least picked up a stick with which to defend herself. The manticore was so close it now sniffed around just below the entrance. Mirabel was trapped. *This may be the end of my journey.* She couldn't believe that the fate of two worlds came down to one hungry manticore and a defenseless woman with a child in stasis. It was so unfair. She was so close. If she was going to die, she wanted to die completing her mission.

Mirabel backed against the wall of the cave, trembling. Then she heard a snort and something pawing at the ground. She couldn't see what it was, but the manticore screamed and backed up. It lowered its front end to the ground, ears back, and hissed. Mirabel gaped as the most beautiful creature she had ever seen came into view. A magnificent horse with golden hooves and outstretched wings stood guarding the cave. She could see brilliant, iridescent white hair under the layers of dust covering its coat. It stood proud, head and tail held high. Its wings were frayed, and it too looked painfully thin. It advanced forward, continually pawing at the ground, flapping its wings, and snorting as it bore down on the manticore. The fight quickly went out of the manticore, and it turned and fled.

The winged horse turned and looked at Mirabel. Its eyes shone like emeralds, and inside the dark circle of its pupils she swore she saw stars. Entranced, Mirabel moved reverently towards it. The horse bent down, kneeling on its two front legs, and bowed its head. Mirabel came forward, one arm wrapped around Maia, the other outstretched to touch this magnificent creature. She placed her hand on the space between the horse's eyes and whispered, "Thank you."

The winged horse looked at her again and she suddenly knew its name, *Neehamad*. Neehamad neighed and bent her head again, gesturing for Mirabel to climb on her back.

Mirabel put her finger to Neehamad's nose and mentally communicated, *One moment, Neehamad. I am honored and I will ride, but I must get my pack*. She went back into the cave and grabbed her pack, placing it on her back. She adjusted the snug with Maia in it, then walked back out and mounted the horse. No other words needed to be said. Their minds attuned, Mirabel knew that Neehamad intended to carry her over the mountain.

Mirabel knew what the winged horse risked to do such a thing, as she was already fragile and weak with hunger. The winged horses were revered on her world. They were intelligent, majestic creatures and it had been rumored that among all her creatures, the Shiashialon had created them last, putting all her love and artistry into these angelic beings. They were mysterious, like the cosmos, wild and free. To see one was to witness the untamed beauty at the heart of being.

Mirabel firmly clutched Neehamad's mane with one hand and protected Maia with her other as Neehamad rose above the trees and headed toward the peaks. At first, the horse gained height easily, but as she rose, Mirabel could feel her labor for her breath under the strain. Neehamad bore her burden with devotion. Mirabel could feel Neehamad's spirit within her, and a bright love enveloped her. In her mind's eye, Mirabel inhaled the life-giving breath of the Shiashialon; the energy of existence.

As they rose toward the peaks, the wind battered Neehamad's wings. She had to battle to keep her course as the gusts pushed them backwards. Each advance now took three times the effort, but Neehamad battled forward, head down, for over an hour before they finally started making their way down the other side of the mountain. Mirabel could once again see the Shialon Tree in the distance, and hope sprang in her heart once more.

Neehamad faltered, weakening with each beat of her wings. Once below the winds, she was able to glide down along the slope, but Mirabel knew she couldn't hold out much longer. In her mind she begged Neehamad to put her down and let her make her way down the mountain on her own, but Neehamad refused. Her breath now came in deep heaves, and Mirabel wept as they finally dropped down to the base of the slope.

Neehamad landed gently, ever careful of her cargo, and then collapsed. Mirabel dismounted and came round to hold the horse's head in her lap, caressing Neehamad's mane. She felt a surge of warm, expansive love, and then Neehamad's spirit was gone. Mirabel hung her head in deep honor of the winged horse and the sacrifice she had made. From her mind connection, Mirabel knew Neehamad was the last of her kind. Mirabel was devastated.

Is there ever a place for joy to live for more than a fleeting moment in my life?

She sat holding the horse's head in her lap for a long time, then got up and covered the body with what boughs she could find from the dying trees. Sorrow or no sorrow, she knew she must head for the Shialon Tree. She did not want Neehamad's sacrifice to be for nothing.

Chapter Twenty-Six

J aney, Matt, and the protesters had gathered at the Shell Ridge Bike Shop and Sports Bar and a raucous celebration ensued. Any excuse for a beer fest was gladly accepted by all the bikers who hung out there, and they had an excellent excuse today.

Janey sat on the sidelines. As outgoing and personable as she was, bars and beer weren't really her thing. She preferred to remain in the background and watch. Sitting at the far end of the bar, she entertained herself by counting how many times Matt was slapped on the back and told, "Dude, you were awesome!" He took it all in with a measure of humility and she could see the playful camaraderie that surrounded him had been built over years. The bikers obviously held him in great esteem. He was their hero from his competition days, and now his hero status was renewed and embellished. He took it all in with a smile and reciprocal slaps on backs. But, despite the revelry, Janey could see the sadness of loss in his eyes and she knew he worried about Mirabel constantly.

Janey closed her eyes for a moment to see if she could feel Mirabel out there in the ether somewhere, but she got nothing.

Perhaps it's too much to expect in the midst of this noisy celebration. She had tried to set aside her uneasiness, but it agitated her, making her shift in her seat and drink more beer than she liked.

A TV had been playing over the bar the whole time and the bartender had been watching it off and on. Janey noticed his attention to the TV suddenly intensify, then he let out a shout. "Hey Matt, did you know you were on TV?"

The noise level in the bar dove suddenly as all heads turned toward the TV and everyone shuffled toward the bar. A few loud conversations kept going until someone yelled, "Shut up! We can't hear."

Janey looked up at the TV and sure enough, she saw Matt standing by the Mother Tree. He bent over and placed an object at the tree's base and looked as if he might be saying vows. She couldn't make out what he was saying, as the film was a little shaky, and looked like it had been recorded on a Smartphone.

After showing the scene at the tree, the camera switched to a reporter who announced, "This is Sue Ellen Joseph at the scene of the large protest in Walnut Creek today. Earlier, you saw the alleged leader of this protest, where I followed him up to this tree in the hills above the club where the club owner, John McNulty, tried to build his new clubhouse. We are working to verify the identity of this leader right now, but we believe he is Matt Gallagher, owner of Shell Ridge Bike Shop and Sports Bar in Walnut Creek, and former winner of several mountain biking competitions in the area. Let's pan back to the scene at the tree. He is placing something at the foot of the tree and it looks like he holds this tree in great reverence. Perhaps this tree is his inspiration for the protest." The background scene switched to the mayor's speech at the club earlier that day. "At any rate, the mayor made an announcement today that the project has been stopped and Jay Reed, the city planner, has been fired. More on this story tomorrow. This is Sue Ellen Joseph at Lime Ridge Open Space in Walnut Creek. Back to you, Dan."

The news moved on to the next story and the noise in the bar picked up again as everyone started commenting on what they had just seen.

"Hey Matt," someone yelled. "Did you know you were being filmed?"

Matt, looking stunned, shook his head.

Someone else chimed in, "Matt, why didn't you tell us you were a tree hugger!"

General laughter broke out and the party went on. Janey knew it was all good-natured ribbing, but Matt appeared decidedly uncomfortable and Janey's sense of unease ramped up a few notches after the report.

Matt walked over to her. "What do you say we get out of here, Janey? I'm done with this crowd for now."

"Yes, let's," Janey sighed in relief. She had been ready to leave an hour ago, but didn't want to take him away from his groupies.

They got in the truck and started toward the house.

"Did you know you were being filmed?" Janey asked.

"I had no idea. I would have chased her out of there had I known. I am not comfortable with that. Now they are making me out to be some kind of tree hugger. I mean, not that I don't love trees, but I am not comfortable with labels...and if they only knew what was at stake."

Janey put her hand on Matt's arm. "I know, Matt. I know." She looked out the window. "I wish we knew how Mirabel was doing, where she is, if she's safe, and if she's getting close. I wonder if we will ever know?" She paused. "Matt, I feel uneasy. I can't explain what it is and I can't contain this to myself anymore. But it's almost unbearable."

"Janey, if there's one thing I know, it's when you feel something, it's a good time to listen. What can I do? How can I help?"

"I wish I knew. Intuition doesn't come with a guidebook. Sometimes you just have to wait. I hate it when it's like that. It makes me feel helpless. This unknowing dread creeps in and won't give me any peace, yet I can't do anything because I have no idea what to do. It's so frustrating!"

"Well, I suppose we could both use a good night's sleep. Perhaps an answer will come tomorrow. Do you still want to go to the grove with me? Maybe being next to the tree will help you find answers."

Janey sighed. "That sounds like good advice. I only hope I can sleep."

"How 'bout I make you some of your famous chamomile tea? You always take care of me; let me take care of you this time. I'll give you some tea and you can sit down and relax."

She smiled and said, "That's the best offer I've had all day!"

• • •

Back at the Marriot Hotel, Jay Reed had also been watching the news. He heard the whole sordid story, from the mayor making an announcement about stopping the project, to pinning the blame on him. *Like I was the one schmoozing with John McNulty.* Not only had he lost his job, but now he had been publicly shamed and betrayed by the mayor. His dreams had shattered into shards at his feet. He had been betrayed by his wife, his best friend, and now the mayor.

He felt completely helpless to do anything, so took another swig of whiskey directly from the bottle. Whiskey was good for days like this. He looked at his bottle. It was getting kind of low and he wished he'd had the foresight to buy two. But before he could get up to go buy another, a reporter named Sue Ellen Joseph came on to talk about the leader of the protest, Matt Gallagher. She reported while the footage of Matt played, showing how he appeared to be worshipping at one of the trees. Jay's rage rose, starting in his gut and burning its way up to his gorge. Then rage mixed with disbelief. There he was, the ruins of his life scattered at his feet, and it was all for some stupid tree! Now it was personal. His life had fallen apart all because of some idiot tree-hugger biker. His rage took on a new focus—Matt Gallagher. *Him and his fucking tree!*

Jay paced the room. Revenge was suddenly on the menu. He owned a gun; maybe he could kill that damned tree hugger. But then he remembered his gun was back at the house and he was too drunk to drive there—and he didn't want to face Sheila after the embarrassment on the news. Sheila had a cruel tongue, and after the scene he had walked into at their house, he was finished with her. *Besides, murder is a possible death penalty.* Even in his drunken rage, he knew he couldn't pull off a murder. But he *could* kill what Matt loved. He *could* murder a tree. After all, that stupid tree was at the center of his troubles, and if Matt worshipped the tree, then killing it would hurt Matt.

He paused his pacing. He had a plan and he didn't feel helpless anymore. He was going to cut down that tree and then start a fire. Perhaps the fire would spread to the club and the whole thing, open space and golf club, would go up in flames, just like his life. Jay finished off his whiskey and devised a plan. First thing in the morning he planned to stop at the hardware store, buy an ax, propane, and some matches. He would get a pack to carry it in, and make his way up to the grove where that tree stood. *Yeah! Take that, Mr. Matt Gallagher.* He called the front desk and asked for an early wakeup call, then stumbled into bed and fell into a drunken stupor.

• • •

Janey and Matt got up early. Janey had squirrels in her stomach from the moment she woke up, and still felt uneasy. Sleep hadn't helped, and if anything her disquiet had increased from the previous night. She still didn't have a clue what was behind it, but her intuition was clearly telling her something. They were eating breakfast when suddenly she knew.

"Matt, we have to get to the tree!"

They left the house quickly. Matt drove silently, deep in his own thoughts. He gripped the wheel hard, and resisted the urge to floor the gas pedal. Last night he wanted to ask Janey to do some kind of ritual around the tree to send hope to Mirabel on her journey. Now it seemed more important to get to the tree as soon as possible. He didn't like how panicked Janey sounded when she said they needed to get to the tree. Right now she was looking out the window, silent and distant.

Matt parked the truck and they both got out. Before they had left the house, Janey had hastily grabbed her Navajo blanket, stuffed it in her pack, and threw in some ritual implements. Now she grabbed the pack from behind the seat and they made their way to the gate. There was only one other car parked in the lot.

Today was a completely different scene from the protest the day before. The project was officially shut down and the equipment had been quickly removed.

Janey and Matt began the hike up the trail. The incline up the first hill was quite steep, and Janey soon started breathing heavily. Matt, on the other hand, was not winded at all and was busy looking around. They walked on in an uncomfortable silence for a few minutes. When they got to the golf course, a new jolt of fear surged up Janey's spine.

"Matt," she grabbed his arm. "I feel a screaming inside me. It's the tree. Oh Matt, we have to hurry."

Matt didn't question her and took off at a run. Janey tried to keep up, but was quickly too winded to go any faster.

"Matt, you go on ahead. I'll catch up. Just get there as fast as you can." With that, she doubled over. Her body was connected with the tree. She didn't know how that had happened, but her insides were screaming with pain and fear. She stumbled on as best as she could.

Matt ran through the torn-up lower grove. He had to slow down to go through the ravine, but scrambled over the rocks and branches as quickly as he could until he came to the middle of the second grove. He paused for a minute, then heard a rhythmic chopping. His heart went to his throat and he pulled himself up the hillside, hand over foot. When he arrived at the top, he came upon a devastating scene. The tree had been chopped down to a stump. Mangled branches surrounded it, and a man with an axe stood at the center of the tangled mess. Matt's mouth formed a scream. "No..." he tried to say, but little sound came out. Then his voice found its strength and he screamed aloud this time, "NOOOOOOO!"

He fell to his knees, covering his face. In this moment, all the hope he had for Mirabel, for himself, and for his baby turned into horror. The happiness from the success of the protest dissolved at the realization that the two worlds were soon to be severed by this tree's demise. He was immobilized.

He watched as the man who had destroyed the tree turned. Seeing Matt, an evil grin spread across his face, and he laughed an empty, throaty laugh. Matt recognized Jay Reed, the fired city planner. His laugh, dead of any humor or passion, finally stirred Matt from his inertia. At that laugh, Matt picked himself up off the ground and surged toward the man. Matt flew into a mindless rage, intending to strangle him.

Jay grabbed the can of propane and doused himself with it. He lit a match, and burst into flames just as Matt clambered over the broken tree limbs and crashed into him. The flames whooshed outward. Matt picked himself up and backed away, trying to shield his face as he stumbled backwards, tripping over the branches. His shirt was on fire. Panicking, he flailed around, trying to put out the flames.

Janey, near desperate now, climbed toward them to the smell of charred flesh. As she crested the hill, she witnessed a screaming conflagration next to the destroyed tree, and Matt thrashing around with his shirt on fire. Sudden, crystal clarity caused her to yell out, "Matt, drop and roll. DROP and ROLL!"

Matt followed her command and she came up to him just as the flames went out.

"Matt, are you okay?"

He nodded his head, but she knew they would need to get him to care as soon as possible. She looked at the burning man and quickly saw there was no hope there. And the flames were spreading rapidly, putting them in danger. They needed to get out of there, and fast.

Janey urged, "Matt, Matt, can you walk? We have to go." She worried that he wasn't going to make it. The skin on his arms and back was scorched and raw and what remained of his shirt stuck to his skin or hung in tatters. She was afraid to touch him.

Janey led Matt down the hill as quickly as she could. She cleared brush out of the way and helped him avoid as many branches and scrapes to his exposed flesh as possible. When she felt they were a safe enough distance from the fire to make a call, she pulled out her cell and called 911. Satisfied that help was on the way, she pulled her blanket out of her pack to protect Matt's exposed burns, sat him down to rest, and continued down to the main trail alone to wait for help. While she waited, she focused her energy to send healing to Matt.

Soon a helicopter flew over the area and dropped water on the burn site. A special fire truck made its way up to where she waited, and she led them on foot to Matt. After calling for helicopter transport, the two firemen performed triage on Matt. When the helicopter arrived, they loaded him on a gurney and Matt was flown to the Bothin Burn Center at Saint Francis Hospital in San Francisco. The firemen examined Janey. Finding no injuries, they let her go at her insistence, but not before she saw them carrying down what remained of Jay Reed's body.

Janey swallowed, sick with dread and sorrow. *We were so hopeful yesterday. Now everything is in ruins.*

She wondered how quickly the world was going to die. The tree was dead. She couldn't quite wrap her mind around it. But, her immediate concern was Matt's condition. She had to get to his side as soon as she could.

Janey made her way down to the truck, drove home, changed her clothes, and switched to her car for the drive into

San Francisco. The drive took forever and she was sick with worry the entire trip.

Chapter Twenty-Seven

$\mathcal{M}$irabel realized she needed to eat before she continued to the tree. She grabbed her pack and pulled out the contents. She was down to the last piece of unleavened bread, and only a few pieces of dried fruit remained. This would be her last meal, as there would be nothing left after a meager breakfast. Her magic water skin, as usual, had replenished itself. Mirabel ate, and drank deeply, then rocked Maia.

"Maia, I think this will be the last day of our journey. Maybe I will finally get to see you awake! At last, I will free you from your bundle." She slung the pack onto her back and the snug over her shoulder, and prepared to set off. Before taking a step, she looked up. The tree was an enormous presence dominating the land around it. Her eyes were drawn to it. From this distance, the bark looked smooth and white. The tree had a huge, broad trunk, rather like a large oak, with immense branches. It was more massive than ten of the great redwood trees she had visited in California, and she gawked, awed by it.

Here the trail toward the tree was broad and easy. She needn't follow the tug in her belly any longer, although it still pulled her more strongly than ever before. Like a magnet, the tree drew her toward it. There was a slight incline, and Mirabel walked for several hours, inching closer, her footfalls nearly silent on the gentle path. Finally, she reached the place where the roots broke above the ground and spread out around the base of the tree, then down the gentle slope. The trail made its way between the roots, and for this Mirabel was grateful, for climbing among and around the roots would have been impossible.

Mirabel stopped and looked up. The tree was stunning. The sheer size of it was impossible. Now that she was close, she could see that the bark gleamed white and had whorls and knots of gold. The trail went between two great branches that swept down to the ground, and she entered the canopy reverentially. When she stopped and looked up, she could no longer see the top of the tree. The air felt cool and pleasant under the branches, and a sweet dew kissed her skin. Her senses were filled with a scent rather like sweet rose, but not quite. Mirabel detected energy in her hands and looked down to find that the shimmering spirals in her palms had awakened. She stared, fascinated by the whirling spirals. They looked like stars and she fancied she could see galaxies and endless cosmic vistas, all there in her palms. She was still quite distant from the trunk, but longed to place her palms on the tree, so she walked slowly toward it, each step a prayer.

The tree emanated love, wildness, and pulsing life all at once. Swept into its aura, Mirabel heard music more beautiful than anything she had ever heard in her life, and soon her movements became part of that music. Finally, she stepped up to the massive tree trunk and placed her palms on the smooth bark. It was alive with energy and pulsed gently, but powerfully. The texture reminded her of leather, so alive and so unlike any other tree bark in her experience. Mirabel closed her eyes and stood silent, filled with reverence, allowing the pulsing music of existence to flow through her while at the same time standing in absolute peaceful and expansive stillness. She opened her eyes. Tears of joy and sadness tracked down her cheeks. This was life, all of it— every feeling, every breath, every birth, and every death.

Overwhelmed, Mirabel had to step back and remove her palms. As she did this, Magdalena stepped out of the tree toward her.

Stunned, Mirabel said, "Magdalena, how are you here?"

"I never left here, my dear."

"But you were in Walnut Creek, by the tree, and before that in the coffee shop. How could you be in both places at once?"

"Anything is possible by the tree, my dear."

They embraced with Maia between them. Then Magdalena pulled away and cupped her hands around Mirabel's face.

"My dear, you have traveled far and it has been an arduous trip. You are so brave and so strong. The blood of your mothers and all of your ancestors flows strong within you. I have waited here for what seems an eternity. It is time. Let us sit under the great bows of this tree and I will explain what must be done. Only you can do this thing—you, the last living daughter of our people. You have brought hope where there was little hope before. You gave birth to a child of both worlds. While she is born of your blood, she was born on Gaia and in that is hope of mending the tear between the two worlds. I am afraid your task is not an easy one, my child, for it will require that you sacrifice your life for the future of both worlds. I would have it otherwise, but the choice is not mine."

Mirabel sat with tears streaming down her face. This was her destiny. There was no turning back.

"A great tragedy has taken place now and the worlds are severed," Magdalena said. "We must act quickly."

"Liouradion, what of Maia, what will happen to her?"

"Maia will be safe with me, but first we must wake her and you must pass your memories on to her. Spread the blanket I gave you here below the tree and carefully remove Maia from your snug. Place her in the bundle on the blanket. I will remove the bundling."

Mirabel did as Magdalena said. She carefully laid out the blanket, straightening the corners, then removed Maia Jane from the snug and placed her on the middle of the blanket. Magdalena unwrapped the bundle and positioned the small, perfect child on the blanket, face up.

"Bring the silver buckeye seed to me."

Mirabel opened the pack, pulled out the silver buckeye, and handed it to Magdalena.

Magdalena placed the silver buckeye to her lips and blew. A magical tone rang out. She blew again and the tone rang out once more. The lock on the buckeye fell off and the buckeye opened. Sitting inside the silver seed was a tiny, pulsing blue light. Magdalena carefully gathered the light in her hands, then used her fingers to open Maia's mouth. She let the light roll off her hands and into the baby's mouth. The light spread from Maia's head, down her neck, and into her limbs. After a moment, glowing with light, she wiggled and opened her eyes. Looking up at Magdalena, she smiled.

Mirabel knelt on the blanket behind Maia and looked at her in wonder. Her beautiful, precious child had an equally precious smile, and suddenly she knew the love of a mother in a way she hadn't experienced when Maia had been in stasis. Joy overtook Mirabel, and she glanced up at Magdalena, beseeching Magdalena to hand Maia over so she could hold her.

"Yes, my dear, take her in your arms and let her feel your love."

Mirabel scooped her up, holding her tenderly at her breast. She looked down into Maia's face, and the child smiled her beautiful smile, searching out Mirabel's eyes and gazing into them.

After a few moments, Magdalena put her hand on Mirabel's arm. "My dear, we must make haste. Place the child on the blanket and place your hands on either side of her head. Stoke the energy in your palms and the memories will transfer."

Mirabel reluctantly placed Maia Jane back on the blanket and did as Magdalena requested. As the memories passed into Maia, the energy moved from Mirabel's heart, down her arms, through her palms, and into the child. It felt like warm water coursing through her and out her hands. It took but a few moments, and then it was done.

"Now my dear, it is time."

Mirabel leaned down and kissed Maia on the forehead, taking one long, last look, then stood and looked at Magdalena.

"Now walk to the tree and place your palms against it once again, and pray to it. Enter the tree's song with all your being and it will bring you inside. To do this, you must shed any fear you have, and let your mind go. The tree will not allow you to enter unless your mind is free and clear. Just enter the song, as I have told you. Allow your whole being to become the song."

Mirabel looked back at Maia. "Will I see her again?"

"Yes, my dear. Just enter the tree and you will see."

Mirabel paused, suddenly afraid.

"Mirabel, just trust! This is what is required of you now. Just trust with all your heart and you can't fail."

Mirabel nodded her head and turned back toward the tree. She walked to it and stood before it. She calmed her mind by opening her awareness, and surrendered to all that existed for her to experience in this moment. She calmly placed her palms on the tree. Energy pulsed through her and she opened herself to the song, dissolving and becoming one with the music. She found herself inside the still center of a galaxy, vastness all around her with millions of stars circling around. She could no longer sense temperature here. She was surrounded by vastness, color, music, and stars. Suddenly, she had the desire to just let go and allow herself to expand and meld with the vastness, but then she felt a *No!* It came from within her, although it didn't come *from* her. Once she had entered the tree and merged with it, she had forgotten Maia and Magdalena on the outside, just as she had forgotten Matt and Janey and her life before. But with that *no*, it all came back to her. And then the Weavers gathered around her. She didn't know how, but she knew who they were and that they had always watched over her and loved her.

The Weavers parted and Mirabel felt another presence. From that presence, instructions came through to her, although there were no words. She just somehow knew what was being transmitted.

"I am the Deep." It paused. "You must awaken the Shiashialon. She has been sleeping long. In her sleep, all things are held, but cannot be renewed, and we have come to the end of this turn. As it was foreseen, she must join me that we might create again. All will be lost, all will be forgotten, all will be renewed."

It paused again and Mirabel waited.

"Take the life in your palms; they are a gift of the Deep. Your child still needs the essence of your life if she is to survive. She will become renewal and wisdom." The instructions continued. "Place your hands on the child and let yourself go into the music. Hold her up before me and let your life flow into her until almost the very last. You must conserve one drop of life inside your being for the journey after. Once the child is filled with life, you may look at her, but you must hand her over to the Liouradion. It will be your farewell. The Liouradion will take her. Know that the child will be cared for and will carry you with her always."

Now Mirabel could see Magdalena holding Maia in front of her. Mirabel remained inside the tree, but at the same time stood by Magdalena's side outside the tree. She placed her hands on Maia as instructed, and allowed herself to be filled with the music. She was no longer solid, but in two places at once. Her life flowed into Maia and she held her up before her, as if offering her to the Deep. The offering was accepted. As she did this, the baby's amazing, gold-flecked, purple-brown eyes gazed at Mirabel with wisdom far beyond her own. Maia knew her and loved her. This prescient child was fully conscious. Mirabel almost forgot to save a drop of life for herself, but she looked into Maia's eyes one last time and Maia reminded her with a silent sigh. No words were needed; the love flowed between them. Conserving her last drop of consciousness, Mirabel stepped back and saw Maia nestled in Magdalena's arms, safe.

The Deep said into her mind, "Now, with your last drop of being, you will know how to awaken the Shiashialon."

Mirabel hung still, deep inside the vastness, now alone. The very last task of her journey was upon her.

Chapter Twenty-Eight

J aney stood by Matt's bed in the burn center. She had to dress in sterile scrubs before entering the room. Matt was sedated. He had third-degree burns on his arm and one side of his body, and he had gone into shock while being transported to the hospital.

Janey could feel the life draining from the world and it was losing color. Everyone else appeared oblivious to it, but she could see the color fading and everything becoming dull. Sound had changed, too. She couldn't quite define it, but everything sounded tinny and dissonant. Inside she could feel her passion dying, and worse, the hope she had always carried inside her heart was dissipating. Even her fear was dulled.

When she had arrived at the hospital, the faces that greeted her were somber. The nurses said little, showed her to the changing room, and wordlessly led her to Matt's room, where they deposited her and left her. There were no words of sympathy; there was no compassion. They were like automatons.

Janey slumped in the chair next to Matt and sat there for hours while the color of the world slowly drained away.

Eventually, the monotonous beeping of the heart monitor slowed and went into a flat line. No one came. Janey sat in her chair without moving as barely visible tears, one at a time, made their way down her cheeks and dropped into her lap.

Chapter Twenty-Nine

The vision of Magdalena holding Maia faded into the galaxy and Mirabel floated at the center, one single point of consciousness holding her there. That single point of consciousness became love, and that love had one desire: to let go and fall. Following that desire, Mirabel let go and fell. She dropped into the darkness below her, through the center of the galaxy, dropping below the galaxy, and still she fell. She fell past the stars until there were no stars, only a black void. She fell until time did not exist and could not be tracked, and still she fell further. Just when she thought she might fall forever, she saw a light in the center of the dark and her love swelled. The only consciousness left of her coalesced into a single, crystal-clear drop and landed in the center of the brow of the Shiashialon...and she awoke.

Chapter Thirty

irabel opened her eyes to a golden, shimmering light streaming through the window, gracing the room with an ethereal magic. At first she didn't recognize where she was, but then her vision began to clear. She lay in a bed in the hospital room where she had given birth to Maia so many weeks ago, but it felt like eons. Matt was standing by her bed, looking down at her, lovingly pushing stray strands of hair from her forehead. Janey stood on the other side of the bed gently rocking and crooning to a tiny bundle in her arms. She looked up at Mirabel and she smiled. Tears sparkled in the corners of her eyes, and a halo of iridescence shimmered around her. She moved toward the bed and handed the bundle over to Mirabel. Mirabel looked down and gazed into the wise, purple-brown eyes of her child Maia and saw the love of the Shiashialon reflected back at her.

Epilogue

A lone doe stood in the center of a burnt grove. Charred remains of the trees were scattered about, and the sun, cresting on the horizon, filtered into the grove, sending gentle rays upon serpentine rocks, which glistened and soaked in the light. The doe bent her head down and gently nuzzled the small sapling that pushed through the remains of the burnt-out trunk of the potbellied buckeye that once dominated the grove. Even at this small size, the sapling's trunk shimmered a dazzling white in the sunlight. Somewhere in a far distant world, a great tree shook its mighty branches and dropped its new flowers. As they landed, a chorus of ringing tones pealed out, sending a harmonious symphony across the world. The desolate land shivered in anticipation. The long-awaited child was awake.

About the Author

Maura McCarley writes both fiction and non-fiction. The Curious Magic of Buckeye Groves is her first novel. Mythology, fairy tales, mysticism and the esoteric have always fascinated her. Maura has longed for magic all her life and often found it by being swept away in a fantasy story. She believes that once upon a time, we humans had greater access to non-physical realities, but have chosen to ignore them. She writes to create a world where magic is possible once again and where the human heart leads.

Maura has an MA in Women's Spirituality from New College of California. Her work is inspired by her relationship to the Divine Feminine, nature and her experiences as a mystic. She lives in Northern California with her family and her two cats.

Visit her author site at:
www.mauramccarley.com